Gisele turned  e fashionable w n.

Jamie suddenly fel t of his coat and jerk him around with a shocking force. She hauled his lips to hers, and he struggled to breathe—drugged instantly by her scent and her softness—as he fought vainly to make sense of what was happening. And then Jamie felt Gisele sigh into his mouth, and he stopped thinking altogether.

"You two should be ashamed!" The words floated over the woman's shoulder as she sailed past them into the yard, where a crested carriage waited for her. Gisele pulled away from Jamie just enough to watch the carriage door swing shut.

"What the hell was that?" Jamie demanded hoarsely. He watched as her gaze dropped back to his mouth. Dear God, he couldn't think when she did that.

"That," she began shakily, "was the Countess of Baustenbury."

He leaned toward her, his mouth close to her ear. "Listen and listen carefully. I will take you inside, and once we are settled, you will tell me why you used me to hide from her. You will tell me who you really are, and you will tell me what or who is waiting for us in London. Understood?"

Gisele nodded.

"And if you ever kiss me like that again," he whispered, "be prepared to finish it."

KELLY BOWEN

I've Got My Duke to Keep Me Warm

WITHDRAWN

FOREVER

NEW YORK   BOSTON

This book is a work of fiction. Names, characters, places, and incidents are the product of the author's imagination or are used fictitiously. Any resemblance to actual events, locales, or persons, living or dead, is coincidental.

Copyright © 2014 by Kelly Bowen
Excerpt from *A Good Rogue Is Hard to Find* © 2014 by Kelly Bowen
All rights reserved. In accordance with the U.S. Copyright Act of 1976, the scanning, uploading, and electronic sharing of any part of this book without the permission of the publisher constitute unlawful piracy and theft of the author's intellectual property. If you would like to use material from the book (other than for review purposes), prior written permission must be obtained by contacting the publisher at permissions@hbgusa.com. Thank you for your support of the author's rights.

Forever
Hachette Book Group
1290 Avenue of the Americas
New York, NY 10104

HachetteBookGroup.com

Printed in the United States of America

First Edition: December 2014
10 9 8 7 6 5 4 3 2 1

OPM

Forever is an imprint of Grand Central Publishing.
The Forever name and logo are trademarks of Hachette Book Group, Inc.

The Hachette Speakers Bureau provides a wide range of authors for speaking events. To find out more, go to www.hachettespeakersbureau.com or call (866) 376-6591.

The publisher is not responsible for websites (or their content) that are not owned by the publisher.

ATTENTION CORPORATIONS AND ORGANIZATIONS:
Most HACHETTE BOOK GROUP books are available at quantity discounts with bulk purchase for educational, business, or sales promotional use. For information, please call or write:

Special Markets Department, Hachette Book Group
1290 Avenue of the Americas, New York, NY 10104
Telephone: 1-800-222-6747 Fax: 1-800-477-5925

For my family

Acknowledgments ─────

My warmest thanks to: my agent, Stefanie Lieberman, for her invaluable guidance and humor; my talented editor, Alex Logan, for making the entire process enjoyable and rewarding; and the entire team at Grand Central for its dedication and expertise.

I've Got My Duke to Keep Me Warm

Chapter 1 ———————————

Somewhere south of Nottingham, England, May 1816

Being dead was not without its drawbacks.

The tavern was one of them. More hovel than hostelry, it was plunked capriciously in a tiny hamlet, somewhere near nowhere. Her mere presence in this dismal place proved time was running out and desperation was beginning to eclipse good sense.

Gisele shuffled along the filthy wall of the taproom, wrinkling her nose against the overripe scent of unwashed bodies and spilled ale. She sidestepped neatly, avoiding the leering gaze and groping fingers of more than one man, and slipped into the gathering darkness outside. She took a deep breath, trying to maintain a sense of purpose and hope. The carefully crafted demise of Gisele Whitby four years earlier had granted her the freedom and the safety to reclaim her life. True, it had also driven her to the fringes of society, but until very recently, forced anonymity had been a benediction. Now it was proving to be an unwanted complication.

"What are you doing out here?" The voice came from beside her, and she sighed, not turning toward her friend.

"This is impossible. We'll not find him here."

Sebastien gazed at the sparrows quarreling along the edge of the thatch in the evening air. "I agree. We need a male without feathers. And they are all inside."

Gisele rolled her eyes. "Have you been inside? There is not a single one in there who would stand a chance at passing for a gentleman."

Sebastien brushed nonexistent dust off his sleeve. "Perhaps we haven't seen everyone who—"

"Please," she grumbled. "Half of those drunkards have a dubious command of the English language. And the other half have no command over any type of language at all." She stalked toward the stables in agitation.

Sebastien hurried across the yard after her.

"The man we need has to be clever and witty and charming and courageous and...convincingly noble." She spit the last word as if it were refuse.

"He does not exactly need to replace—"

"Yes, he does," Gisele argued, suddenly feeling very tired. "He has to be all of those things. Or at least some of those and willing to learn the rest. Or very, very desperate and willing to learn them all." She stopped, defeated, eyeing a ragged heap of humanity leaning against the front of the stable, asleep or stewed or both. "And we will not find all that here, in the middle of God knows where."

"We'll find someone," Sebastien repeated stubbornly, his dark brows knit.

"And if we can't?"

"Then we'll find a way. We'll find another way. There will—"

Whatever the slight man was going to say next was drowned out by the sound of an approaching carriage.

Gisele sighed loudly and stepped back into the shadows of the stable wall out of habit.

The vehicle stopped, and the driver and groom jumped down. The driver immediately went to unharness the sweat-soaked horses, though the groom disappeared inside the tavern without a backward glance, earning a muttered curse from the driver. Inside the carriage Gisele could hear the muffled tones of an argument. Presently the carriage door snapped open and a rotund man disembarked, stepping just to the side and lighting a cheroot. A well-dressed woman leaned out of the carriage door behind him to continue their squabble, shouting to be heard over the driver, who was leading the first horse away and calling for a fresh team.

Gisele watched the scene with growing impatience. She was preoccupied with her own problems and annoyed to be trapped out by the stables where there was no chance of finding any solution. Still, the carriage was expensive and it bore a coat of arms, and she would take no chances of being recognized, no matter how remote this tavern might be.

She was still plotting when the driver returned to fetch the second horse from its traces. As he reached for the bridle, the door to the tavern exploded outward with enough force to knock the wood clear off its hinges and send a report echoing through the yard like a gunshot. The gelding spooked and bolted forward, and the carriage lurched precariously behind it. The man standing with his cheroot was knocked sideways, his expensive hat landing somewhere in the dust. From the open carriage doorway, the woman began screaming hysterically, spurring the frightened horse on.

"Good heavens," gasped Sebastien, observing the unfolding drama with interest.

Gisele stood frozen as the unidentifiable lump she had previously spied leaning against the stable morphed into the form of a man. In three quick strides, the man launched himself onto the back of the panicked horse. With long arms he reached down the length of the horse's neck and easily grabbed the side of the bridle, pulling the animal's head to its shoulder with firm authority. The horse and carriage immediately slowed and then stopped, though the lady's screaming continued.

Sliding down from the blowing horse, the man gave the animal a careful once-over that Gisele didn't miss and handed the reins back to the horrified driver. The ragged-looking man then approached the woman still shrieking in the carriage and stood before her, waiting patiently for her to stop the wailing that was beginning to sound forced. He reached up a hand to help her down, and she abandoned her howling only to recoil in disgust.

"My lady?" he queried politely. "Are you all right? May I offer you my assistance?"

"Don't touch me!" the woman screeched, her chins jiggling. "You filthy creature. You could have killed me!"

By this time a number of people had caught up to the carriage, and Gisele pressed a little farther back into the shadows of the stable wall. The woman's husband, out of breath and red-faced, elbowed past the stranger and demanded a step be brought for his wife. Her rescuer simply inclined his head and retreated in the direction of the tavern, shoving his hands into the pockets of what passed for a coat. He ducked around the broken door and disappeared inside. He didn't look back.

Gisele held up a hand in warning.

"He's perfect," Sebastien breathed anyway, ignoring her.

Gisele crossed her arms across her chest, unwilling to let the seed of hope blossom.

"You saw what just happened. He just saved that wretched woman's life. You said courageous, clever, and charming. That was the epitome of all three." Sebastien was looking at her earnestly.

"Or alternatively, stupid, lucky, and drunk."

It was Sebastien's turn to roll his eyes.

"Fine." Gisele gave in, allowing hope a tiny foothold. "Do what you do best. Find out who he is and why he is here."

"What are you going to do?"

Gisele grimaced. "I will return to yonder establishment and observe your newfound hero in his cups. If he doesn't rape and pillage anything in the next half hour and can demonstrate at least a tenth the intellect of an average hunting hound, we'll go from there."

Sebastien grinned in triumph. "I've got a good feeling about him, Gisele. I promise you won't regret this." Then he turned and disappeared.

I am already regretting it, Gisele thought dourly twenty minutes later, though the lack of a front door had improved the quality of the air in the taproom, if not the quality of its ale. She managed a convincing swallow and replaced her drink on the uneven tabletop with distaste. Fingering the hilt of the knife she was displaying as a warning on the surface before her, she idly considered what manner of filth kept the bottom of her shoes stuck so firmly to the tavern floor. Sebastien had yet to reappear, and Gisele wondered how much longer she would be forced to wait. Her eyes drifted back to the stranger she'd been studying, who was still hunched over his drink at the far end of the room.

She thought he might be quite handsome if one could see past the disheveled beard and the appalling tatters currently passing for clothes. Broad shoulders, thick arms— he was very likely a former soldier, one of many who had found themselves out of work and out of sorts with the surrender of the little French madman. She narrowed her eyes. Strength in a man was always an asset, so she supposed she must count that in his favor. And from the way his knees rammed the underside of the table, he must be decently tall. Also an advantage, as nothing caught a woman's attention in a crowded room like a tall, confident man. Beyond that, however, his brown hair, brown eyes, and penchant for ale were the only qualities easily determined from a distance.

It was the latter—the utter state of intoxication he was rapidly working toward—that most piqued Gisele's interest. It suggested hopelessness. Defeat. Dejection. Desperation. All of which might make him the ideal candidate.

Or they might just mark him as a common drunkard.

And she'd had plenty of unpleasant experience with those. Unfortunately, this man was by far the best prospect she and Sebastien had seen in weeks, and she was well aware of the time slipping past. She watched as the stranger dribbled ale down his beard as he tried to drain his pot. Her lip curled in disgust.

"What do you think?" Her thoughts were interrupted

by Sebastien as he slid next to her on the bench. He jerked his chin in the direction of their quarry.

She scowled. "The man's been sitting in a corner drinking himself into a stupor since I sat down. He hasn't passed out yet, so I guess that's promising." She caught sight of her friend's glare and sighed. "Please, tell me what I *should* think. What did you find out?"

Sebastien sniffed and adjusted his collar. "James Montcrief. Son of a duke—"

"What?" Gisele gasped in alarm. She involuntarily shrank against the table.

Sebastien gave her a long-suffering look. "Do you think we'd still be here if I thought you might be recognized?"

Gisele bit her lip guiltily and straightened. "No. Sorry."

"May I go on?"

"Please."

"The duchy is . . . Reddyck, I believe? I've never heard of it, but I am assured it is real, and the bulk of its lands lie somewhere near the northern border. Small, but supports itself adequately."

Gisele let her eyes slide down the disheveled stranger. "Tell me he isn't the heir apparent."

"Even better. A bastard, so no chance of ever turning into anything quite as odious."

Giselle frowned. "Acknowledged?"

"The late duke was happy to claim him. Unfortunately, the current duke—a brother of some fashion—is not nearly so benevolent. According to current family history, James Montcrief doesn't exist."

Giselle studied the man uncertainly, considering the benefits and risks of that information. Someone with knowledge of the peerage and its habits and idiosyncrasies could be helpful. *If* he could remain sober enough to keep his wits.

"He hasn't groped the serving wenches yet," Sebastien offered.

"Says who?"

"The serving wenches."

"*Hmphh*." That might bode well. Or not. "Married? Children?"

"No and no. At least no children anyone is aware of."

"Good." They would have been a difficult complication. "Money?"

"Spent the morning cleaning stalls and repairing the roof to pay for his drink last night. Did the same the night before and the night before and—"

"In other words, none." Now that was promising. "Army?"

"Cavalry." Sebastien turned his attention from his sleeve to his carefully groomed moustache. "And supposedly quite the hero."

She snorted. "Aren't they all. Who says he's a hero?"

"The stableboys."

"They probably had him confused with his horse."

"His horse was shot out from under him at Waterloo."

"Exactly."

Her friend *tsk*ed. "The man survived, Gisele. He must know how to fight."

"Or run."

Sebastien's eyes rolled in exasperation. "That's what I love most about you. Your brimming optimism."

Giselle shrugged. "Heroes shouldn't drink themselves into oblivion. Multiple nights in a row."

Sebastien leaned close to her ear. "Listen carefully.

In the past twenty minutes, I have applied my abundant charm to the chambermaids and the barmaids and the milkmaids and one very enchanting footman, and thanks to my masterful skill and caution, we now possess a wealth of information about our new friend here. The very least *you* can do is spend half that amount of time discovering if this man is really as decent as I believe him to be." He paused for breath. "He's the best option we've got."

She pressed her lips together as she pushed herself up off the bench. "Very well. As we discussed?"

"Do you have a better idea?"

"No," she replied unhappily.

"Then let's not waste any more time. We need help from some quarter, and that man is the best chance we have of getting it." Without missing a beat, he reached over and deftly plucked at the laces to Gisele's simple bodice. The top fell open to reveal an alarming amount of cleavage. "Nice. Almost makes me wish I were so inclined."

"Do shut up." Gisele tried to pull the laces back together but had her hand swatted away. "I look like a whore," she protested.

Sebastien tipped his head, then leaned forward again and pulled the tattered ribbon from her braid. Her hair slithered out of its confines to tumble over her shoulders. "But a very pretty one. It's perfect." He stood up, straightening his own jacket. "Trust me. He's going to surprise you."

She heaved one last sigh. "How drunk do you suppose he is?"

"Slurring his *s*'s. But sentence structure is still good. I'll see you in ten minutes."

"Better make it twenty," Gisele said slowly. "It will reduce the chances of you ending up on the wrong end of a cavalryman's fists."

Sebastien's dark eyes slid back to the man in the corner in speculation. "You think?"

Giselle stood to join the shorter man. "You're the one who told me he's a hero. Let's find out."

~

Jamie Montcrief, known in another life as James Edward Anthony Montcrief, cavalry captain in the King's Dragoon Guards of the British army and bastard son to the ninth Duke of Reddyck, stared deeply into the bottom of his ale pot and wondered fuzzily how it had come to be empty so quickly. He was sure he had just ordered a fresh drink. Perhaps the girl had spilled it on the way over and he hadn't noticed. That happened a lot these days. Not noticing things. Which was fine. In fact, it was better than fine.

"You look thirsty." As if by magic, a full cup of liquid sloshed to the table in front of him.

Startled, he looked up, only to be presented with a view of stunning breasts. They were full and firm, straining against the fabric of a poorly laced bodice, and despite the fact that they were not entirely in focus, his body reacted with reprehensible speed. He reached out, intending to caress the luscious perfection before him, only to snatch his hand back a moment later when sluggish honor demanded retreat. Mortified, he dragged his eyes up from the woman's chest to her face, hoping against hope she might not have noticed.

He should have kept his eyes on her breasts.

For shimmering before him was a fantasy. His fantasy. The one he had carefully created in his imagination to chase away the reality of miserable marches, insufferable nights, unspeakable hunger, and bone-numbing dread. Everything he had hoped to possess in a woman was sliding onto the bench opposite him, a shy smile on her face. And it was a face that could start a war. High cheekbones, a full mouth, eyes almost exotic in their shape. Pale hair that fell in thick sheets carelessly around her head and over her shoulders.

He opened his mouth to say something clever, yet all his words seemed to have drowned themselves in the depths of his drink. He cursed inwardly, wishing for the first time in many months he weren't drunk. She seemed not to notice. Instead she cheerfully raised her own full pot of ale in a silent toast and proceeded to drain it. At a loss for anything better to do, he followed suit.

"Thank you," he finally managed, though he wasn't sure she heard, as she had somehow procured two more pots of ale and slid another in front of him.

"What shall we toast to now?" she asked him, her brilliant gray-green eyes probing his own.

Frantically Jamie searched his liquor-soaked brain for an intelligent answer. "To beauty," he croaked, cringing at such an amateurish and predictable reply.

She gave him a dazzling smile anyway, and he could feel his own mouth curling up in response. "To beauty then," she said. "And those who are wise enough to realize what it may cost." She drained her second pot.

Jamie allowed his mind to slog wearily through her cryptic words for a moment or two before he gave up trying to understand. Who cared, really? He had a magnificent woman sitting across the table from him, and another pot of ale had already replaced the second one he had drained. This was by far the best thing that had happened to him in a very long time.

"What's your name?" Her voice was gentle.

"James. James Montcrief." Thank the gods. At least he could remember that. Though maybe he should have made an effort at formality? Did one do that in such a setting?

"James." His name was like honey on her tongue, and her own dismissal of formality was encouraging. Something stirred inside him. "I like it." She gave him another blinding smile. "Why are you drinking all alone, James?" she asked.

He stared at her, unable, and more truthfully, unwilling to give her any sort of an answer. Instead he just shrugged.

"Never mind." She tipped her head back, and another pot of ale disappeared. Idly he wondered how she still remained sober while the room he was sitting in was beginning to spin. She tilted her head, and her beautiful blond hair swung away from her neck, dizzying in its movement. "You have kind eyes."

Her comment caught him off guard. He did not have kind eyes. He had eyes that had seen too much to ever allow any kindness in. "I am not kind." He wasn't sure if he mumbled it or just thought it. Inexplicably, a wave of sadness and loneliness washed over him.

"What brings you here?" she asked, waving a hand in the general direction of the tavern.

Jamie blinked, trying to remember where *here* was, then snorted at the futility of the question.

"Nowhere else to go," he mumbled. The accuracy of

his statement echoed in his mind. Nowhere to go, nowhere to be. No one who cared. Least of all him.

"Would you like to go somewhere else, James? With me?" Her words seemed to come from a distance, and with a frantic suddenness, he needed to get out. Out from the tavern walls that were pressing down on him, away from the smells of grease and bodies and smoke and alcohol that were suffocating.

"Yes." He shoved away from the table, swaying on his feet. In an instant she was there, at his side, her arm tucked into his elbow as though he really were a duke escorting her across the ballroom of a royal palace. He could feel the warmth of her body as it pressed against his and the cool silk of her hair as it slid across his bicep. Again he wished desperately he weren't so drunk. His body was dragging him in one direction while his mind flailed helplessly against the haze.

"Come," she whispered, guiding him out into the cool night breeze.

He went willingly with his beautiful vision into the darkness, dragging in huge lungfuls of air in an attempt to clear his head. He pressed a hand against his temple.

"Are you unwell?" She was still right beside him, and he was horrified to realize he was leaning on her as he might a crutch. He straightened abruptly.

"No." He concentrated hard on his next words. "I don't even know your name."

She stared at him a long moment as if debating something within her mind. "Gisele," she finally said.

He was regretting those last pots of ale. Thinking was becoming almost impossible. "And why were *you* drinkin' alone, Gisele?" he asked slowly.

The sparkle dimmed abruptly in her face, and she turned away. "Will you take me away from here, James?" she asked.

"I beg your pardon?" His mind was struggling to keep up with his ears.

She turned back. "Take me somewhere. Anywhere. Just not here."

"I don't understand." Blade-sharp instincts long suppressed fought to make themselves heard through the fog in his brain. Something was all wrong with this situation, though he was damned if he could determine what it might be. "I can't just—"

Jamie was suddenly knocked back, tripping over his feet and falling gracelessly, unable to overcome gravity and the last three pots of ale. Gisele was yanked from his side, and she gave a slight yelp as a man slammed her back up against the tavern wall.

"Where the hell have you been, whore?" the man snarled. "Like a damn bitch in heat, aren't you?"

Jamie struggled to his feet, fighting the dizziness that was making his surroundings swim. He reached for the weapon at his side before realizing he couldn't recall where he'd left it. He turned just in time to see the man pull back his arm to slug Gisele. With a roar of rage, Jamie launched himself at her attacker, hitting him square in the back. The man was barely half his size, and the force of Jamie's weight knocked both men into the mud. A fist caught the side of his head in a series of short, sharp jabs, only increasing the din resonating through his brain. Jamie tried to stagger to his feet again, but the ground shifted underneath him and he fell heavily on his side.

"Don't touch her," he managed, wrestling with the

darkness crowding the edge of his vision. Usually he welcomed this part of the night, when reality ceased to exist. But not now. This couldn't happen now. He had to fight it. Fight for her. Fight for something again. He pushed himself up on his hands and knees. He looked up at the figures looming over him. Strangely, Gisele and her attacker were standing side by side as if nothing had happened. The buzzing was getting louder as Gisele crouched down beside him, and he felt her cool hand on his forehead.

"So sorry," he mumbled, his arms collapsing beneath him. "I couldn't do—"

"You did just fine, James," she said. And then he heard no more.

Chapter 2

Gisele shifted in her chair, tapping the floor gently with her toe. James Montcrief still lay sprawled across the bed, mouth open slightly, his breathing deep and steady. Sebastien had been right. James had indeed surprised her. Her experience with nobility—or those who had been raised as such—had taught her to expect little from men of Mr. Montcrief's stock. But his actions last night had left her with a newfound sense of hope.

She wondered what had made him leap to her defense the previous evening. Perhaps he had a sister he adored. Or some other woman he either respected or was fond of. Somewhere in the journey of his life, he had come to the determination that a man should not be allowed to beat a woman senseless. Even a woman dressed and acting as she had been, a lowborn peasant or worse.

Regardless, Gisele didn't much care how he had come to posses the moral fortitude he had shown in the tavern yard, only that it existed.

She had no sooner finished her thought than the door of the inn's room creaked open and Sebastien sauntered in, taking in the still-snoring heap on the bed.

"Dear God, it smells like a distillery in here." He sniffed

as he approached the bed, bending over in critical examination. "He'll need to be cleaned up and—*erk*!"

A hand had shot out from beneath the cover and grabbed Sebastien by the front of his shirt.

"Who the hell are you?" The voice sounded like gravel.

Sebastien glowered. "*Tsk*. Manners. Language. Perhaps I erred in—"

"Let him go, Mr. Montcrief." Gisele rose from her chair and came to stand near the foot of the bed, leaning casually against the wall.

The hand faltered enough for Sebastien to jerk himself free, fussing over the new and offending wrinkles in his linen. "Barbarian," he muttered, smoothing both his clothes and his hair.

A pair of gritty brown eyes focused on Gisele in confusion, probably wondering how she knew his name. She could see him searching his leaky memory in despair.

"Gisele," she offered. She wasn't in the mood to play games. She had business to discuss, and time was of the essence. "You tried to rescue me last night."

"Um…" He was flailing. "I was…"

"Drunk," she supplied.

"Er…right." He struggled to sit up, and the sheet fell to his waist. Suddenly aware of his nakedness, he yanked the edge of the sheet back up. "Where are my clothes?" he demanded.

"In the hearth." She crossed her arms, watching as his eyes flew to the far wall.

"There's a fire in the hearth," he said dumbly.

"Thank God for small miracles."

"I'm naked!" His tone was one of total disbelief. His eyes widened as he turned back to Gisele. "Who—when—did we…"

"I think he's blushing," Sebastien stage-whispered nastily, still miffed at having been assaulted.

"Oh, God." James dropped his head into his hands. "I don't remember."

Gisele pushed herself off the wall and sat down on the edge of the bed, careful not to allow her eyes to drop too far down. Even though she had seen it all last night when they had stripped him of his foul garments, it had been rather dim, and in the light of morning, the man's broad expanse of muscle was an unwelcome distraction.

"We were not intimate, if that is what you are asking," she said, deciding to put him out of his misery. "Believe me, if we had been, you'd remember." She couldn't resist the last comment. No man should ever lose that much control to drink.

His head snapped up, and his jaw dropped open.

"Now he is blushing," Sebastien sniffed. "Perhaps you should try him out?"

Gisele shot her friend a black look, though she suspected Sebastien was provoking James on purpose.

"What?" Sebastien groused. "There's no call to look at me like that, Gisele. You don't buy a horse without taking him for a bit of a gallop first, do you? Though by the looks of Mr. Montcrief this morning, I'm not sure he'd manage much more than a slow trot." When Sebastien's crude joke was met with utter silence, he raised his voice and continued. "Iain would encourage you to do the same, I assure you—"

"Stop," Gisele interrupted her friend before he could go any further. Goading Montcrief was one thing. But she had no intention of discussing Iain in front of him, nor did she think it wise to bait a muscle-bound behemoth with innuendo. She could tell by the man's rising color that his confusion was rapidly giving way to anger.

"Yes, do stop," James ordered from the bed, flinging the sheet away from him in sudden fury. "I don't know who the hell you are or what the hell you want, but if you wish to rob me, go ahead. For the only things I own you just burned in the fire. If you wish to ransom me, you'll be dead of old age before anyone comes looking." He turned flashing eyes on Gisele. "And you. If you want to try me out, I'll have you every way you can think of and some you can't." He staggered to his feet and drew himself up to his full height, pinning Gisele motionless with his eyes. "Though I don't like an audience. And I won't share."

⁓

Jamie stood with a heaving chest, roiling stomach, pounding head, and a throbbing erection to top it all off. He tried to stare the ice queen called Gisele down, but she seemed utterly unfazed by his outburst.

Perhaps he was still drunk. Perhaps this was a terrible hallucination and soon he would wake up and the world would make sense again. Bits and pieces of last night were starting to come back to him in measured doses.

She had said kind words to him, he thought. Before she took him outside. Before she was attacked. His eyes flew to the man standing on the far side of the room.

"You," he ground out. "You hit her." Another wave of anger surged through him, and he welcomed it as an emotion not felt in a very long time. In fact, emotion of any sort seemed to have become somewhat alien to him.

"I did no such thing," the man sniffed. "She'd beat me bloody if I tried."

Jamie eyed the man suspiciously. He was older, short and slight and, in truth, did not look capable of swatting a fly, much less a woman. Was he this woman's husband? Her lover? Brother? Did it matter? The pounding in Jamie's head increased, and he abandoned his useless speculation.

"Why would you care if he hit me?" The question was deceptively quiet.

He turned back to Gisele and faltered. Her eyes bored directly into his and robbed him of breath. Flustered, he grabbed the abandoned sheet and wrapped it around his waist. His attempt at bluster and bravado had failed, so he opted to sound the retreat and try to salvage the tiny shreds of dignity still remaining.

"It's not honorable."

She frowned. "Even if I were his wife? His property?"

Jamie barked out what might have passed as a laugh. "Forgive me, madam, but you don't seem the type to be anyone's property."

Her lips pressed into a wan smile that didn't reach her eyes. "Why did you stop him?"

He shrugged carelessly. "If a man wants to fight, he should damn well do it against a worthy opponent."

He watched her expression shift.

"Not that you wouldn't be worthy," he added hastily, realizing his last comment hadn't come out quite right. "I'm sure you're plenty worthy. Brave. For a woman, that is." *Stop talking, Jamie.* "You look strong, I mean. But not too strong. Not man-strong. You're still very pretty, of course." He clamped his mouth shut and wished desperately for another drink. "No one should be treated as such."

"Even if I were just a streetwalker? Not even a wife?"

A new fury flooded Jamie's chest. "I've seen a woman of little means crawl out onto a battlefield with nothing but her courage and a handful of shredded skirts to save the life of an officer who lay dying under his horse—and all the while soldiers with titles and fortunes and weapons pretended not to notice. You can't measure a person's worth based on a label society has assigned." He clenched his fists at his side, struggling for control.

A long moment passed, Gisele's eyes not leaving his face. Finally she glanced over at the dark-haired man and gave an imperceptible nod.

"I'll see to the details of our departure." Her companion strode across the room and vanished through the doorway, leaving Jamie alone with Gisele.

"I need you to work for me," she said the moment the slight gentleman had disappeared.

"I beg your pardon?" Jamie was startled out of the remnants of his hostility.

"You heard me."

He pulled the sheet a little tighter around him. "I don't think that would be a good idea."

"You have another offer of employment?" she asked.

Jamie frowned. Of course he didn't have another offer. He had nothing. No job, no family, no woman, no money, no weapons, no hope. And no clothes. He was a broke, unemployed, naked cavalry officer without even a horse to his name.

"You'll have a horse."

Jamie's head snapped up.

"I heard yours was lost at Waterloo. Given your current state of . . . er, affairs, I will assume it has yet to be replaced."

Jamie opened his mouth to reply and then reconsidered.

"I can offer you immediate employment. Fair pay, regular meals, decent lodging, and replacement weapons if you wish. And, of course, something to wear other than a bedsheet."

He thought she might be laughing at him. "Is this a joke?" he demanded, feeling foolish.

Her beautiful face was grim. "I can assure you, this is not a joke."

"I'll take your offer under consideration." He wasn't sure what else to say.

Gisele leaned back against the bedpost but remained maddeningly silent.

"Who the hell was the man who just left?"

The woman inclined her head. "Fair enough. That's Sebastien. A friend."

"Then why did he try to hit you last night?"

"To see how you would react."

Jamie frowned.

"Relax, Mr. Montcrief. I have my answer on that score already." Gisele tilted her head. "May I assume you've been tutored? Sebastien said you're the son of a duke."

"Wha—tutored?" He'd never been so damned confused in his entire life.

"Greek, Latin, history, politics, arithmetic, what fork to use, the steps to a waltz?" she prompted.

"Yes." And how the hell did she know his father was a duke?

"Excellent. That will save us some time."

"And you?" he demanded. "Have you been tutored?" Belligerence was always a good substitute for bewilderment.

She looked at him thoughtfully. "I have, actually. You're the first to ask me that."

It suddenly dawned on Jamie that her speech in no way matched her clothes. While she wore the simple dress of a peasant, her deportment suggested a woman to the manor born. "Who's Iain?"

Gisele had the grace to look startled before her expression softened. "A . . . friend also."

Jamie fought what felt suspiciously like jealousy. "A friend you took for a wee gallop from time to time? Or was it a slow trot?" He wanted the words back the moment they were out. Where had his control gone?

Gisele's beautiful eyes narrowed before she smirked. "It was *never* a trot."

Well, shit. He deserved that. "Who *are* you?"

She smiled at him, the first genuine smile he had seen, and it did strange things to his chest.

"I am . . . just Gisele."

That was helpful. He knew nothing more about her than he'd known last night. Annoyance bubbled up again. "Very well then, Just-Gisele, since you won't tell me anything useful about yourself, would you be so kind as to enlighten me as to what it is you'd like me to do should I accept your generous offer of employment?"

Her smile turned brittle. "Not yet."

"Not yet?" Jamie's eyebrows shot up to his hairline. "How the hell am I supposed to make a decision based on *not yet*?"

The ice queen shrugged. "You'll have to trust me."

Jamie closed his eyes, fighting for patience. "Will I need to steal something?"

"Unlikely."

"Kill someone?"

"Hopefully not."

"Blow something up?"

"You're familiar with explosives?"

His eyes popped open at the undisguised interest in her last question. What the hell kind of woman used the word *explosives* the way most used the word *marmalade*? Or *teapot*?

"Yes?" He was afraid of his answer. Truth be told, he was a little afraid of her at the moment.

"Yes?" she demanded, leaning forward intently. "As in yes, when I'm sober I can make big things go bang at my discretion? Or *yes*, I forgot my powder flask too close to the hearth when I was foxed last night and now the tavern is short a stool and a good cooking pot?"

Jamie knew there was an implied insult in there somewhere, but he couldn't stop the ghost of a smile that touched his lips. "The former. Only once the latter, though it was a bench and a good roast."

Gisele grinned at him, and his world tilted. "Unfortunate."

"Took me two days to get the splinters out of my arse."

An elegant eyebrow arched, followed by an inelegant snort. "Also unfortunate. But it does explain the slightly imperfect condition of your backside."

Jamie willed himself not to squirm at the thought of this woman examining him last night while he was insensible. He cleared his throat loudly. "You haven't answered my question."

"Which was?"

"If I'd need to blow something up."

Gisele tucked an errant strand of fair hair behind her ear and sighed. "I'm not entirely sure."

Jamie threw up his hands in frustration before snatching at the sheet as it started to slide from his nether regions. "Let me see if I understand. You spied on me, set me up, stole my clothes, offered me a job in which I may or may not need to kill someone, steal something, or blow something up. Have I missed anything?"

"Please."

"Please?" He wasn't following.

"My manners have been remiss." He watched in fascination as a glimmer of what looked like fear or possibly despair shadowed her features for the barest of seconds and was replaced by determination so quickly he wondered if he had imagined it. "I—we—need your help. Please." She met his gaze without wavering.

Jamie knew there was likely nothing good behind the door this mesmerizing woman held open for him. He should say no, the promise of money and clothing and food and—dear God—a horse be damned. He should swallow his pride and walk away with his bedsheet and his sanity intact, and he could do that with a simple no.

"Yes."

"You give me your word?"

"Yes." Truly, what did he have to lose? Absolutely, positively nothing. Literally and otherwise.

"Thank you." It was barely audible, but he heard the sincerity behind her words. "But if you work for me, this cannot occur again."

"This?" The bewilderment was back.

"This." She gestured at him and his bedsheet. "You cannot drink yourself to the point of oblivion. To the point where you no longer have control of your actions or your memory. Ever."

Jamie looked away for a moment, something that felt suspiciously like shame snaking up through his conscience. "You're not my keeper," he muttered.

"No," she agreed in a gentle voice he didn't deserve. "I am your employer. And I am making a simple request. Can you accommodate me?"

"Yes," he said tightly.

"Thank you." She was silent for a long moment, and he could feel the weight of her stare as she considered him.

"Why me?" he demanded. "You could have chosen a different man. Why am I here?" He was fairly certain he wasn't going to like her answer, but he suddenly needed to know.

"Because you saved me last night. Few other men of your class would defend a woman they believe is…not a lady."

"I can't imagine you have ever needed to be saved," he mumbled.

"You are wrong," she said quietly. "And you're also wrong if you think this is about me. It's not." She stood, smoothing her worn skirts, gazing down at her hands and looking, for the first time, rather vulnerable. In a fluid motion, she suddenly tossed a guinea at him.

He caught it awkwardly. "What's this?"

"It's called money. People use it to pay for things." She smiled again, and this one reached her eyes.

"What's it for?" Jamie held on to his patience.

"Sebastien will be up shortly to see that you have the necessities and to assist you with whatever you require. If you are not here when he returns, I will understand. The coin is for your trouble and to ensure you will not have to spend the rest of the day naked."

"You should know that I honor my promises," Jamie said, not sure if he should be irate or impressed.

Gisele shrugged. "I would like to think so, Mr. Montcrief. But at the moment, I can't say I really know you at all."

~

The man she called Sebastien did not make an appearance until after the heavy wooden tub had been emptied and dragged from the room. Jamie stood by the dwindling fire, his skin raw from scrubbing. He shivered as his hair dripped cold rivulets of water down his back.

"I hope these fit." Sebastien strode into the room, his arms laden with a pile of clothing. He dropped them onto the end of the bed and assessed Jamie critically. "Had you not felt the need to choke me earlier, I would have had a better idea of your size."

"Had you not felt the need to abduct me last night, I might have been more courteous upon waking."

"Abduct?" The man's brows rose fractionally. "Fancy word for dragging a man insensible from drink off the streets and putting him to bed."

Jamie winced. Well, hell. The man had a point. "My apologies."

Sebastien's lips twitched. "Likewise."

Jamie nodded warily. "Now what?"

Sebastien considered him. "I would suggest a shave."

"Why?"

"Because you look like a man who's been stranded on an uninhabited island for a year."

"I have." The words slipped out before he realized their import. That was the perfect description of his life.

Trapped alone on an island in a vacuum of nothingness. Dear God, when had he become so maudlin? *Probably when you sobered up*, a little voice intoned.

"I see."

Jamie made a bitter sound in his throat. "I doubt you do."

This time it was Sebastien who made the same noise. "You'd be surprised." He paused. "However, on my island, razors and self-respect have been invented. Let me extend the courtesy."

Jamie smiled despite himself. "You can leave it there." He gestured at the table.

Sebastien looked at him in horror. "I think not."

This time he laughed at the man's sincere dismay. "You have so little confidence in my ability to groom myself?"

Sebastien's eyes traveled the length of him, and a dark brow rose pointedly. "I'm sure you're quite capable," he managed diplomatically with answering amusement. "But I insist." He dragged the chair over to the fire. "Sit."

Jamie remained standing as he watched the man rummage through a leather bag and extract a small shaving kit, laying the contents out on the table with a precision that suggested he'd done this countless times. "Am I to trust you with a blade at my throat then?"

Sebastien rolled his eyes. "If I had wanted to kill you, Mr. Montcrief, I wouldn't have bothered to tuck you into bed so nicely last night. Do you have any idea how difficult it was to drag your rather substantial carcass up those stairs? Besides," he added, pulling out a pair of barbering scissors and running his fingers along the edges of the blades, "Gisele already paid for your clothes, and they sure as hell won't fit me. Or her."

Jamie listened to Sebastien strop the razor. "What is Gisele to you?"

The rhythmic sound stopped before resuming. "A friend," came the careful reply. "What did she tell you?"

"Absolutely nothing."

"Yet you agreed to help us. Why?" The sharp smell of soap drifted across the room.

"I don't know."

"Because she's beautiful?"

"No. Well, that might have been a part of it." Jamie grimaced. "She's the first person in a long time who has put faith in me. And she did say please."

"At least you're honest." There was a clatter as Sebastien pushed the small table closer to Jamie. "Now, continuing to look like a beggar will not help anyone, Mr. Montcrief. Sit." Sebastien rolled his eyes again. "*Please.*"

For lack of any other options, Jamie sat.

"Shall we begin?"

Chapter 3 _____

Adam Levire, the Marquess of Valence, was drunk. Normally he did not enjoy the loss of control that accompanied insobriety, but tonight he required a brief escape. He sat alone in his study, fingering the fine crystal and drinking his hideously expensive brandy the way one might gulp cheap ale. The liquor, however, had thus far failed to dull his mounting grief and rage. Four years, and he still felt cheated. Four years and he had yet to get over the loss of his beloved wife.

Gisele had been perfect. He had known the moment he saw her in that dowdy dress at that dowdy country house, surrounded by crude and clumsy country boys. Gisele's father had paraded the exquisite girl about the room as though she were a prize filly at auction. The man's greed for a lofty match was palpable, and during this vulgar display of her own flesh, Gisele was as silent as good manners would permit. But Adam could tell by the set of her chin that every fiber of her being rebelled against the life her father was selling her into. She was a diamond in the rough who, with the help of the right man, could be polished to a brilliant shine.

Adam was already married by then, of course, to a

widow he'd selected for her impeccable breeding and impressive wealth. Luckily, his first wife had been easily dispatched, and the effort had been well worth it. Gisele had become the toast of the ton, the most desirable woman in London, and she had belonged to him.

As it turned out, she'd also had more fire and strength than he'd anticipated, and it had taken him longer than expected to bring her to heel. Adam had needed every ounce of his cunning to shatter the girl's stoic resistance and ferret out her weakness. How ironic that the one chink in Gisele's armor had been his own stepdaughter, Helena. Adam had originally intended to consign the brat to the same fate as her mother, but Helena had been fourteen at the time of her mother's passing, and by then she had shown the promise of considerable beauty.

And there was always value in keeping beautiful things.

Very quickly Helena became the means through which Adam mastered Gisele. He delighted in watching his flawless blond warrior bend to his will just the way a good wife should. Everything in his life was perfect. Until the explosion on the river took not only his treasured wife and sniveling stepdaughter, but a fortune too. And now his financial survival demanded that he replace it.

Adam hurled his glass at the fire, the splintering crystal doing nothing to soothe his nerves. To avoid penury, he had elected to court and fawn over Lady Julia Hextall, whose fair coloring was like a taunt from the grave. The chit was meek and timid and intolerable in all aspects except for the staggering fortune she possessed and her faint resemblance to his lost bride.

Lady Julia's father, like Gisele's, was predictably

thrilled by the prospect of having a marchioness in the family. The vulgar man had only recently inherited his title from a third cousin and was still shaking off the foul dust of his former life in trade. But at least he grasped the value of Adam's venerable name. The girl's brother, on the other hand, was considerably less impressed. No matter. Adam would simply ignore the boy's feeble protests. For now.

This was all Gisele's fault, really. Adam reached into his desk drawer and drew out a miniature portrait, caressing the gilt frame. He ran the pad of his thumb over the surface of Gisele's perfect face, frozen forever.

"Bitch!" he hissed at the painting, then clutched it to his chest, his anguish more acute than ever.

The sad truth was that her death had ruined everything. The fortune in diamonds Gisele had been wearing the night she died was gone forever. And the rest of his money troubles could be traced back to her too. After the accident, Adam's grief had been so consuming that he had lost all interest in the management of his estate and relied on others to see to his investments. He regretted it now, but it was too late. The damage was done.

Moreover, Adam's sudden poverty accounted for but a fraction of his despair. In his private life, he could find absolutely nothing that held his interest. Nothing gave him any joy or pleasure. Not a horse, not a card game, not a woman. Certainly not a woman. He'd brought plenty of them to his bed in the last four years, but rarely could he bring himself to perform. Even using his preferred methods of arousal, he was often left unsatisfied. No one could do for him what Gisele had done.

Adam tried to comfort himself with the thought of

the wealth he would have before the season was out. No amount of money could replace what he had lost, of course, but he prayed that perhaps, in the darkest hour of the night, given enough drink or laudanum to blur his vision, he might mistake Lady Julia for Gisele. His Gisele. And that finally he would be able to reclaim the pleasure he had been denied for so long.

Chapter 4————————————

Not two days in and Gisele already regretted choosing James Montcrief for the job.

She wanted to blame Iain—her former partner—for creating the vacancy in the first place. She would never have needed Montcrief at all if Iain, bless his love-besotted heart, hadn't abandoned their cause in favor of taking a wife. He was undoubtedly married by now, holed up in a tiny Scottish hamlet somewhere in front of a roaring fire, wrapped in warm blankets and his pretty bride. In fairness, none of them had known the Marquess of Valence was courting again until well after Iain's departure for Gretna Green. But Gisele would have suggested—no, insisted—that Iain head north with his love even if they'd been aware of Valence's betrothal at the time. She was thrilled for her newlywed friends, and she wished the couple every happiness.

Which meant she would lay the blame for the entire Montcrief debacle at Sebastien's feet instead.

At the end of her conversation with a sheet-clad James yesterday morning, Gisele had been convinced she had the situation well in hand. He'd accepted her terms of employment with little delay. He was impressive physically, and she had been certain his natural intelligence would right itself as soon as every last ounce of alcohol had been flushed from his brain. In short, Gisele judged James Montcrief as more than capable of seeing his contract through. The man was exactly who and what she required, no more and no less.

So there had been simply no cause for Sebastien to transform James Montcrief into ... *that*.

Even after a day and a half, Gisele was still trying to relate the bearded, bleary-eyed, ale-sodden creature she had hired to the Greek god now keeping pace beside her. Sebastien's ministrations had uncovered a gentleman possessed of both refined elegance and raw masculine magnetism—and she found the whole package too unsettling for words.

Things had been much simpler when Montcrief was filthy and drunk.

His hair, she had learned, wasn't brown, as she had first thought. Today it was more of a burnished gold, and it fell in thick, cleverly styled waves over his forehead. Without his beard he had a wide, pleasing face, with eyes the color of fine whiskey and lashes that any woman would gladly barter her soul to keep. On another man they might have looked feminine. But other men didn't have James's strong jaw. Or the strong shoulders and broad chest. Or the powerful legs. Or the strong forearms—she cut herself off with an inward curse. The man simply radiated strength through every pore. Even his damn horse looked stronger when he rode it.

A cavalry *captain*, the boys in the Nottingham stable had told her with wide, worshipful eyes as she had paced, watching James select a mount with the care of a jeweler examining fine stones. Gisele had always considered herself a fair horsewoman. But the man riding beside her made her feel like the greenest girl poking along on her pony. He rode as if he were part of the bloody beast, and he didn't even seem to be trying. Maybe it was his seat. The way he sat his horse was effortless, his long legs relaxed and balanced. Those same legs were sheathed in riding breeches that left absolutely nothing to the imagination, and Gisele was finding it difficult not to continuously admire the way they hugged his thighs and his hips. Which was asinine, considering she had already seen him naked. One would think that would have been sufficient. But even now she couldn't resist tilting her head, resenting the coat of superfine she knew hid a truly magnificent backside.

"Is there something wrong?" James glanced down at the back of his saddle.

"I beg your pardon?" She jerked upright.

"You're staring."

"I was admiring your horse."

"Oh." He patted his horse's rump. "Thank you."

Gisele averted her gaze from those capable-looking hands, then caught Sebastien's silent amusement as he rode companionably behind them. She scowled at him and returned her attention to her own mount.

"I was lucky. Not so many good ones left. War took too many." James's voice sounded distant, and Gisele wondered if he was referring to horses or men.

"Yes," Gisele agreed to both.

"The horse was expensive." James turned toward her, and her insides traitorously converted to molten liquid under that smoky gaze.

Good God, but this had to stop. She could not afford the distraction. She had given up that part of her life years ago and had never regretted it once. Yet now she couldn't go two minutes without wondering if this man kissed as well as he rode.

"Don't trouble yourself overmuch, Mr. Montcrief. You'll earn it." Gisele returned her attention to the road ahead, despising the way her heart was hammering.

"I would expect no less." James lapsed back into silence. "You're a very good valet," he said to Sebastien presently. "You must be missed."

Gisele turned in her saddle and shot her friend a warning look.

"You certainly weren't a footman before you did, well, whatever it is you do now," James continued on blithely.

Sebastien looked insulted. "No, I most certainly was not."

"Even my father would have been impressed, which is no small compliment. What made you leave your calling?"

Gisele decided to put an end to the fishing expedition before it went too far. While James's tone held a teasing quality, she had no doubt he was probing for real answers. Answers she wasn't ready to provide just yet.

"Since we're on the subject," she interrupted loudly, "why don't you tell us about your father, Mr. Montcrief?"

He gave her a long look, and she knew she hadn't fooled him.

"Your father, Mr. Montcrief?" she prompted again.

He shrugged, clearly yielding, then frowned. "Jamie."

"I'm sorry?"

"Jamie. Please call me Jamie. James was my grandfather's Christian name, and he was a miserable old cur.

No one could stand him. And *Mr. Montcrief* seems utterly absurd given our rather, ah, unique introduction."

Gisele balked. "I don't think such familiarity is appropriate." She didn't relish the idea of calling this man Jamie. It sounded much too intimate.

"And this from a woman who calls herself Just-Gisele?"

"Very well. I suppose you have a point," she capitulated. But she would not be diverted. "I will call you Jamie. If, in return, you tell me about your family."

"Why is it important?" Jamie gave her a suspicious look.

Because I need to know exactly who I'm dealing with. Because I need to know how much you know about London society. Because the life of a young girl might rest on your shoulders, and I need to know how strong they really are.

She shrugged carelessly instead. "It's not. If you would prefer to ride in silence, please, just say the word. I simply thought polite, pleasant conversation would be an agreeable way to pass the time."

Jamie gave her another long look. "My father's dead, you know, so if you're hoping to get to him through me, you're about five years too late."

Gisele made no effort to hide her irritation at Jamie's response. "Suit yourself."

A pregnant silence followed, punctuated only by the sound of hooves thudding on the packed road, and the creak of leather.

"I'm a bastard as well, in case that didn't come up while you were spying on me," Jamie said to no one in particular. "So I stand to inherit naught. No titles, no land, no wealth, no estates. I wasn't lying to you earlier when I said I own nothing."

Gisele slanted him a sideways glance. "Yes, I got that.

If you recall, it was I who paid for your clothes and your boots and your horse and your breakfast." She was gratified to see his jaw clench. "And for the record, I'm uninterested in the lurid details of your conception. All I wish to know is why a man so obviously raised in privilege found himself here. But if you prefer not to talk about it, we can certainly discuss something else. Politics, perhaps? Or religion? How you got the scar on the inside of your left thigh?"

Sebastien guffawed, and Jamie scowled anew.

"Fine," he snapped. "My father was Edward Montcrief, Duke of Reddyck. He had a handful of other titles, most of which are unimportant. He was a good father."

"He saw to it you had an education."

Jamie nodded. "And he bought me my commission."

"Very generous of him."

Jamie nodded again.

"Do you still own it?"

She wasn't sure if Jamie had heard her; he was silent for so long.

She tried again. "Are you still a captain—"

"No. I sold my commission after Waterloo."

A pang of disappointment assailed her. A cavalry captaincy was worth a great deal of money, Gisele knew. He had evidently divested himself of a small fortune in a very short time. *Where did all that money go?* she wondered silently. Given Jamie's condition at the tavern, she supposed the answer was obvious. For some inexplicable reason, the thought of the waste was depressing. She would have liked to believe he was better than that.

"And your siblings? I am assuming there is a new Duke of Reddyck? Do you see him?" Gisele asked.

Jamie's expression froze. "I am as dead to him as my father is. My brother wishes the French had done what he will never have the guts to do himself."

Interesting. She hadn't expected that. Gisele chose her words carefully. "And how would your death benefit your brother?"

Jamie's lips tightened, and he shook his head, clearly having reached the limits of what he was willing to share on that front.

"Have you spent much time in London?" she asked with an air of nonchalance, though, for her purposes, the question was far from casual.

Jamie turned to face her. "London?" He laughed bitterly. "I've spent the last ten years of my life as an officer of the King's Dragoon Guards. I've been too busy stuffing entrails back into the bodies of fallen Englishmen to attend very many London tea parties." He stopped abruptly. "I'm sorry. That was uncalled for."

Gisele shrugged, keeping her face carefully blank. "Do not apologize on my account."

Jamie shifted his reins to his other hand. "The last time I was in London, I—" He stopped again, and Gisele watched a fleeting shadow of pain tighten his face. Then it was gone. "The last time I was in London I was sixteen years old," he said with an obvious effort at civility. "My father took my brothers and me to buy horses." He cleared his throat.

Gisele considered him, wondering what he had been going to say before he had changed his mind and lied.

"And yourself? When was the last time you were in London?" He returned her question.

A shudder coursed through Gisele, catching her unprepared. A vile mixture of bitterness and pain engulfed her, making it hard to breathe for one horrific moment. She bit her lip, furious at herself and her lack of control over emotions she thought she had long ago bested. "Four years," she gritted out. "The last time I was in London was four years ago." And she had been certain then she would never go back.

"Is that where we are going?" Jamie asked, gesturing ahead of them. "We're on the right road for it, anyway."

"Yes," Gisele managed grimly. "We are going to London." She took a deep breath in an effort to regain her composure. "Though we have a stop to make along the way."

⁓

The woman had gone white as a sheet. It would seem that angry, naked men did little to discomfit his new employer, but the merest mention of London had almost been her undoing. It was the first time he had noticed any sort of crack in the ice queen's polished veneer. It had also served as a reminder that he still had no notion of Gisele's true objectives, and the danger of throwing himself behind an unknown cause suddenly hit him with the force of a runaway carriage. He'd completely lost his edge. He'd allowed himself to be lulled into complacency by a good horse, a good haircut, and a fetching woman who had professed her faith in him. The notion of that faith had been intoxicating and humbling and he had embraced it with recklessness.

Or maybe that was the idea.

Perhaps he had just become the victim of a shrewd and cunning woman who had sensed his vulnerabilities and exploited them with the deftness of a puppet master. She had, after all, spied on him and set him up. And aside from admitting she had intentionally duped him in that tavern yard, Gisele had divulged nothing else about herself.

He had no idea who this woman and her companion really were. They could be thieves or spies. Or worse.

He made a quick mental tally of what he did know. Sebastien, he suspected, had been a valet. He was witty and clever and capable of extraordinary things with a straight razor and a pair of scissors. He was clearly a trusted friend to Gisele—Jamie had watched them communicate without words many times.

And as for Gisele, if that was even her real name, he knew nothing. *Nada. Rien.* She was titled, or she had been at one time. He was sure of it. Two days of watching her manners and her comportment, and even the way she handled her bloody horse, had convinced him. All of it was too natural to be feigned, and he would know. Aye, he didn't have the title, but he had suffered through the same lessons thanks to his father. No matter her present dress and appearance, she was not the peasant she pretended to be.

They were still a good ways out from London, so for now Jamie was content to watch and wait. Gisele clearly had some sort of agenda in Leicester, and perhaps whatever he found there would provide him with the answers she seemed so reluctant to provide.

⌒

They skirted Leicester, diverging from the main road that would have taken them into the heart of the town and angling slightly east. Sebastien left them then, dropping back from the pair and out of sight. Gisele waited for the expected questions from Jamie, but none came, though she was aware of his gaze on her, heavy and deliberate. The brooding silence was almost worse than a barrage of questions might have been.

He didn't speak until they had stopped just in front of another tavern, not so different from the one they had left behind outside of Nottingham.

"Where did Sebastien go?"

"He'll meet us later," she told him.

"Are we staying here for the night?" he asked dubiously, eyeing the sagging thatch and the tilting walls.

"No," Gisele answered. "We're not." She dismounted and glanced around cautiously at the yard and its lengthening shadows. There was no one about, but she knew it would be busy with thirsty men once the sun retired.

"Are we eating here?"

"No."

"Then what are we doing?" Jamie slid effortlessly from his own horse, his boots creating twin puffs of dust. He crossed his arms over his chest. "And I want a real answer this time."

Gisele imagined he had cowed men twice his size under his command with that tone. Pity it wouldn't work on her.

"Polly Tuck," she said after a second's hesitation.

"Who?"

"Polly Tuck. Eighteen years old. Lives just over the ridge of oaks we passed on our way here, in a rather isolated cottage. Married for sixteen months to Garrett Tuck, a middling carpenter on the days he's sober. Polly's parents are both deceased, though she has a widowed sister who still lives nearby with her three small children."

"And who is she to you? A friend? Relative?"

Gisele shook her head slowly. "I've never met her."

"I'm not in the mood for guessing games, Gisele. Why are we here?"

She sighed. "Polly's husband has an unfortunate tendency to take out his frustrations at his own shortcomings on his young wife. Usually he uses his fists. Occasionally a rake or a shovel. Once, I am told, it was a chain."

Jamie blinked. "Jesus." His brows drew together. "Can't she leave? Is there nowhere she can go?"

"This is where it becomes difficult. Last fall Polly fled to her sister's. Mr. Tuck hunted his errant wife down, threatened to kill her sister and her children and burn down her home if his wife did not return with him. Polly, of course, returned with him to spare the only family she has left. Polly was beaten beyond recognition for her defiance, though she survived. The baby she had been carrying was not so fortunate."

Jamie exhaled loudly. "The man should be shot."

"Yes." Gisele shrugged wearily. "Though not everyone would agree with you."

"Did you hire me to kill Tuck?"

Gisele slanted him a look. "No. I believe I was clear when I said it was unlikely you'd have to kill anyone. As much as some circumstances warrant it, I am not a murderer. And, I think, neither are you."

Jamie looked away from her, his expression suddenly stony.

"Polly is pregnant again," Gisele continued. "And her desire to protect herself and her unborn child has finally overcome her fear of her husband." She paused. "That is why we are here."

"To do what, exactly?" He turned to face her again.

"To make Polly Tuck disappear." Gisele watched as understanding dawned in Jamie's eyes.

"You've done this before. You and Sebastien. Made women like Polly disappear."

Gisele's gaze had fixed somewhere over his shoulder, and she willed her mind not to slide down into the past where her own dark, tangled memories churned and seethed. "Yes. We create a new identity, a new home, and a new life for the woman and her children, if she has any. England is full of widows, especially in the last few years, and an unknown one arriving in a new town is hardly worth comment."

He watched her, clearly considering her words. "And this is what you hired me for? To help you save this woman?"

"For now, yes."

He was quiet for another long moment, and Gisele wondered if he would press her further. And what she would tell him if he did.

"Very well," he said finally. "Tell me what it is that you need me to do."

Gisele released a breath she hadn't realized she'd been holding. "Nothing you'd likely wish to share with a magistrate," she warned.

"Are you trying to scare me?"

"Maybe." She was serious.

Jamie snorted. "Does it involve explosives?" He gave her a crooked grin.

Gisele pressed her lips together, daring, for a second, to believe that Jamie Montcrief was the man she needed him to be. "Not this time," she replied, meeting his gaze.

"I gave you my word," he said, suddenly grave. "And I'll keep it."

"Saints be praised." A coarse voice interrupted whatever Gisele would have said next. "You're right on time. Good thing or I'd have to kill the bastard myself."

Gisele turned to find a wide woman bearing down on them, her red hair tied in a messy braid and her apron stained with ale and grease.

"Hello, Martha." Gisele greeted the woman warmly before she schooled her expression. "And no one is going to murder anyone. We've discussed this." She paused. "Polly hasn't changed her mind, I trust?"

The tavern keeper's flushed face creased. "She's as scared as all hell, but she's more scared of what will happen if she stays. She wants this child to live."

"Good." That was the most important part.

Martha's eyes flickered past Gisele to Jamie. "Where's Iain?"

"Unavailable." She didn't want to get into a long explanation that would require her to detail Iain's departure and the method of Jamie's recruitment. "This is James," Gisele continued purposefully. "He's here to help. James, this is Martha. She owns and runs this establishment. It was Martha who contacted me on Polly's behalf."

Jamie gave Martha a brief bow. "A pleasure," he replied.

"*Hmph.*" The tavern keeper eyed him skeptically. "A gentleman." She said it as though it were a disease, and in any other situation, Gisele might have found it funny.

"Not his fault," Gisele replied. "I can assure you, James is quite up to the task."

Jamie's eyes flew to her own, contemplative and assessing.

"*Hmph.* If you say so." Martha suddenly rummaged in

the pockets of her apron and leaned close to Gisele. "The Darling brothers left this for you here this morning," she whispered. She passed Gisele a small scrap of paper.

Gisele read the note in a glance. "All in order." The two brothers were nothing if not brief and to the point. She nodded to herself in satisfaction.

"Tonight then?" Martha asked, interpreting her gesture correctly.

"Yes. Everything is in place." The arrangements for Polly Tuck had been made weeks ago, long before the news of the Marquess of Valence's engagement had reached her. No matter her haste to get to London, Gisele would see this through first. She'd never forgive herself if she didn't and something happened to the girl.

The tavern keeper nodded. "She's been waiting but I'll make sure she's ready. Thank you, Miz Gisele, for coming. For what you do."

Gisele smiled briefly. "Everyone needs a little help sometimes."

Martha put her hands on her substantial hips. "You ever need anything, you know you just need ask. Anything at all."

"Thank you."

"Now you best be on your way. Place will fill up soon. The things you asked for are around back. And you were never here."

⁓

The first time Gisele had helped a woman disappear, her pulse had pounded uncontrollably and her heart had been in her throat the entire time. It had been nearly a week before she had stopped looking over her shoulder, convinced that both she and the woman she'd helped escape were not being hunted like crippled foxes. Nearly four years later, the underlying fear still existed, though Gisele was glad for it. It kept her alert, and it kept her from making overconfident mistakes.

Which is why they were waiting for complete darkness, huddled against the unseasonable chill and concealed in a copse of trees.

"How many?" Jamie asked into the soft whine of the wind. It was the first thing he'd said since they had left the tavern and collected their horses.

She didn't pretend to misunderstand. "Dozens over the years."

"How do they know where to find you?"

Gisele stared at the light from the tavern windows just visible through the foliage. "Through people like Martha. I have other... contacts in different places. York. Nottingham. Liverpool. Bath. A few others."

"London?"

Gisele felt her body tense. "Yes."

"What's in London, Gisele?"

"Let's concentrate on one thing at a time," Gisele deflected. She wanted to trust him. And she did, to a point. But Gisele hadn't survived as long as she had by placing reckless faith in near strangers, no matter how gallant and decent they might seem at the outset.

The wind gusted, and she shivered. Beside her, Jamie shifted so that he blocked the worst of the chill, and she could feel his warmth through the fabric of her clothes. She resisted the insane urge to lean into his heat and lay her head against the solidity of his chest. Instead she pulled her cloak around her more tightly.

The rattle of wheels on the road became audible above the stirring leaves and Gisele watched as a tinker's cart came into view. Two men were perched up on the wide bench at the front, the walls of the cart swaying behind them with the ruts on the road. She glanced up at the ever-darkening sky.

"Almost time," she murmured as the cart rolled past.

Chapter 5 ———————————————

Gisele wasn't a spy. Or a thief.

Part of Jamie, the part that wanted to believe his instincts had been intact when he'd agreed to work for this woman, felt nothing but relief. He wasn't sure what she was, exactly, but this crusade Gisele seemed to have embraced—the one he was now part of—was certainly noble enough, if not skewed slightly outside the law. Which went a long way in explaining her reticent nature.

It did not, however, explain where Gisele had come from and why was she here, pretending to be something and someone she wasn't. Further, it did not explain why she became as taut as a bowstring every time London was mentioned.

An owl screeched somewhere in the darkness, and Jamie returned his attention to the road they'd been traveling now for a good ten minutes. They'd emerged out of the trees and headed back north again, toward the oak-lined ridge, and, he surmised, toward the Tuck residence. He sighed. Regardless of the puzzle that was the woman who called herself Just-Gisele, he would certainly help Polly Tuck, if only because it was the right thing to do.

The night was cloudless, affording the moonlight the ability to touch the earth with a pale illumination. His horse suddenly lifted its head and pricked its ears, and at the top of the ridge, he saw the tinker's cart that had passed them earlier. It was pulled off to the side of the road at the entrance to a narrow lane, though there was no one in sight. Jamie tensed, wary and suspicious.

Beside him Gisele seemed oblivious. She glanced around her once more before guiding her horse directly alongside the cart. The animal standing patiently in its traces nickered softly in greeting.

"Gisele," Jamie warned, angling his horse next to hers, reaching for his blade. He didn't like the feel of this at all.

"It's all right," Gisele said softly, reaching out to put a restraining hand on his. "They're friends."

A man suddenly materialized from somewhere near the mouth of the lane and Jamie jerked, startled. He watched as Gisele slid from her horse and gave the man a quick embrace. "Thank you for this," he heard her say.

"You know you don't need to be thanking us, Miz Gisele," the man said.

"It is out of your way."

The stranger waved his hand impatiently. "Hardly. Just happy the timing worked out as it did." They were speaking quickly and urgently. "My brother's down there now seeing to things. Best hurry."

Jamie dismounted from his own horse. Aside from the cart and its driver, the road was completely deserted, as was the lane leading down to the cottage, and Jamie suspected this hour had been chosen deliberately, when there was little chance of witnesses. The smell of woodsmoke was sharp in the air, and somewhere in the darkened pastures a sheep bleated. He caught a glimpse of a weak light near the end of the twisted lane that led down from the road, betraying the existence of a tiny cottage, half hidden behind a screen of bushes.

Gisele was untying the heavy pack she had lashed to her saddle. Jamie moved to help and took it from her, hefting it over his shoulder. He could feel the stranger's attention shift to him, though the man made no effort to introduce himself, nor did he ask Jamie's identity. Gisele, likewise, remained unapologetically mute, collecting the reins of both their horses and passing them to the silent man.

"Tie them in those trees on the far side for us, please?" she asked. "Where they can't be seen from the road. Ground's too soft to be taking them down the lane. They'd leave tracks that would need to be explained later."

"Of course."

"I'll send her up with your brother."

"We'll take good care of her."

"I know you will." Gisele touched the man's shoulder. To Jamie, she said, "Follow me." She didn't wait for a reply from either man, simply started down the lane, treading along the edges where the grass grew thick. Jamie fell in behind her, careful to do the same.

It was like a perfectly scripted play, he realized. One that had been performed many times, and he wasn't entirely sure if he should be impressed or alarmed.

"Who are your friends?" he asked.

"Men who are familiar with every back road and trail from London to Edinburgh. They've helped me many times before. They'll take Polly with them, safely away from here."

Maybe Gisele should have been a spy. She had answered his question without answering anything at all.

"Where's Sebastien?" he tried.

"Treating Mr. Tuck and all his friends to rounds at Martha's tavern. No one is likely to leave when ale is flowing on someone else's coin." She came to a stop at the door of the tiny cottage. Her eyes met his, gleaming in the gloom. "But that doesn't mean we have time to waste. I need you to do exactly what I say, and I need you to do it quickly. Understood?"

"Yes."

"I need you to pull down as much thatch as you can from the edges of the roof and bring it inside. Or straw if you can find it in the back shed. The drier the better."

Jamie blinked. "Thatch?"

"Yes. And do it quickly." Again Gisele didn't wait for an answer, simply took the pack from Jamie's hands and ducked through the door into the run-down cottage.

It took Jamie less than three minutes to assemble a good-size pile, and he pushed into the pitiful dwelling, depositing his load inside the door. He found Gisele standing in the center of the room, her pack open at her feet, a pair of gleaming scissors in her hands. A discarded dress lay on the floor and a painfully thin woman stood in front of her, dressed in boys' breeches and a loose shirt. Her knotted hair fell along the sides of her face and down her back in a dark mass.

Gisele grabbed a handful of the woman's hair. "Don't move." The scissors flashed, and a curtain of hair fell to the floor unceremoniously.

Jamie tried not to stare at Polly Tuck's face but he couldn't help himself. Even in the weak light offered by the sputtering fire, he could see the left side of her cheek was a mass of discolored bruises. Her left eye had swollen closed altogether. A gash, crusted with blood, ran along her hairline. He felt his jaw clench.

Gisele snipped a few more times, leaving the woman with a rough but passable haircut. She bent and picked up a well-worn hat. "Put this on. It'll hide your face, and if anyone asks, you got into a fight. Scraps between boys are unremarkable. Expected, even."

A movement caught his eye, and a man stood from where he had been crouched behind the table near the small hearth. It was difficult to tell in the shadows, but he looked like an exact copy of the man waiting up at the top of the lane. He met Jamie's eye briefly and tipped his head before turning to Gisele. "I need her ring."

Polly twisted a band off her finger and dropped it in Gisele's palm.

"Are you ready to do this?" Gisele asked the woman quietly. "Because once you leave, there is no coming back."

Polly put her hand on her abdomen, the swell almost unnoticeable, especially under the bulk of her shirt. "Yes." Jamie heard steel in her answer.

"Good." Gisele tossed the ring to the waiting man, who bent, disappearing again briefly behind the table. She turned back to Polly. "There is a woman who is expecting you in York. You will live with her for as long as you require, certainly until the baby is born. She'll help you find a means to earn a living and take care of your expenses until then. You're not the first to come through her door, nor will you be the last. Do you understand?"

Polly offered Gisele a brave smile and wiped a hand across her eyes. "Yes," she said.

The man near the hearth had moved and picked up a warm jacket from the table. He held it out for Polly, gently helping her into it.

"Time to go," Gisele said.

"Thank you," Polly whispered, giving Gisele an impulsive hug. Over Gisele's shoulder, her one eye that still opened met his. "Thank you," she whispered again, this time to Jamie. He simply nodded, swallowing the urge to protest that he hadn't really done anything. And then, without a backward glance, Polly and her guide were gone into the night.

Gisele was already emptying the rest of the pack, lining up jars of what looked like lantern oil.

"You're going to burn the place?" Jamie asked in sudden comprehension.

"To the ground."

"Why?"

"Fire is best whenever possible. It's all-consuming, and it destroys any evidence that may be left behind. It has the added benefit of becoming a very public tragedy, making believers out of an entire community as opposed to a single man." Gisele's voice was grim.

Jamie stared at her before moving closer to where she crouched. "Believers of what? I don't—" He froze as he caught sight of the spectacle laid out in front of the hearth. "What the hell is that?"

A skeleton lay across the floor near the meager fire, the eyeless sockets of a skull staring sightlessly in his direction. Polly's abandoned dress had been draped over the torso and legs and, with a morbid horror, Jamie saw the glint of the ring Polly had relinquished placed carefully on a bony digit.

Gisele barely glanced up at him. "It's one thing to set a fire in the hopes someone believes a soul has perished in it. It's another to convince them wholly. Polly Tuck needs to die tonight in order to live."

Jamie gaped first at the bones, some with sinew still holding them in place, and then at Gisele. "Jesus. Is that really necessary?"

"While it is unlikely Garrett Tuck would ever be able to find his wife, it's always better if one such as he never has reason to look. And there are the others to consider as well."

Jamie raked his hands through his hair in agitation. "Others?"

Gisele was twisting the lids off jars with clinical precision. "Mr. Tuck already threatened Polly's sister the first time she ran. What do you think might happen now if he believed she survived and he went looking?"

Jamie was struggling to comprehend the pure cunning that was unfolding before his eyes. This wasn't a cleverly rehearsed play, it was a tactical campaign, planned and plotted by a web of individuals beyond the scope of his imagination.

It made the fine hairs on the back of his neck stand up. "And your nameless friends just happened to have a body in the back of their cart?" he demanded.

"The Darling brothers are devoted purveyors of fine specimens for the advancement of the medical research field," Gisele said calmly as she stood, a jar in her hand. She dumped the contents over the table, where it splashed and soaked into the skirts of the abandoned dress. The overpowering scent of lantern oil assaulted his nose. "They are in possession of any number of bodies."

Holy hell. It took Jamie two tries before he was able to

utter a sentence. "They're resurrection men?" He was rapidly revising the list of questions he would be demanding answers to when he wasn't in the middle of committing a multitude of felonies in a wretched cottage on the edge of Leicester. "Body snatchers?"

"They do not snatch bodies," Gisele said, sounding impatient. "They collect those that remain unclaimed from prisons or workhouses or any number of unfortunate situations. What they provide has helped surgeons and physicians save the lives of patients everywhere. Soldiers included." She paused. "And tonight it means a woman and her child will survive. Don't you dare think I take that lightly." She stalked over to the pile of rotting thatch Jamie had brought in and kicked it across the dirt floor before she upended the contents of another jar over the mess. The smell of oil in the cramped space became suffocating.

Jamie stared at her. "Are you insane? You've trusted a woman to the care of two criminals."

Gisele's face flushed visibly, even in the dimness, and her eyes flashed. "I've sent a woman away from a criminal in the care of two good men," she hissed. "Men who have done, and will continue to do, everything in their power to see Polly to safety. Men who will see her to a place where she will never have to suffer again the way she suffered at the hands of the one person who should have protected her."

Jamie didn't have an answer for that. His declarations of chivalry yesterday morning suddenly seemed laughably naïve now that he found himself standing in the stark reality of his ideals. She'd given him fair warning, and though he'd listened, he hadn't heard her.

Gisele was still watching him, as though waiting for him to respond. "Do you wish to leave, Jamie?"

"Leave?" He jerked.

"You can keep the horse. Consider it payment for services rendered. I only ask that you do not speak of what you saw here tonight. For Polly's sake."

Jamie stared at Gisele, something angry and defiant rising within him. She expected him to run—to just fade away in the face of adversity and complication. Dammit, was that the kind of man she thought him to be? Given where and how she had found him, he supposed it probably was. If he was honest with himself, it was exactly what he had done a year ago.

But he would not do it, not this time.

With deliberate movements he stalked over to the struggling fire in the hearth and withdrew a burning stick from the edge. He thought of Polly and the abuse that had hurt her but had not broken her. He thought about the child she'd lost and the one she would have a chance to know, thanks to what Gisele had done and the risks she'd taken.

Jamie retraced his steps to where Gisele stood in the doorway and came to stand directly in front of her, forcing her to look up at him. Without taking his eyes from hers, he tossed the flaming stick into the pile of oil-soaked thatch. "No, I would not like to leave."

Something shifted in her eyes, and the corners of her mouth curled slightly. For one wild moment, Jamie wondered what she would do if he kissed her right then. To prove to her just how much he wanted to stay. The urge to taste her was almost overwhelming.

Behind him the fire caught and began to lick greedily,

smoke beginning to curl. He touched his finger to the side of her cheek. "I gave you my word. And I don't scare that easy."

⁓

They'd ridden hard all that night, stopping only once to water their horses. Sebastien had caught up with them some miles south of Leicester, and he hadn't spoken, though he wore a look of satisfaction. Jamie was quite certain that this wasn't the first time Gisele and Sebastien had spent a night on the backs of horses, putting distance between themselves and suspicious circumstances to avoid thorny explanations.

Yet as they traveled south, in the direction of London, the vague sense of unease and urgency surrounding the pair seemed to grow, not lessen. It was a disturbing sensation for Jamie, and it was not unlike the one that plagued men on a battlefield waiting for dawn to reveal an enemy that had amassed before them under the cover of darkness.

Jamie watched Gisele now out of the corner of his eye as they handed their horses over to the stable hands at the inn where they'd finally stopped. All of them desperately needed food and a few hours of rest, as did their horses. She and Sebastien had inquired about rooms at two other guesthouses, smaller, ramshackle establishments farther outside of town, but neither had had any vacant chambers to offer. This one, in the heart of Northampton, was bigger and busy, with quite a few carriages and mail coaches waiting in its sprawling yards.

Jamie could see that neither of his companions was happy about having to seek shelter at these finer lodgings. Gisele was visibly nervous, her eyes darting across the court as if searching for something or someone. Before she'd even dismounted, she'd pulled the hood of her cloak all the way over her head despite the warmth of the late-morning sun.

He eyed Gisele again as she preceded him toward the narrow entrance to the inn and grimaced. Jamie could only assume it was their proximity to London that had her so on edge, and it was unnerving, especially after what he'd witnessed last night. Had Gisele committed a more serious crime in London? Something that would earn her a place on a scaffold should she ever return? Was Jamie now risking the same fate by accompanying her?

Sobriety had reestablished his sense of self-preservation, for better or worse, and no matter how altruistic Gisele's motives might be, keeping his own head attached to his neck had become a priority. Just as well that they'd stopped. He'd have his answers here, before they went another step closer to London.

A commotion just inside the door interrupted his thoughts. A shrill female voice pierced the air, haranguing an unseen group of servants. The accent was refined but the volume and manner of the tirade were just the opposite. Gisele stopped in her tracks and began edging backward. Jamie heard Sebastien swear under his breath as he too veered away from the entrance. A second later, the harridan responsible for the disturbance erupted from the doorway in a froth of embroidered green silk.

Gisele hit Jamie's chest with a thump, turning desperately away from both the fashionable woman stalking toward them and the bevy of maids and footmen clutching bags and lapdogs in her wake. Sebastien had dropped to his knee, head turned away, adjusting a boot that didn't need adjusting. Jamie glanced down at Gisele, who was looking up at him with wide, panicked eyes. They were trapped between the side of the inn and the crush of people behind them. Two of the tiny lapdogs started yapping hysterically, and as Jamie gaped alternatively at the foul canines and the bellowing woman, he suddenly felt Gisele's hands curl into the front of his coat and jerk him around with a shocking force.

His hands hit the rough wall on either side of Gisele's shoulders as she slid her fingers from his coat to his face and hauled his lips to hers. He struggled to breathe— drugged instantly by her scent and her softness—as he fought vainly to make sense of what was happening. And then Jamie felt Gisele sigh into his mouth, and he stopped thinking altogether. He pressed her back into the wall, his body tight against hers, deepening the kiss. Every ounce of blood he possessed traveled immediately to his groin. Her fingers coiled into his hair, and her own breath hissed in response to his, and had they been anywhere else but where they were standing, Jamie would have taken her then.

"You two should be ashamed." The words were spit in their direction loudly enough to be heard above the din of the barking dogs. "Baseborn, common rubbish!" The last floated over the woman's shoulder as she sailed past them into the yard, where a crested carriage waited. A footman rushed forward to open the door of the conveyance, and the lady stomped haughtily inside.

Gisele pulled away from Jamie just enough to watch the carriage door swing shut. She closed her eyes and rested her head on his chest, breathing hard. Jamie reached down and tipped her chin up, forcing her to meet his eyes. "What the hell was that?" he demanded hoarsely.

Gisele's eyes were heavy, her lips swollen, and her breathing still uneven. He watched as her gaze dropped back to his mouth. Dear God, he couldn't think when she did that. He tipped her chin up again.

"That," she began shakily, "was the Countess of Baustenbury."

Jamie narrowed his eyes. "Not good enough."

Gisele let her hands slide from his hair. "I know. I'm sorry." Her arms dropped to her sides.

"Are you?" He made no effort to move, keeping her pinned against the wall and ignoring the people pushing past them.

A flash of heat touched her expression before she bit her lip. "Not entirely."

Bloody hell. He'd wanted to know how she tasted, and now that he did, he wasn't sure that he'd be able to keep himself from doing it again. And again. With a supreme effort of will, Jamie ran a finger along the hood of her cloak, tucking a piece of pale hair back into its depths. He leaned toward her, his mouth close to her ear. "Listen and listen carefully. I will take you inside, and once we are settled, you will tell me who the Countess of Baustenbury is and why you used me to hide from her." He paused, his voice deceptively quiet. "You will tell me who you really are, and you will tell me what or who is waiting for us in London. Understood?"

Gisele nodded.

"And if you ever kiss me like that again," he whispered, "be prepared to finish it."

Chapter 6

When Gisele had been young, before everything had happened, she'd known desire. It had been the blacksmith's son, strong and gentle and as innocent as she in the ways of women and men. They'd shared only fumbling kisses and shy, stolen touches, but she'd discovered sensations that had left her flushed and wanting.

She'd thought that part of her dead, battered into submission by cruelty and perversity, and until now, she'd given it little thought. Until she had let Jamie Montcrief into her life. Until Jamie had taken her kiss and turned it into something that had scattered her wits and reignited something deep within. He'd made her feel that desire again, that reckless thrill deep in her belly that urged her to risk everything for more.

Gisele paced across the little rented room in agitation. She had panicked when she had seen the countess bearing down on her, but the woman was one of the biggest gossips in London, and a cruel one at that. She would have recognized Gisele in a heartbeat, and everything Gisele had done and was attempting to do would have unraveled just as quickly.

Both she and Sebastien should have anticipated that

they would encounter old acquaintances on this journey, and they should have had a plan of action in place. Kissing Jamie was not a good plan at all. Not if she wanted to retain her concentration and focus. And ultimately her life.

For in that moment, when Jamie had kissed her, when he had let go of his hesitation, Gisele had abandoned her own vigilance. The countess had ceased to exist. The inn, the yard, the carriages, the *world* had impossibly ceased to exist. She had never been kissed like that. By anyone.

"Was he as good as he looks?" Sebastien's voice had her whirling to the door in alarm.

"Shut up," she snapped.

Sebastien stood in the doorway, his arms crossed, smirking unrepentantly.

"It was a mistake," she declared with far more conviction than she felt.

"Didn't look like one."

Gisele pinched the bridge of her nose. "I didn't know what else to do. The countess was right there."

"Yes, she was." Sebastien closed the door gently behind him, his teasing tone disappearing. "And it's going to happen again. Next time it will be an earl or a viscount or even—"

"I know," she mumbled miserably.

"You must tell him everything, darling. It's only been two days, but I have a good feeling about him. I don't think you will find a better champion."

"I don't need a champion!" she scowled. "I am not some helpless princess waiting in a tower for a knight to rescue her from the terrible dragon!"

"No, you did that all on your own," Sebastien replied

quietly, lowering himself to a wooden chair and leaning forward.

"With a little help." She gave him a weak smile.

"Let James Montcrief in, Gisele. If not for you, then for those others who do need a champion. How many times does he need to prove himself to you?"

Gisele looked away.

"If you don't tell him, I will," Sebastien warned. "For he's a liability to us otherwise."

"I—" A knock on the door interrupted whatever ridiculous objection she might have thought to make at that point.

Sebastien rose and pulled the door open.

"Is everything all right? I heard raised voices." Jamie stood in the doorway in his shirt-sleeves, his coat over his arm, brushing stray bits of hay and straw from the garment.

"Where were you?" Gisele asked.

"Stables. Seeing to the horses."

"There are stableboys for that."

Jamie shrugged unapologetically. "Old habits die hard."

Sebastien slid past Jamie into the narrow hall. "I'll leave you two alone. You have a great deal to discuss." He gave Gisele a meaningful look.

Gisele glared at Sebastien's retreating back, and then, recognizing the futility of that, she transferred her glare to Jamie.

"Don't." Jamie carefully laid his jacket over the back of the chair Sebastian had just vacated. "You don't get to be incensed or anything approaching righteous. Instead, you get to be pleasant and accommodating and *informative*."

Gisele took a deep breath, making a swift catalog of the information she would need to share with Jamie. Sebastien was right, as usual. She would need to tell Jamie the whole sordid story as much as she was loath to do it. But Iain was off-limits.

"Let's start with this Iain," Jamie said conversationally, settling his bulk into the chair. He made a show of making himself comfortable, but the planes of his face were like granite. "I've got all day."

The small room shrank further. "Ask me a different question."

"Fine. Is Iain your husband?" Jamie stretched and put his hands behind his head.

"That's not a different question."

"Yes it is. And it's a simple one to answer, requiring only a yes or a no. I'm not interested in his favorite color or if he enjoys bread pudding. I want to know what he has to do with you, and therefore with me. I'd like to avoid pistols at dawn and all that."

Gisele almost stomped her foot in frustration. "No," she bit out.

"No, he isn't your husband, or no, you won't answer?"

"He isn't my husband." She somehow managed the words through clenched teeth.

"Then he's your lover."

Gisele closed her eyes, a familiar resentment beginning to simmer. "No."

"Yet that's not what you implied earlier." He wasn't giving her any quarter. "Were you lying then? Or are you lying now? For I don't like being used by another man's mistress."

Gisele stared daggers at Jamie. "You're a bastard."

"I believe we've already been over that," he said flatly, his expression intense and unforgiving. "Who is he to you?"

"A friend."

"*Friend?* Mother of God, but I've come to despise that word. It means nothing."

"Truly, Jamie, Iain has nothing do to with you. You don't need to understand that part."

"Then tell me about the parts I do need to understand." He paused. "Like last night. It was another one of your damned tests, wasn't it?"

"No." She turned away, but not fast enough.

"Stop lying to me. You wanted to see how far I could be pushed outside the boundaries of the law."

"What?" She spun in startled confusion.

Jamie leaned forward, his eyes slitted. "You didn't need me last night at all. You were perfectly capable of doing what we did on your own." He paused. "More than capable. Masterful, in fact."

Gisele was struggling for words.

Jamie seemed to mistake her silence for agreement. "I'm left to wonder then, what you could possibly need me for in London. Certainly not to rescue another country maid." His nostrils flared. "I will not be used as a convenient scapegoat for whatever diabolical crime you have committed in London."

Gisele stared at him. "That's why you think I need you?"

He rose to his feet. "What am I supposed to think? You're terrified at the idea of returning to London— terrified that you might be recognized. Yet you're on casual, nay, *cordial* terms with men who collect bodies for a living. And let's not forget I watched you burn a cottage to the ground with such a skilled efficiency I know you've done it many times before."

"I did that to save a woman who would have been dead within a year had I not!"

"Then I ask why? While it may have been noble, why go to such extremes for a woman you've never even met? I have to assume, Gisele, that what you did—what you do—is to atone for something in your past. Something terrible. What did you do in London, Gisele?"

"I got married," she said savagely, suddenly furious he had forced her into this before she was ready.

A charged silence filled the space between them.

Jamie sat back down with a thump. "You're *married*?" It came out as an accusation.

"Not anymore."

"You're a widow?" His tone softened slightly.

"No. I'm…" She trailed off, searching for the right words.

"Divorced?" He was incredulous now.

"No."

"Then what?" he demanded. "What the hell are you?"

Gisele looked directly into his eyes. "Dead," she whispered. "I'm dead."

Chapter 7 ———————————

Of course she was.

It explained everything. Given everything that had transpired in the last twenty-four hours, he felt like a fool for not having figured it out sooner. A lady—and she was a lady, of that there was no doubt—did not learn how to do what she had done last night at a fashionable finishing school. She would have learned to do what she had done last night from experience.

He moved past Gisele to the far side of the room, noticing the dust motes dancing in the bright ray of sunshine slanting through the window and across the floorboards. He took his time, trying to make sense of this peculiar conversation, a jumble of questions vying for his attention.

"What's your name?" He decided to start with the easiest. "Your real one."

Gisele watched him with guarded eyes. "I was born Gisele Whitby. When I married, I became Lady Valence."

"Valence?" A stirring of recognition hummed somewhere in his brain. "The Marquess of Valence?" He was trying to remember where he had last heard the name mentioned.

Gisele's face was unreadable. "Correct."

Jamie gave up trying to tease out the memory. "You are—were—his wife?"

"Correct."

"But now you're not."

"No." Her answer was tight, and the way she held her body put him in mind of a horse ready to bolt.

Very slowly he moved behind her and guided her into a chair, feeling the tension and stiffness rolling off her in waves. He wanted her settled before he asked his next question.

"Why?" he pressed.

She drew a sharp breath but didn't immediately respond. "He was...unsuitable," she said after a time.

"Unsuitable. Care to expand?" He kept his voice low, removing any inflection from his tone.

"The marquess was...not my choice, but then, I never imagined I would have the luxury of choosing. My father was a striving country gentleman whose greatest aspiration in life was a better listing in Debrett's. By the time I was sixteen, I was known in our county as an *exceptional beauty*." Gisele's voice was thick with contempt. "I was a priceless asset for a man such as my father, and I knew very well what would happen when I came of age."

"He married you to Valence?"

"Yes." She studied her hands. "Valence seemed benign enough at the start. He was never anything but polite and charming in public, well-liked by those he met. But after, in private, he was...cruel. Violent. Vicious." She shrugged carelessly as though she were describing how she liked her tea, but Jamie wasn't fooled for a second.

"To you?"

A brittle smile preceded a humorless laugh. "Yes. He had some very specific ideas as to the duties and responsibilities of a wife. The marquess seemed to enjoy my dissent and took great pleasure in correcting what he perceived to be my rebellious nature. When I resisted him, he quickly learned that his powers of persuasion over me were greater when it was Helena, his stepdaughter, who was threatened."

He paced to the window, his jaw clenched. "I see."

"I couldn't kill him. I won't deny I fantasized about it, but I would most certainly have been caught, and then Helena would have been left alone. I was the only family she had left, and she needed me."

"So you faked your own death instead." Jamie felt another tug of recognition and knew the memory he sought was right on the edge of his consciousness.

"He would never have stopped looking for us. For me. He would have hunted me to the ends of the earth if he thought there was even the slightest possibility I was out there—somewhere—drawing breath. My husband was exceedingly fond of me, you know." She gave a tiny, mirthless chuckle.

A picture of a newspaper page—folded and mailed to one of his fellow officers—suddenly popped into Jamie's mind's eye, the text accompanied by a drawing of a massive explosion on the Thames. "You blew up a boat," he whispered, turning to her.

Gisele looked up at him in surprise. "Yes."

"The Marchioness of Valence and her stepdaughter were killed in the blast," he recalled in wonder. "The barge sank to the bottom of the Thames, along with a fortune in diamonds. Nothing was recovered, with the exception of a few charred pieces of the vessel."

"Your memory is sound. But the newspaper reports

might have been a little off," she said wryly, and Jamie was relieved to hear that a small degree of normalcy had returned to her voice.

"Why the need for such extremes? Surely your father would have protected you?"

"My father?" Her brow rose in mock astonishment. "I told him. Six months after my wedding I told him exactly what was happening to me. And do you know what my father said?"

Jamie was suddenly quite sure he didn't want to know.

"He told me to be glad I had a husband with such important connections and titles. He reminded me how much he had sacrificed to get me to where I was. And he chided me for being a whining shrew and ordered me to learn to accommodate my husband's wishes. 'All men have needs,' he said. 'And the only reason you were put on God's green earth was to meet them.'"

"That's reprehensible. I'm so sorry."

Gisele frowned, puzzled. "Whatever for? It had nothing to do with you. I took care of it in my own way. Though I did have some help."

"Sebastien."

"Among others."

"Iain."

"Yes. Iain Ferguson has been my friend since I was four years old. We grew up together until he went to war, and I"—she faltered slightly before recovering—"and I became Lady Valence."

Jamie leaned against the sill. "And where is Iain now?"

A genuine warmth touched her features. "He's getting married. To Helena."

"Your stepdaughter?"

"Yes." She looked at Jamie in that direct way of hers. "Iain and I were never lovers," she said. "At the time I escaped, Iain had just come back from the war in Spain, and we were both broken and wounded, just in different ways. I'd like to think our friendship healed us both."

"I see."

"Thank goodness. Does that mean we can now lay the topic of Iain Ferguson to rest?"

"God, yes," Jamie said vehemently.

"Good." Gisele stood and joined him at the window. "Because Valence is getting married again. The wedding must be prevented, and I need your help to do it. That is why I hired you."

Jamie nodded. "You need my help to make the bride disappear? Like what we did for Polly Tuck?"

Gisele sighed in obvious frustration. "It's not as simple as that. I can't make anyone disappear who doesn't want to. Society is completely ignorant of the nature of the marquess, as is his intended bride and her family. His fiancée has no reason to believe she is in danger. She has no reason to walk away from this marriage."

"So you don't have a plan?"

"Not yet." Her forehead creased. "I only know Sebastien and I can't do it alone. I cannot reenter London society, obviously, because I'm supposed to bc dead, and Sebastien, as you've guessed already, was a sought-after valet before I escaped. He is bound to be recognized as a servant, which limits his access to Valence's elevated social circles. That is where you come in."

"I have little experience with the ton, Gisele."

"Exactly. Your obscurity will serve us well, I think. You can essentially become whoever we need you to be."

Jamie wasn't sure he liked this strategy, but he let it slide for the moment. "Who is the girl the marquess is set to marry?"

"Lady Julia Hextall. Daughter of the Earl of Boden. She comes with a spectacular dowry, a must for Valence, since he lost most of his own fortune to the bottom of the Thames."

"And when is the wedding?"

"In seven days."

"Seven days!" Jamie spluttered. "How the hell are we supposed to thwart a wedding that's set to take place in a week?" His voice had risen a full octave, but he didn't care. "They've probably started decorating the church already."

Gisele scowled at him, eyes glittering. "I only just found out about it myself," she said. "I haven't exactly been an avid reader of the London social pages since escaping from my gilded cage."

He scowled right back. "You're mad. What could *I* possibly do to stop this marriage in seven short days?"

Gisele considered him. "You could ruin the bride. Seduce her and make sure you're caught doing it. That would render her unmarriageable, at least to a marquess."

Jamie blanched. "You can't be serious. I will not ruin an innocent girl's reputation. While I understand it might save her from whatever danger Valence poses, society will rip her to shreds. She'll be destroyed anyway."

Gisele was grim. "I've met her, Jamie. She's like a pretty porcelain doll. She'll never...she won't be able to..." She cursed under her breath, flailing for words.

"Jesus Christ, what did Valence do to you?"

"Doesn't matter."

"Gisele—"

"I said, it doesn't matter. What matters is that he doesn't do it to someone else."

He watched as she unclenched her fingers with deliberation. It was clear she would say no more on the subject, and they were both silent for several long minutes.

"If we run out of time, you may have to kidnap Lady Julia," Gisele said suddenly. "She won't go willingly, but her reputation can be preserved if you do it right."

Jamie looked to the ceiling. "If I do it right? There is no right way to kidnap someone, Gisele, and the result will be the same as if I ruined her. There has to be a better solution than that."

"Fine. You could marry her yourself." Gisele crossed her arms.

"I beg your pardon?"

"You could marry—"

"Yes, that's what I thought you said." Jamie was staring at her now in shock. "I was trying to give you the benefit of the doubt. That you hadn't lost your mind altogether."

"It would work." She had completely ignored his last words and was considering him in the way he imagined she might evaluate a prize bull at a country fair. "We would just need a few selected family members to stumble upon a romantic interlude that has gotten a little out of hand. There would be some talk, of course—that will be unavoidable—but she wouldn't be ruined by any stretch of the imagination. You could certainly do worse, all things considered." She looked at him expectantly.

"No," he growled, annoyance starting to weave its way into his disbelief.

Gisele huffed before turning back to the window. She grew pensive as she pressed her palms to the sill, obviously lost in deep thought. "What if you just made her fall in love with you instead?" she asked suddenly. "Ply her with pretty words and empty promises. You wouldn't need to do anything untoward, only make her believe in your tender feelings enough so that she calls off the wedding on her own."

Jamie didn't much care for this farfetched idea either, but it was a sight more appealing than the others.

"I suppose I could try." He hesitated. "But I warn you, I haven't had much experience playacting. I don't know that I would make a convincing Romeo."

"Well," she sighed, "perhaps you'll surprise yourself and discover you have a natural talent for the stage. And if not, I doubt a botched performance will matter very greatly to Lady Julia. You are *quite* irresistible just as you are, you know." Her cheeks suddenly colored. "Ah, I mean, objectively speaking, you hold great, um, appeal," she stammered. "For young, sheltered society girls, that is. As a war hero and, er, all that. The debutantes will swoon, I promise you."

Jamie's lips quirked as he watched her scramble in verbal retreat. "But an experienced woman such as yourself would never succumb to my pedestrian allure. Is that what you're trying to tell me?" He couldn't resist teasing her, if only to draw forth some healing laughter. Everything in the past Gisele had just revealed had exacted its toll, and Jamie sensed a terrible weariness beneath her mask of determination.

"No, there is little danger of that," Gisele assured him evenly, displaying a disturbing amount of control for a woman who had seemed entirely flustered seconds earlier. "I'm sure you realize now that what happened between us in the courtyard was all for show. I am as indifferent to you as I would be to any other man. You were convenient, that is all."

Convenient? That stung. He'd been called a lot of things in his life, but *convenient* had never been one of them.

He frowned. The kiss they had shared earlier had been no less than shattering for him. Was he really to believe the feeling was one-sided? No, he concluded, it couldn't be. Or at least, he fervently hoped not. And he damned well wasn't going to accept her declaration of indifference without testing his theory. At least a little.

He stepped forward so that their bodies were almost touching, and watched her reaction. Gisele's eyelids immediately dropped to half-mast, and her breath hitched audibly. *Indifferent, my ass*, he thought fiercely. Before his own rapid breathing betrayed his intent, he continued his assay.

"Then you are a very skilled actress, Gisele." Jamie's voice was now muted, his tone honeyed even to his own ears. "For you seemed to find me much more than *convenient* earlier. Perhaps you should reveal the secret of your convincing performance so that I might better snare Lady Julia?"

"Don't be obtuse, Jamie." Gisele had doubtlessly intended these words to sound harsh and dismissive, but they left her lips like a whisper of silk.

Encouraged, but still unsure, Jamie brought his hand softly to her cheek. He waited, heart pounding, for a protest that never came. And neither did Gisele move away—out of sheer stubbornness or something else—as he trailed his fingers down the side of her face. So, without giving either of them an opportunity to reconsider, he wrapped his hand around the back of Gisele's neck, pulled her across the last inches, and claimed her mouth.

Chapter 8

Gisele melted into Jamie instantly. Later he would reflect that it might have been his own body that had dissolved into hers, but the order of things was unimportant, really. He felt her arms snake around his neck, and he let his own hands roam down the curve of her back, feeling the strength and heat that lay beneath the fabric of her dress. His mouth moved to the hollow at her throat, and he could taste the salt on her skin, feel her pulse hammering beneath his lips. He had never wanted a woman so badly in his life.

He flexed one arm around Gisele's waist and lifted her just enough that her toes left the ground. He stumbled backward, bringing the two of them heavily onto the chair, and pulled her weight on top of him so that her long legs straddled his lap. He shoved her skirts up, sliding his hands along the tops of her thighs, and then around her arse, and then, with one swift and unforgiving tug, he slid her closer so that the cradle of her hips slammed into his arousal. They both groaned, the intimate contact rendering him motionless with pleasure. But only for a blink. He rocked into her once, twice, a third time, until they had established a rhythm that sent sparks traveling through his limbs and caused pinwheels of light to flash behind his half-closed eyes.

Gisele threaded her fingers through his hair and arched her back, driving her hips against his straining cock with even greater force. He grew impossibly harder as her head tipped back, her silken hair cascading down into his lap and brushing opulently over his arms.

With one hand Jamie brought Gisele's lips back to his and kissed her deeply, their tongues meeting in a cadence more languid than the pulse of their bodies. She met him stroke for stroke as his other hand found the neckline of her bodice. Reverently he cupped one breast through her gown, but it wasn't enough. Not nearly enough. He dragged his mouth from hers even as he frantically pushed the material of her dress down. He took a nipple into his mouth and sucked and was rewarded by the feel of her fingers curling into his scalp.

Jamie slid his free hand between them then, down beneath Gisele's skirts. He caressed her through the opening of her pantalets and then smoothly slid a finger into her core. She was slick and hot and shockingly tight. He was touching and tasting and thrusting—all in one maddening and unrelenting rhythm. Soon her entire body spasmed, clenching and compressing around him with a blinding intensity as her breath hissed against his ear.

Gisele collapsed against Jamie's chest. She lay panting for a minute as he pressed light kisses to her exposed neck. His erection was still straining at the fall of his breeches but he was loath to move, instead taking fierce satisfaction at the pleasure he had wrung from the woman cradled in his arms. Neither of them stirred nor spoke for what felt like millennia.

Then Gisele placed her hands on Jamie's thighs and slowly rose to her feet. He felt the loss of her body acutely but couldn't form the right words to call her back. Instead he surveyed her movements as though in a trance, watching as she took two large steps backward and began to put herself to rights with methodical concentration. Her face remained hidden by her hair even as she made a final adjustment to her bodice and let her arms drop to her sides.

When she did finally raise her eyes to look at him, Jamie felt something black and miserable claw through his chest. Gisele's face was expressionless. The stare she offered him was empty.

"You've proven your point," she said tonelessly.

"My point?" He felt as if someone had gut-punched him.

"That you hold a great deal of . . . allure. To any woman. A fine audition, indeed."

Jamie shook his head in an effort to clear it. Not an ounce of his passion for her had been feigned. How could she think otherwise?

"But please know that I do not require a repeat performance," she continued grimly. "I left this part of my life behind a long time ago. So save your charms for the Lady Julia. She will need them more than I."

Jamie opened his mouth to argue, but before he could formulate a protest, they were both startled by a few sharp raps on the chamber door. Wordlessly Gisele crossed the room and admitted Sebastien, who staggered in, his arms supporting a large tray heavy with food and drink. Jamie immediately moved to help him.

The valet looked pointedly between Jamie and Gisele, a silent question aimed at both.

"Jamie knows everything now," she said simply.

Sebastien looked to Jamie for confirmation, and Jamie inclined his head, hoping Sebastien would interpret the flush of Gisele's countenance as having been wrought by emotional conversation and nothing more.

"Thank God," Sebastien said, sounding enormously relieved. "I was afraid it was going to be a very long day." He sat at the small table and picked up a knife.

Jamie observed Gisele from the doorway, but he made no move to join his companions at their meal. God, but he wanted this captivating woman. And not just physically, though the feel of her body against his had been so very right.

She was intelligent and brave and beautiful, and the idea of having a woman like Gisele Whitby want to be with him made him almost dizzy with longing. But he should know better than to covet things he didn't deserve. He had absolutely nothing to offer her, other than his pledge of assistance, whatever that might be worth. For the first time in his life, Jamie regretted his lack of fortune and title, two things he might have wielded with power and purpose on her behalf.

Gisele still wanted his help, but she wanted him to keep his distance. She'd been quite clear on that score, and Jamie truly had no idea how he was going to manage it. Her touch had branded him somehow despite her claimed indifference. He wondered how long Gisele's mark would burn him or what he might do to bury the lingering heat. Jamie sighed heavily.

Sebastien was wrong. It *was* going to be a very long day.

Chapter 9

They rode into London late the next afternoon under a blanket of sullen gray clouds, the wind chasing leaves and dust through the winding, twisting streets. The spring warmth of the previous evening had fled, leaving a pervasive chill that darted and bit through the seams of Gisele's cloak.

"How much farther?" It was the first thing Jamie had said to her in over an hour.

Gisele watched him from the corner of her eye, guilt and unhappiness nudging at her conscience. She'd hurt him yesterday, she knew. She'd seen it on his face when she'd dismissed him, after he had left her shattered and senseless and reeling. It had taken everything she had to retreat from him and demand distance, but what had happened in that room last night could never happen again.

She didn't fear the physical intimacy. It was the power Jamie Montcrief had over her—his ability to reduce her to a desperate mess of wanton recklessness with a simple touch—that was unacceptable. He made her lose control. Her desire clouded her judgment and allowed her emotions to control her decisions. It was too dangerous, not only to their mission but also to her own carefully reconstructed sense of self.

The problem was that she still very much needed his help. So the best she could do was disassociate herself from the undeniable attraction she felt toward this man. He had been right about one thing. She could be a very skilled actress.

"Not too much farther." She kept her tone light, determined to recapture a professional and cordial partnership. To recapture *control*. "Did you wish to stop for something?"

"No." He was watching her now. "Is this wise?" he demanded suddenly. "You being in London? How recognizable are you, exactly?"

She bit the inside of her cheek. "I'm not sure," she answered honestly. "I was the Marchioness of Valence. I died in a spectacular explosion hundreds of people witnessed. But that was four years ago, and the ladies and gentlemen of the ton tend to care only for the gossip sitting conveniently in front of their noses. I suspect their memories of me are cloudy at best."

"Yet Sebastien left ahead of us so there would be no chance of you two being seen together."

"It is better if we are not, I think. If Sebastien is recognized and I am standing right beside him, it's that much easier for a keen eye to connect us both to Valence."

Jamie was frowning at her now. "So he was Valence's valet. He must have known what was happening to you."

Gisele twisted in her saddle to look at him, ruthlessly suppressing a surge of dark memories in order to keep her voice even. "Yes. He knew. Sebastien helped orchestrate our escape."

"And did no one wonder at his sudden disappearance immediately following yours?" Jamie sounded critical.

"He didn't disappear immediately," Gisele said, not liking his tone. "He stayed long enough to make sure Helena and I were declared dead. He organized and planned our funerals. Made sure there were no loose ends. When enough time had passed, he left."

Jamie grunted at the information and eyed the looming specter of Westminster in the distance. "Who else?"

"Who else what?"

"Who else in London knows the Marchioness of Valence isn't dead?"

"The Duchess of Worth. The Dowager Duchess of Worth," she clarified. "And her limited staff."

"A duchess?" Jamie's forehead wrinkled. "Why?"

Gisele shook her head. "That is not my story to tell. But she was the only one who saw me. Truly saw me and understood what was happening."

"How did she know?"

"My gown ripped one night at a ball. She hustled me off to repair it before Valence understood what had happened. She saw...I couldn't..." Gisele floundered for the right phrase, aware Jamie was watching her closely. "She saw some marks that my supposed clumsiness could not explain."

She could see a muscle working alongside Jamie's jaw as he returned his attention to his horse. The shadows were getting longer now and casting strange shapes across roads that narrowed and widened in intervals. An occasional cart or hackney drove past, interspersed with people hurrying to their destinations before darkness fell.

"And no one else suspects? Friends or others you might have been close with?" he finally asked.

"I didn't have friends. I was not allowed out in public without my husband. Attempts to socialize in secret resulted in consequences I do not care to recall."

Jamie face darkened further. "So it is the Duchess of Worth we are paying a call to then." His words were clipped.

"Yes."

"Does she even know we're coming?"

Gisele tipped her head. "I sent her a message from Nottingham so she'll be expecting us at some point. Sebastien should have arrived at her town house already, and he will inform her we're not far behind. But it doesn't matter. She is the closest thing I have to family, and family always looks after their own."

Jamie made a noise in his throat. "Not always. Sometimes they do not rise to the occasion."

Gisele was startled at the raw pain in his words and surmised he must be referring to his estranged brother. "Your brother is a fool for—"

"It doesn't matter. Let's hurry."

⁓

The sky was drifting toward darkness by the time Gisele stopped. Here the streets were wider, the buildings set in neat squares with expanses of garden and parks breaking up the urbanity. Lanterns hung at the entrances of the expensive townhomes, illuminating each well-appointed doorstep in the encroaching shadows. The homes were tall, most with facades of brick wrapped around the ground floor and giving way to columns soaring up three stories to the eaves. Somewhere someone was playing the pianoforte, the music escaping into the night through an open window. Despite himself, Jamie was impressed. This was a London he had never seen.

"Wait here," she said, dismounting and passing the reins of her horse to him.

He watched as she glanced furtively up the street, but nothing moved save a cat darting across the pavement. Quickly she opened the wrought-iron gate and hurried down the stairs to the servants' entrance. He could hear the report of her knuckles on the door, and then the area was flooded with light as the door was opened. There was a rush of low voices he couldn't make out, and then the door closed and Jamie could see Gisele coming back up the stairs, trailed by someone.

"Joseph will see to the horses," she said to Jamie by way of explanation. "There's a stable in back next to the coach house. You can follow me."

Jamie eyed Joseph dubiously, doubting the boy's ability to manage a mouse, much less two horses. He was no more than fifteen or sixteen, and even the proper livery he wore could not hide the fact that he was painfully thin. His cheeks were hollow and sharp, his eyes overlarge in his face. His hair had been slicked down, but the occasional piece stuck up at the back in defiance, giving him a slightly disheveled, childlike appearance.

Reluctantly Jamie handed his reins over to the youth and watched as the boy led the two horses away.

"Er, shall I offer my help to the lad? He looks a little peaky," Jamie ventured.

"Good Lord, no," Gisele assured him. "Joseph was the best damn horse thief in all of London. If there's anything he knows, it's horses."

"Horse thief?" Jamie croaked, watching the rump of his beloved roan disappear into the passage toward the mews in back. He would have sprinted after the boy and the animals, except Gisele was pulling him insistently toward the townhome.

"He's retired," she explained as if this made all the sense in the world. "He's Her Grace's coachman now."

"Coachman?" he parroted dumbly. "Why?"

Gisele led him down the stairs, not bothering to look back. "He's brilliant with horses, of course. Now come inside. It's getting cold."

She pushed the door open and a flood of warmth and light enveloped him. He trailed after her, still trying to understand the last part of the conversation. She led him through the cramped but well-organized space, delicious smells wafting from somewhere up ahead, distracting him and reminding his stomach it had been too long since he'd eaten. They passed a scullery, deserted at the moment, and a darkened laundry room, also empty. Narrow doors lined the hall, concealing what must have been the wine cellars and pantries. Abruptly the hall widened into an open space dominated by two large trestle tables.

Standing in the center was a mountain of a woman who had stopped dead in her tracks at their appearance. In her arms she clutched a half dozen heavy butcher knives.

"Miz Gisele?" She set the knives down on the table with a crash. Her face creased with delight, and she barreled forward, coming to envelop Gisele in a smothering hug. Jamie blinked and took a slight step back, eyeing the woman's thick forearms and massive shoulders. The woman looked as though she might be able to lift an entire bullock by herself.

"Never thought I'd see you step foot in London again." The woman drew back, pushing strands of brassy blond hair back under her cap and straightening her stained apron.

"Neither did I," Gisele said with what sounded like real regret. "Is Sebastien already here?"

"Aye. He's helping ol' George with them books in the study upstairs. Her Grace's son was sniffin' around the other day. Sebastien was always a better hand at creative accounting."

Jamie was fighting hard to keep his face impassive. Creative accounting? What the hell did that mean? He glanced sideways at Gisele, but she registered no surprise.

"So the duke's been prowling about?" Gisele was asking.

"Aye. Prob'ly wondering if his mama's lost her mind fer good."

"Just as well to keep him thinking that."

"Aye." The woman nodded sagely.

"Is Her Grace home?"

"Aye, she just returned not a half hour ago. I believe she's jus' changing."

"She didn't know exactly when we were coming," Gisele told her.

"No matter. Jus' happy yer here." The woman nodded her understanding even as her sharp gaze suddenly locked on Jamie. "Who are you?" she asked without preamble but with a great deal of suspicion.

"Margaret, this is James Montcrief. He is working with me. Margaret is the duchess's cook."

Margaret crossed her muscular arms over her boundless chest and studied him openly. Jamie forced himself to meet her shrewd gaze steadily, realizing with a start that the woman's eyes were level with his own.

"A pleasure, ma'am." He hoped he sounded suitably respectful. He honestly didn't like his chances should this Goliath take exception to him.

"*Humph*," she grunted by way of greeting, before turning back to Gisele. "Iain married yet?"

"I imagine so."

"'Bout time," the cook mumbled. "He'll make that girl happy."

"Yes," Gisele agreed.

Margaret picked up one of her knives and ran a finger expertly along the edge of the blade, silent in consideration. "You come up with a plan yet on how we ought to stop that bastard Valence from gettin' married again?"

"Not quite yet." Gisele was avoiding Jamie's eyes.

Margaret sniffed. "Well, if you get desperate, Miz Gisele, I have favors owed me. A man can vanish these days, you know. A large is worth nearly ten guineas now, an' the surgeons are payin' up front and not askin' stupid questions."

Jamie's mouth dropped open. He hadn't thought very carefully about where he might find the connection between the former Marchioness of Valence and the two resurrection men she called friends. But never in his wildest imaginings would he have guessed it lay in the kitchens of a dowager duchess.

"No." Gisele put a hand on the woman's arm. "The Darling brothers offered the same. But I'd never ask that of you even if the risk were not as great."

"Ah, well, I figured you'd say as much." Margaret tapped the tip of the lethal blade against her palm and sighed with what sounded like regret. "You'll let me know if you change yer mind?"

"Of course," Gisele assured her.

The cook began collecting the rest of her abandoned knives. "If yer hungry, help yourself to the leftovers," she told them. She waved her arm in the general direction of the kitchens and the pantries. "We just had cold meats and bread and cheese tonight on account Her Grace was out. Got a few more chores left afore the day's done or I'd fix you something."

"We'll manage quite fine on our own."

"*Humph.* Very good then." Margaret grunted her assent and, with a final arch look at Jamie, lumbered up the wooden servants' stairs.

Jamie watched her go, realizing his mouth was still hanging open. He closed it with a snap.

"Are you hungry?" Gisele asked him, poking her head into a pantry.

He was, but in light of the last few minutes, the inconvenience now seemed rather inconsequential.

"What the hell is going on here?"

"I'm looking for the cheese," came her muffled voice as she rummaged in a pantry.

Jamie sank unfeelingly onto one of the benches. "Cheese?" he muttered.

"Did you want some?" She reappeared triumphantly, a large round in her hand. Her expression changed as she caught sight of him. "Are you ill?"

"Who are these people?" he managed.

"What people?"

"Margaret, for one."

"She's the cook."

"And before that?" he barked.

"What do you mean?" Her eyes were wary.

"Pugilist? Assassin? Body snatcher?"

"Ah. Margaret used to own a flash house."

Jamie stared. "Of course she did. Until she *retired*, I must assume."

Gisele looked at him curiously. "Yes."

"Her references must have been stellar."

"Don't be an ass."

"Almost as good as the references the horse thief submitted when applying for his job as coachman. Or the secretary upstairs in the study who is working on creative accounting."

"George spent eighteen years in the Royal Artillery. He only does the books as a favor to Her Grace. While he's adequate at balancing sums, he's most accomplished at making things explode."

"Because every duchess needs an artilleryman on staff," he mocked.

Gisele carefully placed the cheese on the table. "Is there a point you'd like to make?"

"What the hell are these people doing here, Gisele?"

"Their jobs. Which, by the way, they are exceedingly good at."

Jamie lurched to his feet. "I despise it when you do this," he fumed.

"What?"

"Get all cryptic. And secretive. How the hell am I supposed to help you when you continually refuse to explain anything?"

She regarded him steadily, as if wrestling with something in her mind, before sitting down opposite him. "Do you not think there might be people who would seize the chance to reinvent themselves given the opportunity? That if they could, they would alter the circumstances fate forced upon them?"

Jamie stared at her, uncertain if she was talking about the servants or herself.

"I owe the life I have now to the duchess," Gisele said, answering that question. "And so do the people who work here. Like me, they have pasts, yet it is only their present which truly matters. And like me, they are doing their best to make that present count for something good."

"Good? The cook just offered to have the marquess killed and sold for dissection!" he hissed.

"I can't think of anyone more deserving," Gisele muttered darkly. She looked up at him, a strange amusement dancing in her eyes. "Are you suggesting I reconsider her offer?"

Jamie sat back down with a thump and rested his head in his hands. "How can you find any of this *funny*?" He peered at her through his fingers.

"Because the alternative is unacceptable. And I—all of us—have come too far to ever go back."

Jamie dropped his hands. "But you are. Going back, that is," he clarified. "You're here now. In London."

Gisele looked down at the scarred surface of the table. "Four years ago the only thing I wanted was to escape. To escape with Helena, somewhere where we could never be found. But now..." She trailed off inaudibly.

"Now?"

"Now it is my responsibility to make sure what happened to me doesn't happen to Lady Julia. Now I am no longer afraid."

He could hear the determination in her voice, and

something inside his chest turned over. A sudden need to touch her, to make her feel protected, blindsided him. He cleared his throat, not liking the thickness that had gathered in it.

"Our responsibility."

"What?"

"You said *'my* responsibility.' I corrected you. It's *our* responsibility to see this to the end."

Gisele stared at him, her eyes suspiciously bright.

"You're not in this alone," he said evenly. "You hired me, remember? And I'd like to keep the horse. I've grown quite attached to him." He gave her a solemn smile. "Provided he's still here next time I go looking."

She laughed, and that beautiful sound was worth everything.

"Thank you."

"You're welcome." Jamie couldn't look away from her. "Gisele—"

"Her Grace wishes to see you both upstairs."

Sebastien's voice made him jump. Jamie hadn't even heard him come into the room.

Gisele sprang to her feet and hurried to where Sebastien stood watching them. "How was your ride in?" she asked her friend.

"Uneventful. Yours?"

"The same."

"Good."

Jamie heard the importance of that simple exchange and the relief underlying it.

"I heard laughing," Sebastien suddenly said, looking confused.

"I was being informed of the benefits of creative

accounting," Jamie explained, hoping to get a reaction out of the man.

"Hmm-mm." The valet appeared not to have heard him and was instead eyeing Gisele with speculation.

Gisele was already halfway up the stairs by now, clearly eager to see the woman she had called family. "Let's go. Her Grace does not appreciate being kept waiting."

⁓

The manor house Jamie had grown up in had been large, but it had also been a country home and had served its purpose with understated practicality. There was nothing practical about his current surroundings. He found himself in a gleaming hall, white tiles polished to such a sheen beneath his feet that he could see his reflection. Towering columns of alabaster boxed in the room, and chandeliers and sconces dripped and glittered with crystal and light. Large vases were set into niches along the walls and added a blaze of color. The main staircase soared up and away on the far end, a confection of glossy marble and wrought iron that beckoned guests onward and upward. Even the ceiling was a dizzying kaleidoscope of plaster moldings and color.

Gisele had barely given the chamber a glance, but now she stopped to wait for Jamie.

"You're either stalling or stunned." She sounded entertained.

Jamie gestured to the grandeur around them. "I've never been in a room quite so…"

"Ostentatious?"

"Useless."

Gisele snorted. "It's what is expected, of course, and

certainly from a duchess. Many people put a great amount of importance on possessions such as these."

Jamie didn't miss her implication. "The duchess not being one of them?"

Gisele only smiled.

"She must be rich."

"Obscenely." Her smile widened into a devilish grin. "Now come." She moved toward a door set into the side of the hall, opening it and gesturing for him to precede her. "After you."

Cautiously Jamie stepped into a drawing room and was instantly swallowed by a profusion of gold, yellow, and dark wood, all brought to life by an abundance of candelabras and the glow from a well-lit fire. The furniture was French, beautifully carved pieces upholstered with lavishly patterned fabric. His feet sank into a deeply piled rug, butter-yellow in color and matching the swaths of yellow silk hanging against the walls, tied artfully with gold cords. He barely noticed any of this.

What he noticed was the chickens.

Glass chickens, porcelain chickens, and clay chickens. Jeweled chickens, gilt chickens, and silver chickens. Poultry fashioned from wood and pewter and bronze covered every surface. A dozen mounted roosters in their full plumage perched on the mantel of the fireplace, the flames reflecting devilishly in their beady glass eyes. A fat hen was embroidered on a large cushion propped on the settee, and a profusion of smaller cushions were placed in its wake, each graced with the image of a fuzzy chick. A mirror hung over the fireplace, and Jamie took an involuntary step closer to ascertain that it was, in fact, eggshells adorning the edges.

"Close your mouth, Jamie. It is unbecoming." Gisele pulled the door shut behind them with a gentle click.

Jamie did a slow circle. "I don't know what to say."

"Well, think of something fast because I would imagine—" Gisele didn't finish her sentence before the door opened again and a woman swept in with the grandeur of a queen.

She was nearly as wide as she was short, and her white hair was piled on top of her head in a style Jamie hadn't seen in fifteen years. Her gown, however, was cut to the height of fashion and embroidered intricately with gold thread, and the jewelry she had on would have made a monarch or a thief salivate.

The woman turned to face them, and that was when Jamie saw the chicken under her arm. This one, however, unlike its comrades, was very much alive.

"Close the door," she ordered, and Gisele obeyed. "This is Iain's replacement?" The elderly woman took out a quizzing glass and held it to her eye, examining Jamie from head to toe.

"Yes."

"Very good." She nodded her approval. "Handsome, although if he closed his mouth he would be more so."

Jamie snapped his jaw shut for the second time in as many minutes.

"His name?"

Gisele stepped forward. "May I present Mr. James Montcrief. Mr. Montcrief, this is Her Grace Eleanor, the Duchess of Worth."

"Pleased to make your acquaintance, Your Grace," Jamie said carefully, sketching a polite bow.

"Montcrief?" The duchess's voice cut through the air

with the command of a general's. "*Captain* James Mont-crief? Of the First Dragoon Guards?"

"Formerly, Your Grace." Jamie cut a glance at Gisele, who was frowning slightly.

"Have you met?" Gisele asked.

"No. Not until just now." The duchess stuffed the pro-testing hen unceremoniously into a cage, not taking her eyes off Jamie. She came around the settee and took Jamie's hand in her own. "An honor, Captain Montcrief. It is not every day one gets to meet a true hero and not a peacock stuffed into gold braid who can't ever get the story straight twice."

Jamie flinched. "It is *Mister*," he clarified, "and while I thank you for the sentiments, I am not a hero." Certainly not to the men who had died under his command. "War produces survivors, not heroes."

"*Psht.*" The duchess ignored him. She turned a specu-lative eye on Gisele. "Did you know who he was when you hired him?"

Gisele was looking slowly between Jamie and the duchess. "I'm not sure I know who he is now," she said.

"I see." The speculation was focused back on Jamie. "You didn't tell her."

"Gisele—ah, Miss Whitby is aware I was a cavalry officer, Your Grace." Jamie stood ramrod-straight, won-dering with a trepidation bordering on dread what it was the duchess thought he should have disclosed. "She is also aware I sold my commission after Waterloo."

The duchess ignored him. "Captain Montcrief is a highly decorated cavalry officer. He was promoted twice to the title of captain—not by purchase, but by his com-manding officers for gallant conduct. Rare and telling."

"You told me your father paid for your commission," Gisele said to Jamie.

"He did," the duchess answered for him. "As a cornet."

How the hell did the Duchess of Worth know that? More bewildering, why would that information be of any interest to her?

"The circumstances of war being what they are, Your Grace, there were regrettably a large number of vacancies that required filling. My promotions were a matter of convenience." Jamie did not want to have this discussion.

"Poppycock," the duchess disagreed pleasantly. "You were promoted because you were one of the few who knew the value of discipline on the field." She released Jamie's hand and motioned him over to a large wardrobe. She released the catch and the doors swung open, revealing a mass of maps pinned to the interior and shelves filled with neatly ordered files, each bound with string and labeled with a date and a location.

Jamie stared, recognizing the maps for what they were immediately. Battle plans, maps of topography and troops. Details of numbers and units and regiments. Arrows drawn in colored ink showing advances and retreats. Infantry, cavalry, artillery. A map of Quatre Bras and Waterloo hung prominently near the top, but Jamie made no move to step any closer. He knew each rise and hill and rock of those bloody fields. He felt the terror, the suicidal recklessness, the despair, and the guilt course through him all over again. He could smell the stench of burned powder and burned flesh, of guts and death, hear the sobs and screams of dying men and dying horses. He had no interest in going back, literally or figuratively.

The duchess riffled through a stack of loose papers

until she found the one she wanted. "The First Cavalry Brigade acquitted themselves well in their initial charge of d'Erlon's left flank. Why in God's name did they not stop?"

There was no judgment in the words, just a blunt, detached curiousness. How could he respond? How could he describe how inexperienced English cavalry officers, drunk on the taste of victory, had recklessly spurred their men over a shattered French infantry toward enemy lines? Jamie had tried to stop them, a desperate, futile attempt to turn them back. But in the end, two brigades of Englishmen on exhausted, bloodied horses had been cut off from British lines, and the French lancers who had been waiting beyond the thick smoke for their own taste of slaughter had descended like vultures.

Jamie fought to curb the anguish that welled up at the memory and tried to answer the duchess with the same blunt detachment that had characterized the question. "Most of the officers' horses, Your Grace, had more intelligence than their riders."

The duchess grunted. "Wellington implied the same thing. Said there was even one regiment that came back with only twenty out of the three hundred and fifty it had started with. Is that accurate?"

"Yes." He pushed the word out through gritted teeth. Goddammit, but he needed a drink.

The woman made a notation on the paper with a stub of a pencil. "A hobby of mine," the duchess said. "Perhaps someday I'll write a book. Regardless, your name was oft mentioned in the propaganda doled out to the civilians in London to assure us that England's domination of the world was always well in hand." She was watching him keenly, though not without some sympathy. She replaced her paper and closed the doors, and the snap of the latch was like a gunshot in the space.

Jamie didn't trust himself to speak and instead only nodded.

"I can see the resemblance now," she said. "I met your father during my first season, you know. Only once, but I remember him well. Your grandfather had just brought him to London to find a bride."

Jamie grasped the change in topic with alacrity. "My father always maintained the journey wasn't a total loss. He enjoyed the horse races and sales," he offered weakly.

"I am glad he found something to enjoy, for I have never met a man more miserable and heartsick in my life." The duchess tipped her head in memory.

"It ended well," Jamie replied, aware Gisele was giving him a strange look.

"Not for you," the duchess said, her sharp, shrewd look back.

"I have no complaints. I've wanted for nothing in my life."

"Your grandfather's obstinacy cost you the title."

"My grandfather was a tyrant. And he died alone and unhappy."

"Stop," Gisele finally interrupted. "I seem to have missed something."

The duchess cut her eyes to Gisele, then back to Jamie. "My, my, but you really have been holding out."

"You said you were a bastard," Gisele said.

"I am." Jamie sighed. "By law."

"By law? What does that mean?"

"It means I was born out of wedlock. It means my father married my mother after I was born."

"Your mother was the Duchess of Reddyck?"

"Yes."

Gisele was frowning fiercely at him. "How long after you were born were they married?"

Jamie heaved another sigh, aware the duchess was still watching him like a hawk. "Two hours."

"Two *hours*?" Her voice rose incredulously.

"What does it matter?" Jamie asked. "As you so delicately assured me on another occasion, you are not interested in the lurid details of my conception. It changes nothing."

"Ah, but there you are wrong." The duchess was tapping a bejeweled finger against her chin. "You, Mr. Montcrief, are teetering on the fine edge of the peerage. Regardless of the law, you are still the eldest son of a duke and his duchess."

Jamie scowled. "Not relevant. I have no designs on the title," he said. "Ever."

The duchess cut him off with a wave of her hand. "But it is, Mr. Montcrief. It is very relevant, given the circumstances." She turned to Gisele. "Mr. Montcrief's father had fallen in love with the daughter of the brewer from the village nearest his estate. He fully intended to marry her and informed his own father, the duke, of his plans. The duke forbade it, threatened to have the girl's family ruined and run off should the young man proceed. Within a fortnight, Reddyck had rented a townhome in London and thrust his son into the full lunacy of a London season with the sole intention of finding a *suitable* bride for the future duke."

"And?" Gisele had perched herself on the edge of a chair. "He did, I am assuming?"

Jamie threw up his hands in defeat.

"Of course he didn't. Over the duration of the season, Mr. Montcrief's father came to the conclusion he couldn't live without the beautiful girl he had left behind. He bought a fleet horse, procured a special license, and rode as fast as he could back to the love of his life, intending to marry her, his father's wishes be damned."

"So what happened?" Gisele's brow was creased.

"He didn't ride fast enough," Jamie said wearily.

"He didn't ride fast..." She trailed off, looking at him in horror. "She was already pregnant and he didn't know?"

"No. She didn't tell him, afraid of what the old duke would do to her, her family, and her unborn child if he thought she was trying to trap his son into marriage."

"How could he not know she was pregnant?"

"He was away for almost the entire season," the duchess reminded her. "Who would have told him? He had no way of knowing."

"Bloody hell." Gisele slumped back in her chair before looking up again at Jamie with speculative eyes. "So the current Duke of Reddyck is your younger brother. Your full brother."

"Yes," Jamie replied curtly.

"If he had a patron of significant rank and with his exemplary military service, Mr. Montcrief would be welcome in any club and any establishment he should choose." The duchess gazed at him speculatively.

"It gets him in." Gisele was speaking urgently. "Into a world even Iain couldn't get into."

"To do what, exactly?" Jamie asked, to remind them he was still in the room.

"I don't know," Gisele admitted, more to the dowager than to Jamie. She bit her lip and gestured in Jamie's direction. "I had thought originally that I—we—would come back and just stop this wedding. But..."

"It's not enough, is it?" Eleanor spoke softly.

"No. It has to end. Otherwise the cycle will continue. Even without Lady Julia, there will be another. And another." The statement was bleak.

The Duchess of Worth turned an assessing eye on Jamie. "How committed are you to helping Miss Whitby?"

Jamie frowned. "I am unsure of your meaning, Your Grace."

"Miss Whitby seems to think you are genuine in your commitment to the terms of your...employment. But what she has done and continues to do is to defy convention and custom and law, and there are many, many people who will not and cannot accept this breach of constancy. If we are to go forward here, I must determine if you are a man who will be able to see this to the end."

Jamie felt his irritation surge as he met the duchess's eyes squarely. He had tolerated this entire charade for far too long, and his nerves were raw. "You called me a war hero," he said hoarsely, "when I walked in. But war is not a game of chess pieces that can be righted once they get knocked over. Every man who fought beside me and never made it back from the battlefield wasn't a statistic for me to note in a ledger. He was someone's hero too—a brother, father, husband, or son, no different from me, and we struggled and bled and sacrificed together." He forced himself to take a deep breath and temper his tone, aware his voice had become ragged with emotion.

"Perhaps I'm not qualified to offer an opinion on the edicts of marriage, but I am of the mind a wife should be no different. Your own heroine at your side who might share the sacrifices, the struggles, and the victories. My mother was my father's greatest ally and he her most fervent supporter. She was never made to suffer abuse or depravity simply because, by law, she became his property on their wedding day."

A long silence descended in the room, broken only by the sound of a piece of coal shifting in the grate.

The duchess swallowed and cleared her throat. "Thank you, Mr. Montcrief, for your honest and candid answer. That will suffice." She paused. "And you have my apologies, for whatever it's worth."

Jamie rubbed his face with his hands, feeling suddenly exhausted. A week ago he had been in the middle of nowhere, lost to himself and to everyone around him. There had been no need to examine his principles or his beliefs under such a bright beam, or any light at all for that matter. He had been anonymous, numb, and miserable. And it had suited him fine. He had deserved nothing more. But now he'd been forced to start living again. And it was strange and painful. The constant guilt was still there but it was now accompanied by a sense of purpose. And the hope that maybe—just maybe—by embracing this cause, he would somehow, in some small way, make amends for his past failings.

The duchess had moved to the mantel, fingering the plumage of one of the mounted birds. "Do you know why these are here?" she asked Jamie suddenly.

"Your Grace?" He was startled by the abrupt change in topic.

"The chickens." She gestured to the hen in the cage and the room around her in general.

Jamie stepped closer to the fire. "One might assume it is because you enjoy the company of poultry."

The duchess smiled then, and Jamie caught a glimpse of the beauty she must have been as a girl. "One might assume that, yes. But I am interested to hear what it is you assume, Mr. Montcrief."

Jamie continued to hold the duchess's gaze, recognizing the question for the test it truly was. "Very well, Your Grace. One might also then conclude that the Duchess of Worth is starting to slip in her dotage. That her mind is not as sharp as it once was. That she has developed eccentricities that, because she is a duchess, must be tolerated. Strange behavior in a great lady that has become expected and never questioned. And with careful planning, it can also help camouflage certain righteous—but forbidden—pursuits that would shock polite society, or perhaps even land a person in prison."

A slow grin of approval spread across the duchess's face. "Heavens, if I were thirty years younger."

Jamie couldn't help the faint, answering smile that touched his own lips. "You flatter me, Your Grace."

The grin slowly faded, replaced by a cold determination. Her voice dropped to a whisper, one that Gisele could not overhear. "Has she told you what Valence did to her, Mr. Montcrief?"

Jamie shook his head slowly. "She has told me a great deal, but no, she has not confided in me the specifics. I am trying to imagine."

"You can't."

Jamie felt chilled despite the stifling room.

"Valence needs to be stopped, Mr. Montcrief. Lady Julia has no idea what that man is capable of. Society has no idea what that man is capable of, and that is what makes him dangerous."

Jamie considered her words, the venom in them unmistakable. "Given the conversation of the last minutes, Your Grace, I must, in turn, ask what your stake is in this. Why help a woman of no relation to you? Then or now?" He was direct and unapologetic.

The duchess smiled a sad, tired smile and was silent for a long moment. "When Gisele was first brought to London, she reminded me a great deal of myself. Innocent, trusting, dazzled by the sparkle and trappings of unimaginable wealth. Yet sometimes beneath that glittering facade lies an ugliness never exposed to the world, for if it were to be uncovered, the shame and the humiliation would be intolerable." She looked past Jamie at Gisele, who was watching them. "I never had the courage to do what she did. I endured and hid my shame from my children and friends until the day my husband died. Do you understand?"

"Yes." Jamie knew how much those words had cost her.

"Good." The steel was back in her voice. She moved back toward Gisele. "I had prepared myself for the task of creating a wealthy gentleman out of Iain's replacement, one who might move freely along the edges of polite society so as to best determine how to orchestrate Valence's downfall. You, however, Captain, have exceeded all expectations. The very pedigree you have successfully ignored for so many years will become our ammunition.

I will be arranging the triumphant return of a war hero, and not just any common war hero. Captain James Montcrief, after all, is not only a courageous, valiant leader of men, but he is the son of the late Duke and Duchess of Reddyck, who were, I've just remembered, dear friends of my youth." She glanced sideways at Jamie. "Prepare yourself to embrace the role, Mr. Montcrief. We all have our regrets, but the next sennight is not the time to dwell on whatever yours may be. Understood?"

Jamie nodded, the enormity of what he was getting himself into beginning to become clear.

The duchess was pacing now. "It would not only be natural but expected that I would welcome Mr. Montcrief with open arms when, after years of faithful service to His Majesty, he has returned to enjoy all the pleasures London can offer." She picked up a tiny silver chicken and stared at it. "I might be considered peculiar but I still have the power to unleash an eligible bachelor upon society in a style few others will ever achieve. Expect to become the gallant cavalryman convention demands. Can you do that, Mr. Montcrief?"

"Yes." Jamie forced the word out.

"Excellent. There is a suite of rooms waiting for you at the Albany."

"The Albany?"

"A suitable address for the image we are creating. My nephew occupies the suite when he is in London. He is, however, in India or some other untamed place at the moment and is not using it. It is family money that pays for the suite, and therefore it is family who may decide how it's used in his absence."

"Of course," Jamie murmured.

"The apartment also includes two attic rooms for servants. A gentleman of substantial means, such as yourself, will have a valet at the very least to see to the details of his personal and public life, not to mention his wardrobe."

"Sebastien."

"Yes. You will also employ a housekeeper, though she will be invisible in her role." She swung around to face Gisele. "As much as it would please me to have you stay here, I cannot risk it. There are too many who come and go who still might remember the stunningly beautiful and elusive Marchioness of Valence, and short of locking you in *my* attics for the next few nights, I can't avoid the risk of an inopportune encounter with a wayward guest. But you need to stay close. Of everyone, for better or worse, you know Valence best. If we are going to expose him, we will need you and the information you possess."

Jamie felt overwhelmed. Everything seemed to be happening incredibly quickly.

"And when will this occur?" he ventured. "The triumphant return of . . . ah, a retired cavalry officer?"

"War hero," she corrected. "And you will be presented tonight."

"Tonight?" Jamie straightened. "As in . . . tonight-tonight?"

"We'll need to work on your comprehension skills," the duchess chided lightly. "The Countess of Baustenbury is hosting a ball. She does it every year, and it has grown into quite the event."

"The Countess of Baustenbury?" Jamie refused to look at Gisele.

"Do you plan on echoing me for the remainder of this discussion?"

"No," Jamie sputtered. "It's just . . ."

"You are acquainted with the countess?" The duchess was watching him curiously.

"Not exactly. Why this ball?"

"The marquess will be there," Gisele said quietly. "Invitations are rare and exclusive. Two things that are irresistible to him."

Eleanor turned to Jamie. "I wish you to meet the man. I want you to see him, to speak with him, insert yourself into his world."

"To what end?" Jamie felt something cold lodge in his chest.

The duchess's lips thinned. "We will determine that. But for now, we will concentrate on making you visible, and most importantly, making your presence both desired and required at every club and crush in this city."

"I cannot believe I will be so coveted."

Eleanor drew herself up. "Your looks will get you noticed, though you already know that. Your job tonight, Mr. Montcrief, is to be charming and polite to every woman in attendance, whether she is eighteen or eighty. You will be humble and witty and cordial to every man to whom you are introduced, and if they ask for a war story, you will give them one, whether you wish to or not. Let me take care of the rest." She paused. "I will bring my carriage to collect you myself at ten o'clock sharp. You will be dressed in a manner best left to the expertise of Sebastien. My son is of the same build as you—I will have him send over something appropriate until you can obtain a wardrobe befitting your role. Any questions?"

Jamie was beginning to feel a little as if his life had spun completely out of control, and the feeling was not sitting comfortably. "No."

"Very good." She glanced at the clock on the mantel. "I would suggest you retire to your new lodgings and familiarize yourself with their location and amenities. And I would suggest you do that soon. Ten o'clock is not that distant."

"Of course."

"Until tonight then, Mr. Montcrief?"

"I'll be ready, Your Grace."

For what exactly, he had no idea.

Gisele waited until the door had closed behind them before turning on him. "Were you ever going to tell me?"

"About what?" Jamie asked, feeling utterly drained.

"The truth about your family? Your captaincy? Any of it?"

"What difference does it make? I have given you my word to help you, and I intend to see this through. I should think that would be enough."

Gisele watched him steadily. "I just wish I had known the whole of your history before we visited the duchess. I was blindsided in that room."

"Oh, pardon me, did you want me to be honest?" he mocked in disbelief, the emotional turmoil of the last hour finally snapping what remained of his patience. "Like the way you've been honest with me?" He thought he saw her flinch but he didn't care. "Every scrap of information you've given me I've had to beg and tease and draw out of you in the manner one might pull a bone away from a hungry dog. I still don't even know what it was your husband did to you and what it is I'm supposed to stop from happening again!" He stopped, breathing hard. "I'm working on assumptions and blind faith, Gisele. You, of all people, cannot *dare* condemn my lack of transparency!"

She looked away.

Jamie cursed. "I'm sorry."

"Don't be." Her words were dull. "You're absolutely right."

He ran his fingers through his hair, at a loss for an appropriate response. What he wanted to do was kiss her. Sweep her up into his arms and carry her to the ends of the earth, where he would spend the rest of his life making her forget every terrible thing that had ever been done to her. But she didn't want that from him—that she'd made very clear. She'd fought her own way free from her past. And if he was any sort of man at all, he would respect that.

He wished she'd yelled at him instead of backing down. Hysterics would be easier to manage than her quiet retreat. He should not have said what he'd said but Gisele had pushed him into a darkened corner so filled with unbearable guilt and regret that he'd wasted a year of his life trying to drown it all in drink.

Gisele turned and walked to the door, her expression completely unreadable. "We should hurry," she said, her voice lacking any discernable emotion. "We have a great deal to accomplish before ten o'clock."

Chapter 10 _____

The Albany apartment was more spacious than Gisele had anticipated. Manicured as carefully as those of the townhomes they had just left, the exterior of the building exuded understated money and exclusivity. The interior was no different. Stepping through the door of the suite, Gisele found herself in a simple but expensively appointed hall where a fire was struggling to establish itself. Sebastien, efficient as ever, had already ordered coal brought up, water heated, and the windows cracked open to dissipate the mustiness of a space unused for too long.

Alone she continued her exploration into a masculine-looking drawing room of sorts housing an expansive desk, a modest settee, a comfortable leather chair, and a small sideboard topped with cut crystal decanters and glasses. Bookshelves covered the entire wall behind the desk, and Gisele let her fingers glide across the spines, leaving faint trails in the dust. Drifting toward a set of double doors, she peered into a bedroom tastefully decorated in cream and dark blues. A heavy bed dominated the center of the room, flanked by an ornate armoire. On the other side, a narrow door led to a dressing room where she could see the corner of a large hip bath in which water already steamed.

She returned to the hall to find Sebastien and a porter struggling to deposit a large crate just inside the door. The valet looked harried and harassed.

"Where is James?" he demanded, the moment the porter had left and shut the door behind him.

"In the stables." Gisele shrugged and toed the edge of the crate with her shoe.

Sebastien said something inaudible under his breath and pulled out his timepiece.

"Would you like me to fetch him?" Gisele asked with little enthusiasm. She and Jamie had barely exchanged a dozen words since leaving the duchess's.

Sebastien collapsed into one of the upholstered chairs near the fireplace and waved his hand in defeat. "An hour," he muttered.

"I beg your pardon?"

"In an hour Her Grace's carriage will pull up outside this building. At which time she expects James to be *spectacular* and *irresistible*. Her words, not mine."

"I have faith," Gisele told him warmly, trying to cheer him up. "For you are a miracle worker."

"As much as I appreciate your pretty flattery, my dear, I must point out I have nothing to work with," Sebastien despaired. "No clothes, no shoes, and no James."

A sharp rap on the door interrupted his lamentations, and he heaved himself out of his chair to answer. A footman in fine livery stood in the doorway holding a long, bulky box.

"The Duke of Worth sends his regards," the servant said pleasantly. "He has sent over a number of items at

Her Grace's request for"—he consulted a card—"Mr. James Montcrief. He does hope they will suit, and he looks forward to making his acquaintance this evening." His oratory complete, the footman deposited the box into Sebastien's arms and retreated back out into the night.

Sebastien marched the box into the bedroom, where he placed it on the bed, mollified somewhat by the delivery of the clothes if not the man he needed to dress. Gisele wandered in after him, watching as the valet began to extract evening wear with near reverence.

"The man might be a rogue, but he certainly knows how to appoint himself." Sebastien picked up a black evening coat and admired the cut.

"Who? The Duke of Worth?"

"Yes."

"Margaret told me he was snooping around Her Grace's house the other day."

Sebastien snorted. "He was probably just trying to make sure there was still enough money in the coffers to keep him in racehorses," he said. "I don't think the duke would have the smallest idea of what he was looking at even if someone were robbing the family blind and leaving a trail of coins and silverware out the front door."

Gisele's forehead wrinkled. "I'm trying to remember him."

Sebastien laid out two different cravats on the counterpane with admiration. "Sinfully handsome, perhaps a little self-absorbed, and as far as I can tell, not at all interested in the business end of his title. But generous to a fault." He held up a pair of evening pumps and stroked the black leather with a happy sigh. "And he has a superb sense of style."

"What the hell are those?" Jamie growled from behind Gisele.

She jumped and spun, her heart leaping in her chest.

"Nice of you to join us," Sebastien said, eyeing in dismay the bits of straw and hay that once again clung to Jamie's clothing. "And they're shoes."

"For leprechauns?" Jamie asked.

Gisele snickered despite her efforts to remain silent.

"For *gentlemen*." Sebastien pinned both of them with a glare.

"Dear God," Jamie muttered. "If you expect me to wear those, I'm going to need a drink. Or six."

"No, you need a bath," Sebastien corrected.

"Why?"

"Because you smell like a horse. And even though you will likely dance with ladies tonight who do indeed look like horses, that does not mean *eau d'equine* will curry you favor with anyone. No pun intended."

Jamie was frowning fiercely as he surveyed the clothing on the bed.

"I'll bring you a drink once you're in the tub," the valet offered.

Jamie looked up with reluctant interest. "You will?"

"Yes. I'm not above bribery. Now go and get clean like a good boy. I'll be in to shave you right away."

Jamie sighed in defeat before he pushed past Gisele on his way to the dressing room. His eyes met hers briefly before they skittered away.

"Are you two not speaking?" Sebastien asked the moment the dressing room door closed behind him.

"I don't know what you mean." Gisele backed out of the bedroom, unwilling to have this conversation.

"Darling, you're a terrible liar. At least to me."

She stopped in the doorway, caught. "Jamie's mother was the Duchess of Reddyck. His parents were married after he was born." She paused. "And he didn't purchase his captaincy. He was promoted. As it turns out, he really was a war hero."

"And?" Sebastien had a perplexed look on his face.

"And what?"

"Why are you telling me this? As interesting as this trivia might be, honestly, what difference does it make?"

Gisele sighed unhappily. "That's exactly what Jamie said when I berated him for not telling me before." She leaned her forehead against the wood. "God, I am such a fool."

"Ah." Sebastien left the far side of the bed to face her and nodded sympathetically. "Fool, no. Unfair, yes." He raised a dark brow. "It sounds as though you owe James an apology." He turned back to the clothing. "But you can't do it now. I have"—he checked his timepiece again—"only forty minutes to create *spectacular* and *irresistible*."

Gisele nearly laughed. Despite her earlier encouragement, no miracles were necessary. Jamie unshaven and naked was stunning enough.

"I fail to see anything amusing about this," Sebastien grumbled. "So if you are only here to entertain yourself at my expense, please get out."

Gisele dropped him a mocking curtsy and retreated, leaving the valet to his fervent comparison of waistcoats.

She busied herself unpacking the contents of the crate still in the hall. Candles, bricks of hard soap, towels, extra bed linens, and bottles of whiskey and brandy. Blacking, brushes, and small tins that Gisele could only guess as to their contents and purpose, but nevertheless had been designated as necessary by a valet who took his job very seriously. The mundane work gave her time to consider both Jamie's and Sebastien's words, and she squirmed as she did so.

Sebastien had said she'd been unfair, but that was kind. Gisele had been far worse than unfair. Wasn't she the one who had lectured Jamie on the unimportance of one's past when the present counts for more? And then to accuse him of not being honest about the events in his life when it truly mattered naught...

She glanced toward the bedroom doors, still tightly shut as Jamie prepared himself to face the unforgiving judgment of the ton. Gisele knew very well he would spend a large portion of the evening reliving the horror of Waterloo for the idle entertainment of aristocrats. He would undoubtedly need to provide an explanation about his title, or lack of one. Things he'd probably never expected he'd have to do when he agreed to help her.

Would she do the same if their roles were reversed? If it were Jamie who needed her help? Help that would require her to explain the abuse she'd suffered at the hands of her husband? Or relive the flames and the freezing water of the Thames? Would she sacrifice that personal privacy in order to keep her word? She didn't have an easy answer, and for that she was ashamed.

God, but she owed Jamie an apology of epic proportions for her hypocrisy. And she would add another equally large *mea culpa* for her selfishness.

Gisele was hurrying back to the drawing room, resolute and determined, when the bedroom doors swung open. She stopped short as Sebastien emerged looking smug and extremely pleased with himself.

"May I present to you, my lady, Mr. James Montcrief."
He bowed with a flourish and moved aside as Jamie
stepped out from behind him.

Gisele felt the ground give way beneath her, and she
sat down hard on the wide leather chair. "Oh" was all she
managed.

He was dressed in the very height of fashion, a look
that was somehow cavalier yet perfect all at once. Black
tailcoat, a pearl-colored waistcoat, and a cleverly tied cravat so blindingly white it couldn't help but emphasize his
rich complexion and unyielding jaw. Modern black trou-
sers hugged powerful legs, his muscular calves encased
in black silk, and the sleek look was finished with a fashionable pair of thin leather shoes. His dark golden hair
fell over his forehead in thick, careless waves, begging for
fingers to run through it. There was a slight flush in his
cheeks from his bath or his shave or both, bringing attention to those exotically colored eyes.

Gisele had never in her life seen a man as physically
breathtaking as the one standing before her.

"*Oh? That's all you have to say? Really?*" Sebastien
demanded. "Tell me you don't feel the need to throw
yourself at his splendor. Or swoon at his feet?"

Gisele was still trying to find her voice.

Jamie had no such problems. "I want my boots back,"
he growled.

"Over my dead and bloodied body," Sebastien replied,
peeved. "Only a boor dances in boots."

Gisele rose slowly from her chair and came to stand
directly in front of Jamie. His eyes were guarded, his
thoughts unreadable.

"If you are worried about dancing, perhaps I might

have the pleasure of this one?" It would be the only opportunity she would ever have to dance with this man, and despite everything, she would not squander that.

"Practice. Excellent idea," Sebastien sniffed. He hummed the opening bars to a waltz. "I'll leave you to it while I put the rest of the clothes in order before they are ruined forever. The bedroom looks a little like we've been robbed."

Jamie hesitated before he held out his hand, and Gisele wondered if he was going along with this idea out of duty or kindness. She placed her hand in his, and he encompassed it in his warmth, while his other hand slid around her waist. A thrill coursed through her.

"You approve." He glanced down at his clothes. "I am suitable?"

"You are stunning." She didn't see any reason not to state the obvious.

He gave her a slow smile, dropping his guard, and she forgot to breathe. Lust flexed through her, leaving her throbbing and damp. He led her into the first steps.

"When I learned this dance, it was considered the height of indecency," he whispered. "Scandalous." His fingers traced a slow circle at the small of her back.

"Times have changed." God, but he was making it hard to think. "Though if you waltz with a debutante like this tonight, you'll still find yourself married by tomorrow morning."

"I have no desire to waltz with a debutante," he said quietly.

"But you will." *Because I've asked you to*, she added with silent remorse.

"Yes."

She gathered her courage. "Jamie? I need to apologize."

He stilled. "No, you don't. What I said earlier—"

"Stop." She pulled back and searched his eyes. "When I asked for your help, I had no idea this would become so...personal. I, more than anyone, understand what it is like to try to forget, and I never intended for you to have to return to places better left behind. For that I am truly sorry." She fingered a button on the front of his coat. "Your past is not mine to appraise or censure. I promise I will not do so again. The mere fact you are still here after everything..." She trailed off. "Your presence speaks louder than words ever could. Thank you, Jamie."

His hand tightened on hers, and he pulled her back into him. She could feel the hard strength of him beneath the fine clothes, and she leaned into it, laying her head against his chest, for the first time truly believing everything would be all right.

"You're welcome," he whispered, his mouth inches from hers.

"Ahem." Sebastien cleared his throat. "Her Grace's carriage has arrived."

Gisele stepped away from Jamie with acute regret. The valet was waiting behind them, gloves in hand.

Jamie raised Gisele's fingers to his lips and kissed them softly. "Thank you for the dance, Miss Whitby," he said formally. "It was an honor."

"Good luck," Gisele said, fighting an irrational urge to burst into tears. Dear God, what was wrong with her? "Keep in mind what I said about your waltzing." She tried to make her voice light but was fairly certain she had failed miserably.

"Of course." Jamie squeezed her hand and then let it go, following Sebastien out into the hall.

Gisele heard the murmur of voices, and then the door opened, a draft of chilled air curling itself through the apartment before the door shut behind them. She wrapped her arms around herself, turning slowly. Without Jamie she felt a little adrift, and she wondered when that had happened. She squared her shoulders, ignoring the sharp feeling of loss. It was late, she was tired, and there was no longer any reason for her to stay. Morning would arrive soon enough.

She went in search of her own room in the attic.

Chapter 11 ———————————————

The Duchess of Worth escorted Jamie into the ballroom, and as he heard his name announced with hers, the conversation stuttered before resuming. They were certainly getting their fair share of stares, which showed a peculiar mix of mild curiosity and undisguised assessment. He wondered idly if it was he or the duchess generating such looks. She was, after all, carrying a chicken.

Eleanor took Jamie's arm and plowed ahead into the crowd, smiling and murmuring vague greetings as she went, but not stopping to talk to anyone. Eventually she reached the far side of the room and paused, slightly out of breath.

"Well," she puffed, "I would think everyone has had a glimpse of you, without getting a good look. They'll be circling soon."

"Your Grace?" Jamie looked around with forced casualness, noting the soaring ceilings, the countless candles mounted in antique chandeliers, and the hundreds of people reflected in the surfaces of the tall windows surrounding the ballroom.

"We'll allow them to come to us. War heroes, and

spectacularly irresistible ones at that, do not chase company. They *allow* others into their presence."

Jamie scoffed. "That is the most ridiculous thing I have ever heard. I'm not the bloody Prince of Wales."

"Ah, but perception is everything, is it not?" She hefted the chicken under her arm with a small smirk. "Trust me."

Jamie nodded.

"Now listen carefully, Mr. Montcrief, for this may be the last time I will have a chance to speak with you for quite a while. The marquess will be somewhere in this crush, and you will, at some point, be introduced. Take his measure, befriend him if you can. And as for Lady Julia, while I do not expect you to sweep her off her feet, there is no reason you shouldn't give her pause. Can you do all that?"

Jamie glanced around, girding himself. "Yes."

"Good. My son will join us shortly," the duchess predicted. "One glimpse of our feathered friend here, and he'll be in full damage control mode, so just play along. He may not be the most ambitious man in the room, but he has a good heart. And he is a *duke*. And that, Mr. Montcrief, will serve you very admirably in the short term indeed. Do you understand?"

Jamie nodded again.

"Mother." A voice carried over the din as if on cue. "There you are."

Eleanor plastered a beatific smile on her powdered face and turned to face the man approaching them. "Worth, darling," she beamed.

Jamie would have guessed him to be a duke, if only for the mass of moon-eyed daughters and covetous mothers he left gasping in his wake. Even without the title, however, the man cut a dashing figure. Tall and lithe with dark eyes and dark hair, he moved with the innate confidence of a man at ease in his station. He had a devil-may-care look about him, dimmed slightly by trepidation that mounted as he got closer to the duchess.

The duke obediently stopped and kissed his mother's hand, and Jamie watched his eyes bulge as he considered the hen.

"Mother, is the chicken necessary?" he asked in a long-suffering voice. "I thought we had discussed this."

"Did we?" Eleanor asked absently. "I don't remember."

Her son ran his hand through his thick hair, and Jamie was torn between the urge to laugh and the urge to feel sorry for him.

The duke straightened, and his eyes alighted on Jamie. "You must be Mr. Montcrief." He took in Jamie's clothes with a sudden grin. "By God, but you look better in that coat than I ever did."

"I doubt it, Your Grace," Jamie said sincerely. "My thanks for the loan. I'm afraid I was ill prepared for an event of this nature so soon after arriving in London. I will rectify the deficiencies of my wardrobe as soon as possible."

The duke waved his hand. "No, no. Please keep the clothes. I have plenty. And they really do look better on you."

"Very generous of you, Your Grace."

"Mr. Montcrief, this is, of course, my son, His Grace, the Duke of Worth. I thought the two of you might get on," Eleanor said happily. "Mr. Montcrief likes horses too, dear, though I do declare, if you spent as much time with our stewards as you do in the stables, we'd all be richer than sin."

The duke rolled his eyes. "That is why I have stewards, Mother. So I don't have to do"—he waved his hand, quite obviously ignorant of the work performed by the dukedom's estate managers—"whatever stultifying things stewards are meant to do," he finished. "And we already are richer than sin." He frowned and lowered his voice. "Speaking of which, Mother, I was at your home the other day looking at your ledgers."

The duchess put a hand to her bosom. "I didn't know such tasks interested you, dear."

"They don't."

"Then why on earth were you looking?"

"I heard that you sold another diamond last week."

A look of genuine annoyance crossed Eleanor's face. "Did you indeed? It would appear I should be taking my business and my diamonds somewhere more discreet in the future," she muttered under her breath.

"Mother, you don't need to sell your jewels. If you are worried about money, I can lend you my own man to put things in order. I do not know why you insist on keeping that relic of a secretary on staff. And while we're on the subject, may I also state your cook scares the bejesus out of me? Wherever did you find her?"

"I never worry about money, dear," Eleanor assured her son with a negligent laugh. "Any more than I worry about my staff. The truth of the matter is, I've decided I no longer care for diamonds. Too garish. At my age, something more subtle is more appropriate."

The chicken under her arm squawked loudly, drawing the attention of a number of people standing around them.

The Duke of Worth cringed. "I worry about you, Mother. On your own like this."

"Oh, *psht*. That is very sweet of you, Worth, darling, but your concern is unfounded. I am quite fine. And I am hardly on my own. Why, I've even hired a companion."

The duke made a show of peering around the duchess. "Is she invisible?"

"Oh, she's here somewhere."

Jamie frowned slightly. He and Eleanor had been the only occupants of her carriage. If the duchess had brought a hired companion to the ball, the woman certainly hadn't arrived with them.

"Is she at least more refined than your cook?" Worth asked in frustration.

"What's wrong with my cook?" The duchess patted her hair.

"Oh, dear God." The duke looked at the ceiling before turning back toward Jamie. "My mother mentioned you served, Mr. Montcrief," he said, changing the subject with what sounded like desperation. "I believe she said infantry."

"Cavalry, Your Grace," Jamie corrected.

"I can never remember the difference," the duchess grumped.

Jamie was overcome by a coughing fit. The duke just looked pained.

"Mr. Montcrief has just retired. He was an admiral or some such thing. Weren't you?" Eleanor smiled brightly at the two men.

"A captain, Your Grace," Jamie supplied with a straight face. "In the King's Dragoon Guards."

"Household under Somerset and Fuller?" the duke asked.

"Yes, Your Grace."

"A shame about Fuller."

"Indeed. I was on the field with him. He was a great leader." Jamie's voice carried so much conviction he nearly convinced himself.

"Yes, yes." Worth was making a pointed effort to ignore the hen that was now struggling and scattering feathers on the floor. "If you might accommodate me, Mr. Montcrief, I should like the privilege of introducing you to a number of men who will find your experiences of interest."

"Of course. I would be obliged."

"Yes, Worth, dear," the duchess encouraged. "Mr. Montcrief has yet to get out and about town. Do introduce him, will you? I know how you boys like your political war talk."

Worth gave Eleanor an aggrieved, if fondly tolerant, smile. "Nothing that would interest you, Mother. Can I fetch you a refreshment before I take my leave?"

"No, no. I see Hettie over there. She's been staring this way since we arrived, so I'd best pay my respects."

The duke hesitated, seemingly torn between concern for his mother and a desire to escape.

"Go along now, dear." She made a shooing motion with her hand.

Her son sighed. "Very well then. Mr. Montcrief? If you care to join me? I believe I might find you a decent vintage and an even better card game."

Jamie inclined his head, shooting a quick glance at the duchess. Just like that, he was now under the personal escort of one of the highest-ranking men in the room. Eleanor winked at him before bustling off toward a group of gray-haired women who had indeed been staring for quite some time.

"Please excuse my mother," the duke muttered to Jamie as he moved away. "She does have her eccentricities."

Jamie grinned at the duke in an effort to put him at ease. "Her Grace has been exceedingly good to me since I arrived in London. Both my parents spoke highly of her generosity and decency. A fondness for avian accessories is easily overlooked."

Worth adjusted his own cravat in the stifling room, his posture visibly relaxing. "If I may be so bold as to ask about your form of address?"

"My—ah, of course." He chose his words carefully. "My father was forced to defy his own sire to marry the girl he loved, and while it makes for a very romantic tale, his tardiness in doing so cost me the title. I, however, chose not to dwell on what cannot be undone and instead used the circumstance of fate to serve my country. I enlisted."

The duke was nodding. "Very admirable."

"I never intended it to be admirable, Your Grace, only practical. I would have made a ghastly cleric."

"God forbid." The duke snickered, then slanted a glance at Jamie. "I applaud a man comfortable with who he is. One cannot always judge a man by the actions of his parents." Worth winced.

"Truer words cannot be spoken," Jamie agreed gravely.

"Now come, let me make some introductions."

Over the next hours, Jamie's head was spinning with names and titles. In almost all cases, the expected pretentiousness of the other guests dissolved at the mere utterance of the word *cavalry* or *captaincy*, or the name

Uxbridge or *Somerset.* Occasionally Jamie was shocked that it was his own name being recognized. It had been almost a year since Napoleon had been defeated, and Jamie never would have imagined the events of Quatre Bras and Waterloo were still being dissected over and over in parlors, cardrooms, and ballrooms. He had no desire to relive any of it, yet kept Eleanor's advice in the back of his mind. His own contributions to the discussions were modest and obliging, but always prompt.

He also followed Eleanor's directive when he was pressed to dance with a multitude of women who were bejeweled, beribboned, and wholly forgettable. Jamie kept his conversation polite and proper to a degree bordering on the absurd, yet the reactions he received from his partners ranged from shy giddiness to blatant sexual invitation. He ignored it all and returned each female to her appropriate chaperone with a bland smile of thanks.

His current partner was one of the shyly giddy ones, and though he did his best to put the young woman at ease, she was unable to respond to anything without blushing violently and mumbling. The dance ended, and with relief, Jamie excused himself from the clearly disappointed girl, only to be hailed by a young man he had briefly met earlier. Tall, blond, blue-eyed, affable. *A viscount perhaps?* Jamie thought, frantically searching his memory.

"Lord Huston," he said, the name coming to him at the last second.

"Mr. Montcrief." Huston looked faintly amused and embarrassed all at once.

Jamie realized there were two women hovering just behind the lord and that both were watching him keenly.

"May I present to you my sisters, Lady Julia Hextall and Lady Viola Hextall. They began pestering me for an introduction as soon as they discovered we were newly acquainted. My apologies for their persistence." The viscount shot them an exasperated, brotherly look.

Both sisters swept Jamie a graceful curtsy, and his heart skipped a beat. So this was Lady Julia. The girl Gisele was risking everything to protect. And in an instant, dowry notwithstanding, Jamie understood why the marquess had picked Lady Julia as his bride.

While her sister was buxom and brunette, Lady Julia bore a striking resemblance to Gisele, albeit a paler, more delicate version. She was exactly as Gisele had described—a pretty porcelain doll with flaxen hair, alabaster skin, and appealing features.

"Not at all, my lord," Jamie replied. "The pleasure is mine." He was pleased at how casual his voice sounded. "Had I realized you were related to such exquisite creatures, it would have been I begging for an introduction."

Both sisters smiled prettily.

"Huston is my courtesy title," the viscount explained. "My father is the Earl of Boden."

"Ah, yes, of course. I am afraid I am still becoming familiar with London society." Jamie pretended to be struck by a revelation. "Then I must offer my felicitations, Lady Julia, on your upcoming nuptials to the Marquess of Valence."

He watched in interest as Huston's face darkened. Jamie raised a brow. It would seem that at least the viscount was not as naïve as Gisele feared.

"Thank you, Mr. Montcrief," Julia was saying. "I am looking forward to the wedding."

Jamie chose his words deliberately and carefully. "Well then, before marriage claims another beautiful bride, perhaps I may be so bold as to ask for the honor of this dance? That is, of course"—he looked over at Viola—"if your sister would do me the honor of the next?"

"Of course," Huston answered for his siblings before either could respond.

Jamie held out his hand to Julia as a quadrille ended. The orchestra began another waltz.

"You look lovely this evening, Lady Julia," Jamie said.

"Thank you, Mr. Montcrief."

"Are you having a good time?"

"Yes, thank you, Mr. Montcrief."

"Do you enjoy dancing?"

"Yes, thank you, Mr. Montcrief."

Jamie fought the urge to roll his eyes.

She allowed Jamie to lead her into the first steps of the dance. Her hand felt tiny and fragile in his, so at odds with Gisele's steady strength. She was perfectly proper and appropriately distant, and Jamie cast about for a way to crack her politesse.

"Is it a love match?" he tried.

Julia looked up at him in shock. "I beg your pardon?"

Well, that was a marked improvement, he thought.

"Your marriage," Jamie clarified, smiling bashfully. "It's just that my parents married for love, and some-day I hope to be able to do the same. I'm sorry if I have offended you."

Julia smiled faintly at him and inclined her head. "Then your parents were very lucky," she said softly. "But

I can assure you, Mr. Montcrief, my father has made a careful selection in a husband for me. Marriage to the Marquess of Valence is a superbly suitable arrangement for our family." A brittle edge had crept into her tone.

"What about you?"

"It's the same thing, isn't it?"

"It doesn't have to be." Jamie looked deep into her eyes and tightened his hand on hers.

Lady Julia blushed to the roots of her hair and dropped her gaze. "This is a highly inappropriate and pointless conversation, Mr. Montcrief," she mumbled. "I would appreciate it if we ceased speaking of the matter."

"Of course. My apologies," Jamie said, feeling slightly foolish and a little frustrated. It would appear it was going to take more guile than he possessed to successfully seduce Lady Julia. The girl was the very picture of stalwart discipline and propriety.

They finished the dance in silence, and Jamie returned her to the care of her brother, Lady Julia's eyes fixed firmly on the floor.

The viscount watched them approach with what looked like grim satisfaction. "Splendidly danced, Mr. Montcrief, Julia."

"Thank you, my lord." Jamie handed Julia back to her brother, then turned his attention to Viola. "I believe you owe me a dance," he said with a gallant bow.

He endured another quadrille and returned the second Hextall sister amid the expected platitudes. Huston, looking relieved he had completed his familial duty, steered Jamie toward the rear of the ballroom, clearly headed to the cardrooms.

"Your sisters are lovely," Jamie said conversationally.

"Yes, they are," he agreed with distraction. "Thank you for consenting to dance with them. The acquisition of your attentions seems to have become something akin to a competition this evening amongst the ladies. My youngest sister was quite insistent she required an introduction."

"I'm flattered. Lady Viola suggested I might join you both on an outing to Hyde Park."

"I bet she did." Huston slanted Jamie a sardonic look.

"With your father's permission, of course."

The viscount grunted. "She could do far worse than a cavalry officer. I must say, you seem like a decent sort, Montcrief."

Jamie winced inwardly, forcibly reminding himself that the stakes necessitated the deception. The viscount, however, had left him the perfect opening. "You are not pleased with the prospect of Lord Valence becoming your brother-in-law."

Huston stopped, his blue eyes troubled. "I didn't say that."

"You didn't need to."

Huston's mouth pressed into a thin line. "It is an advantageous match."

"For your father. Or so I've been told."

His lips thinned even further. "I just…" He trailed off indecisively.

"Don't want to see her hurt," Jamie finished for him.

"Yes." The viscount blew out his breath. "Sometimes I think I am losing my mind. Seeing danger where it doesn't exist."

"Danger?" Jamie wondered out loud.

Huston looked back up at him uncertainly. "She will be the marquess's third wife."

Jamie pretended ignorance. "But that is hardly unique. There are many who marry multiple times because of the death of their spouse."

The viscount wavered, coming to some sort of decision. "You will hear this anyway, so it might as well come from me."

Jamie gave him a puzzled frown.

"His first two wives died...badly."

"Badly?"

"They both drowned. The first one in a pond on his estate grounds and the second one in an explosion on the Thames."

"Good Lord." Some of the shock in his tone was not fabricated. He had never asked Gisele how Valence's first wife, Helena's mother, had died. "But surely these were accidents?" He would have wagered everything he owned that Helena's mother had not died accidentally.

"My father assures me they were. But..."

"You are not so certain."

Huston looked around in alarm. "Please don't repeat that. Valence would call me out for something like that."

"Touchy, is he?"

"Quite."

"It is very admirable you care about your sister's happiness as you do. You are only human to be concerned." Jamie used his most reassuring voice.

Huston grimaced. "I should not be troubling you with such frivolities."

"Nonsense. Your sister's well-being is not a frivolity."

The viscount smiled at him ruefully. "Have you met him? The marquess?"

"No."

"Well, perhaps when you do, you can tell me if my concern is misplaced."

"Of course. What specifically bothers you about his person?"

Huston shrugged helplessly. "I can't put it into words exactly. He just seems...off."

"Off? As in you think he might prefer the favors of men instead of women?"

Huston's mouth made a perfect O.

"I forget myself." Jamie bent his head. "I beg your pardon. I've spent too much time in the rough and have not yet mastered the subtleties of society-speak."

The viscount seemed to recover. "No," he said, smiling despite himself. "It's refreshing. But I am quite certain he's not a lover of men. He was utterly obsessed with his last wife."

"Obsessed?"

"To the point it made others uncomfortable. She was a...*possession*." His eyes were unfocused in memory.

"I see."

Huston shook his head, bringing himself back to the present. "Enough of this dismal talk. I am in desperate need of a drink. Care to join me?"

"Sounds like just the thing," Jamie agreed, and allowed Julia Hextall's brother to lead the way, turning his words over in his mind.

The good news was that Huston's instincts were better than most, and he had serious reservations about the marquess, which might make him a useful ally. For now, Jamie would do what he could to fan the flames of those reservations with his own. Gossip in society was not unlike the speculation that ran rampant through the ranks on the eve of battle. Controlled and directed by the officers, it made a useful tool. Men needed to hear what they wanted to believe, and Jamie had had plenty of experience leaking information to troops.

Like that the enemy had inferior numbers. Or guns. Or cavalry. Its officers were inept and disorganized, its horses starving, its gunners blind, its infantry cowards, its shot ruined from the damp. Aye, he had been seasoned at making men believe anything that would bring them the courage to do the unthinkable.

The cardrooms were crowded, though the tables were less so, giving evidence most of the men had simply come to escape from the dance floor and wives or matchmaking mothers. Smoke hung heavy in the air, drink flowed freely, and the atmosphere was one of boisterous conversation and joviality.

The Duke of Worth was already ensconced comfortably at the center table, and he broke into a wide grin when he caught sight of Jamie. "Well, if it isn't our sacrificial lamb. Wherever did you find him, my dear Huston?"

"Cowering behind a potted palm," the viscount joked.

"Ah." The duke's eyes danced, and he leaned toward Jamie. "Then it's no wonder you two ran into each other. When Huston and I were but boys, I'm quite sure the only foliage he thought he would need to take cover in was the tall oak variety when we hid from our schoolmasters. But now poor Huston is set to inherit an earldom and the potted palm is one of his favorite haunts at these social functions."

Huston made a face at his friend. "Just wait until your sister returns from the Continent and you are forced to escort her about a ballroom. Then you too will learn to appreciate the convenience and the safety of the potted palm. Otherwise you will end up like Mr. Montcrief."

The duke shuddered in mock revulsion. "You have danced with everything wearing a gown, Montcrief," he snorted, looking Jamie up and down with a wink. "Luckily, your handsome coat shows little sign of fatigue."

"I did not wish to risk social suicide by accidental exclusion," Jamie defended himself, allowing a little innocent indignation to creep into his words.

"Lord Almighty, do not apologize to us," the duke laughed, well on his way to a state of happy intoxication. "Every set you dance is one Huston and I need not." Worth pulled out a chair next to him and gestured for Jamie to sit. "But God help you at the next rout, Montcrief. Every mama not shopping exclusively for a title will have her daughters paraded out before you can manage a drink. Speaking of which—" He snapped his fingers and a servant bearing a tray of decanters and bottles materialized, and tumblers were distributed and filled.

"We are playing vingt-et-un," Worth said, draining half his glass with gusto. "Mr. Montcrief, this is Lord Braxton and Lord Grey." He waved his hand at two young men seated to his left, then gestured across the table. "And Lord Valence."

It caught Jamie off guard, the disclosure oddly anticlimactic.

Slowly he turned to face the Marquess of Valence, unsure of what to expect. Horns and a tail and maybe cloven hooves. At the very least a hunched troll more at home in a cave than in a ballroom. Yet all he saw before him was...ordinary.

The marquess was of average height with average brown hair and average features. A person who would get lost in a crowd and whom no one would remember. He was common in build, perhaps a little thick around the middle, dressed expensively and impeccably in evening clothes, but otherwise completely, utterly unremarkable.

"A pleasure, Mr. Montcrief," the marquess said pleasantly. "I understand you are new to London?"

"I am." Jamie found his voice just in time, concentrating hard on keeping his expression neutral.

"And what do you think so far?" Valence asked, gesturing in the direction of the ballroom.

"It is certainly full of...beauty," Jamie replied.

"You are looking for a wife then?"

"Possibly," Jamie allowed, as if he'd put thought to the notion. "Please accept my congratulations on your own upcoming marriage. Lord Huston tells me you are engaged to his sister."

"Indeed I am." Valence raised his glass in a silent toast to the viscount.

Huston's face tightened perceptibly, and he formed an answering grimace.

"You must be looking forward to it." Jamie shifted in his chair.

"Indeed. Lady Julia possesses an abundance of charms any man would appreciate."

The Duke of Worth guffawed, oblivious to the subtle, strained undercurrents. "Any you'd like to share with us?"

"Sod off, Worth." Huston elbowed his friend with

enough force to cause the brandy to slosh over the rim of the duke's glass. "I'm her brother and I'm standing right next to you, remember?" The viscount forced a laugh, making a significant effort to appear relaxed, but Jamie could feel the animosity seeping out around the edges.

Worth laughed. "Thank God for that. I suppose that means we'll have an excuse to see *this* marchioness from time to time then."

An awkward silence fell across the table. All eyes fixed on Worth.

The duke, foxed as he was, recognized his gaffe. "That is to say, Lady Julia will make a superb hostess. She is, er, the quintessence of social accomplishment—"

"What His Grace is trying to say is that Lady Julia will not avoid the social scene as my last wife did," the marquess said smoothly, rescuing the floundering duke. But his eyes were cold.

"I cannot believe that, my lord." Jamie chuckled mirthlessly, finding an opening. "I have yet to meet a woman, whether lady or laundress, who does not revel in the chance to shine, even if only in the company of her friends."

The attention of the table's occupants shifted from Worth to Jamie, and the duke, released from his blunder, shot Jamie a grateful look.

The marquess leaned back in his chair, assessing Jamie with a fleeting look of malice. Jamie lifted a brow in challenge, and Valence's anger was snuffed immediately, replaced with a curtain of bland politeness. Jamie felt the hairs along the back of his neck rise.

"Your sister, Lord Huston, does not posses the arrogance

and condescending nature of my last wife." The words were like poisoned darts, disguised as flattery.

Jamie froze, forcing his eyes to the floor so they couldn't betray him.

The marquess continued. "I do not like to speak ill of the dead, and certainly not of my late wife, for I loved her very much. But the truth of the matter was that she preferred her own company to that of others whom she considered lacking in both beauty and intelligence equal to hers. As much as I tried to encourage her to kindness, she made it very difficult most days."

Jamie felt rage unlike anything he had ever experienced. It rose from the pit of his gut to compress his lungs in his chest and contract every muscle in his body. Slowly he raised his eyes, afraid that if he didn't move something, he might implode.

"And that is exactly why I never intend to marry," the young Lord Braxton scoffed with authority from across the table, finally joining the conversation. "Who knows what kind of woman you're going to wind up with once she's got her hands on your title? No matter how fair of face she might be."

His friend made a face. "You would have married her too, if you'd seen her. She was known through all of England as an incomparable. She was superb."

Jamie hadn't taken his eyes off the marquess.

Valence was staring into his glass, and he flinched at the careless words. "Yes," he breathed. "She truly was . . . spectacular." Genuine grief etched grooves deep into his brow.

"Well, cheer up, man," the duke said. "For you get another chance at it." Worth waved a servant over and glasses were refilled. "Let's get on with some fun, shall we?" Worth began dealing cards, visibly relieved to be dismissing the topic of the late Marchioness of Valence. "Huston, Montcrief, are you in?" he asked, distracting Jamie.

Jamie nodded, forcing his rage and his hatred aside, the void filling instantly with a bitter determination. His hands clenched, and he imagined wrapping his fingers around that fleshy neck and watching the marquess slowly choke. Except he'd be pulled off before he had the satisfaction of seeing the bastard dead, and that would benefit no one. Violence now would accomplish nothing. Jamie would bide his time as he'd been instructed to do. He took another deep breath, fixed what he hoped was an amiable expression on his face, and reached for his cards.

"Have you played before?" Huston asked Jamie discreetly.

Jamie nearly snorted before catching himself. He had learned the game a week into his enlistment and had honed his skill through thousands and thousands of hands. As an officer Jamie had encouraged his men to play, a welcome distraction in miserable climates and camps, his only caveat being no money was ever allowed to exchange hands. In his life Jamie had won enough pebbles and seashells and sticks to build several moated castles.

"I am somewhat familiar with the game, yes."

The first hand was dealt.

⌒

Sixty minutes later Jamie found himself with one remaining opponent, Lord Braxton, sitting opposite him. All the other players had dropped out in defeat, though they remained at the table, enthusiastically watching the two contestants. In fact, the game had drawn a small crowd, all observing with bemused interest.

Young Braxton, Jamie had learned in the course of the game, was the eldest son of the Duke of Havockburn. The boy was eighteen, entitled, and seemed to think himself invincible. As the last hand unfolded, Jamie played his cards out with his usual detachment, knowing very well Braxton had no chance of winning based on the cards already played and the cards on the table before them and in his hand. He upped his wager slightly, and Braxton pulled at his collar.

"No," Braxton said.

"I beg your pardon?" Jamie paused in question. The conversation around them dipped in volume, and two dozen men leaned forward in interest.

The young man consulted his cards and broke into a gleeful smile. "I increase your bid."

Until now the men had been playing for paltry amounts of cash, probably out of unspoken deference to Jamie and the assumption he did not control vast wealth.

"My lord, the amount of the maximum bid has been set." *And for good reason*, Jamie thought. *To keep loose cannons like you from losing your family's money.*

"I wager you my new team and curricle that I will beat you in this hand."

An interested murmur rippled through the spectators.

Braxton's companion, Lord Grey, gave him a horrified look. "You know what happened last time! Your father would never countenance—"

"Oh, do shut up," Braxton complained, taking another swig of his drink.

"My lord, may I caution you against such a move?" Jamie was groping for tactful words that would keep this boy from making a mistake while allowing him to save face. "Even if I agreed to such a wager, I regret to say I have nothing of equal value to stake."

Braxton shrugged carelessly. "You're a cavalryman. You have a horse."

"Yes, but—"

"That'll do. Now are you going to play or are you going to turn tail and run, Mr. Montcrief?"

Well, hell, Jamie thought. Now the young imbecile had painted him into an impossible corner. He had given Jamie the options of seeing the hand through or being labeled a coward in front of the cream of London society.

He sighed. "Very well, my lord," he said with a great show of reluctance. "As you wish."

Braxton grinned with arrogance and gratification and then proceeded to get thoroughly trounced.

The silence at the table was absolute as Braxton stared down at the cards in horror. A polite scattering of applause reminded Jamie of their audience.

"You won," Braxton said in disbelief.

"So it would seem, my lord," Jamie replied wearily.

"Well." The young man had gone a peculiar shade of green. "I will have your winnings delivered to your address in the morning if that suits." His words were forced.

"Yes, about that. I must confess, my lord, I do not have the means to keep or maintain such a luxury," Jamie stated baldly. "If I may be so bold as to suggest an alternative arrangement that would better suit?"

Braxton nodded weakly.

Jamie gave the men around him an easy smile. "Perhaps simply the loan of your team and your curricle for the next fortnight? I may wish to invite a certain lady out for an afternoon, and if I am lucky enough to get her consent to accompany me, I'm quite certain she will not agree to riding on the rump of my gelding." This earned Jamie a round of laughter. "You would be doing me the favor, Lord Braxton."

"Of course." The young man collected whatever tatters of his dignity remained. "Please send word to my father's house whenever you wish to use the team. I will make sure they are readied and brought around at your direction without delay."

Jamie nodded his head respectfully and watched the young man flee the cardroom. The other occupants of the table made ready to take their leave as well.

"A pleasure, Mr. Montcrief. Do enjoy your stay in London." The Marquess of Valence rose to his feet and nodded at Jamie, his friendly words offset by his calculating expression as he excused himself from the table.

Jamie watched the man depart, distracted when the Duke of Worth slapped him on the shoulder.

"Bloody well played, Montcrief." The duke grinned. "If ever someone needed a bit of a setdown, Braxton was due. Let's do this again."

Jamie had no idea what *this* referred to, but he nodded all the same.

Worth gave Jamie another friendly thump and then drifted away into the heavy haze of smoke.

Jamie rubbed his aching eyes, the smoke and the noise and the heat finally getting the better of him. He needed some air.

"That was well handled," said Huston under his breath as Jamie rose. "Braxton, I mean."

Jamie simply shrugged.

"His father would have cut him off for good, if he hadn't killed him first." The viscount followed him out of the cardroom.

"I take no pleasure in making anyone look the fool. Even if they might deserve it from time to time."

"What did you think of Lord Valence?" Huston asked abruptly.

Jamie stopped, turning to the viscount. "I think you are right to be worried," he said quietly with perfect truth.

The viscount's eyes clouded, his face troubled.

"Ah, there you are, Mr. Montcrief." The words were breathless. "Good evening, Lord Huston."

"Your Grace?" Jamie stared in startled confusion at Eleanor, who had materialized at his side. Only this time, along with her chicken, she had a slim young woman in tow. The missing companion, Jamie surmised, noting the woman's subdued gown and simple hairstyle.

"Mr. Montcrief, Lord Huston, may I introduce Miss Jenna Hughes. She is my very capable, very charming companion."

Miss Hughes was surprisingly tall, with ink-black hair, ice-blue eyes, and impeccable manners.

"A pleasure," she said in a low throaty voice, dropping into a curtsy.

"I'm sorry I missed you earlier."

The duchess looked up at Jamie sharply, but Miss Hughes only smiled an enigmatic smile.

"I was regrettably detained," she replied easily, amusement dancing in those pale eyes.

Jamie let that slide, not having the energy to even begin to consider what secrets the lovely Miss Hughes might be concealing. She was, after all, employed by the duchess.

Eleanor cleared her throat and stepped closer to Jamie. "I hear you saved Havockburn's son the humiliation of losing his father's pride and joy tonight."

Jamie blinked.

"Oh, come now, Mr. Montcrief. The card game has been over for at least three minutes and the gossips are much faster than that." She leaned in conspiratorially.

"I'm glad my actions seem to have prevented any premature deaths," Jamie said, still a little taken aback.

Eleanor grunted her amusement and then turned her attention to the viscount. "You're looking very handsome tonight, Lord Huston. Tell me, how are your sisters this evening?"

Huston was uncertainly eyeing both the chicken and the duchess in turn. "They are well, thank you, Your Grace."

"Your family must be frantic preparing for the wedding."

"My mother is quite busy these days, indeed."

"Now, which one is Valence taking? The dark one or the blond one?" the dowager asked absent-mindedly. "I can never remember."

Huston recoiled at her phrasing, but answered her anyway, as etiquette dictated. "Lady Julia, Your Grace. She is fairer than our other sister."

"Of course, of course." Eleanor waved her hand. "I remember now. She looks a great deal like his last wife, does she not?"

Huston cleared his throat. "There is a resemblance, Your Grace."

"Lord Valence is most unlucky in love," Eleanor

mused. "Both of his wives dying so young and so *tragically*. Heavens, I still remember the explosion that killed his last one. You could see the fireball for miles! I do hope your sister fares better."

The viscount looked shaken. The hen squawked loudly, and Huston jumped.

"I believe my mother needs me," he managed. "If you would excuse me, Your Grace? Mr. Montcrief, Miss Hughes."

Jamie waited until he was out of earshot. "You just scared the shit out of him, Your Grace."

"*Tsk*. Mind your mouth. You are not in the barracks, Mr. Montcrief." Eleanor's vapid expression vanished, and she frowned. "And he should be scared. No one wants to hear the truth. But perhaps they can be led to their own conclusions."

Jamie glanced at Miss Hughes, who was still standing discreetly behind the duchess.

"Miss Hughes is well aware of all our conclusions, Mr. Montcrief," Eleanor assured him. "But thank you for your prudence." She paused. "What did you think of the marquess?"

Jamie didn't really know the man at all, yet he knew what he'd done, knew what he was, and he hated him. And from that, Jamie recognized the need for caution and restraint. He forced himself to think rationally.

"He is smart. Exceedingly manipulative. Everyone seems to accept his outwardly pleasant mien, and therefore they have no reason to doubt him when he says that the late marchioness lived in virtual isolation by choice. He gives the impression that Miss Whitby refused to associate with the other ladies of the ton, believing herself far superior to them."

"I am aware." Two angry slashes of color had risen in Eleanor's cheeks.

"It would seem he has worked hard to perfect an image that deflects suspicion. Which tells me he understands that if his depravity were to be revealed, he would be ruined. But Valence will not be pulled into convenient confessions. He is too clever for that."

"Indeed." The duchess was tapping her fingers on her skirts, pensive.

Jamie nodded, trying to put his impressions into words. "The mention of Gisele's name disturbed him. In his own twisted way, he loved her, and..." He trailed off thoughtfully. "And I think he still does."

Eleanor was frowning fiercely. "After the explosion, Valence became a recluse for nearly a year—overcome by a grief that I do not doubt was genuine, as repugnant as it seems. His finances slid into ruin. It is wholly possible he is still fixated on her."

"Is that something we can exploit?" Jamie asked.

"Perhaps."

"How?"

"I don't know." Eleanor hefted her chicken again with distraction. "I'll think on it. Sometimes clarity can be better achieved with a new dawn," she mused. "But for now, I would imagine there is little else that can be accomplished tonight." She paused before giving Jamie a sideways look. "At least anything you haven't already accomplished."

"Your Grace?"

"You've danced with everyone in a ball gown."

Jamie winced. "So I've been told."

"You've been the epitome of polished elegance. You've

proven yourself clever at the card tables. You've saved a duke's son from making an ass out of himself, and that I couldn't have arranged better myself if I had tried. And"—she paused with a twinkle in her eye—"you've been brave enough to be seen with a crazy old bat like me." She patted his sleeve. "Dashing, gracious, sharp, humble, and likable. Your name was on everyone's lips tonight."

"Thank you, Your Grace. I'm happy to hear the evening was a success. I think." The strain of the past day suddenly crashed down around him, crushing him with a bone-numbing exhaustion. He pulled out his shiny new timepiece and checked it. "Do you think it would be acceptable for me to leave? It's nearly three."

"A fashionable man would not consider leaving until well after three," she chided. "Perhaps four."

Jamie sagged. He wasn't sure he could keep up the draining act for another minute, much less another hour. His cravat was choking him, his shoes were crippling him, and the heat had melded his shirt to his back. He was tired of dancing, tired of smiling, tired of thinking. Tired of talking about a war he wanted to forget, tired of pretending he was the hero he wasn't, tired of trying to be someone who didn't exist.

"But, should I create a diversion, you would be more than justified in slipping out and returning home. My coach will be in the line on the north side. Just make sure you tell my coachman to return to collect me."

Jamie shook his head. "I should escort you home."

The duchess laughed loudly, her shoulders shaking. "Very few leave with whom they arrived with, dear. And I have the company of Miss Hughes now anyway." She considered him. "No, you head home. We'll speak again very soon."

"But how—"

Jamie didn't get to finish his sentence before the duchess grasped the hen in both her hands and launched the bird into the air. The squawking chicken veered frantically about the ballroom before coming to land on the head of a dour-looking woman. Instantly the matron began screaming as her husband lunged and tried to swat the bird out of her headpiece. No fewer than four drinks were dropped, glass shattering on the floor and creating a slippery surface that sent two men and one woman sprawling. The Countess of Baustenbury fainted dead away, reducing a pink upholstered footstool to kindling. More screaming ensued, and with determination the orchestra increased the volume of its piece to be heard over the commotion.

"You may go now, dear," Eleanor whispered to Jamie.

The last thing Jamie saw before he slipped out the front door and down the wide stone steps was a footman, hanging by one arm from the balustrade of the grand staircase, waving an appropriated walking stick at the hen, which was now serenely roosting in the center of the Countess of Baustenbury's elegant crystal chandelier.

〜

When Jamie let himself in the door of the apartment, the remnants of a fire still glowed in the hall's hearth. He prodded the coals with the poker in an effort to create a little more heat to combat the increasing chill. Kicking his ridiculous shoes off and leaving them wherever they came to rest, he padded into the drawing room.

A faint light filtered in through the windows from the lamps on the street outside, enough for Jamie to see that the room was as empty as it was silent. He moved into the bedroom, and even though he hadn't really expected her to be there, disappointment still stung as he gazed down at the undisturbed bed. He'd not realized it at the time, but now he understood he'd not been in a hurry to leave the ball. He'd been in a hurry to come home. To Gisele.

For a foolish moment, he considered seeking her out. She had a room in the attic somewhere, and he didn't imagine it would be that hard to find. She'd want to know what had happened tonight. She'd ask him whom he'd met and how he'd gotten on. She'd ask him what had been said and what had not. She'd want to know about her former husband.

Jamie wanted to tell Gisele he understood so much more now. She hadn't been married to Valence—she'd been imprisoned in a carefully constructed cage of isolation. And all the while, the marquess, with all his smooth social graces and easy lies, had remained untouched.

He understood Gisele's fate had been directed by men too many times. First by her father and then by her husband, and it had taken extreme measures for her to finally free herself from that oppression. She had apologized to Jamie tonight for prying into his past, but he understood now it had never truly been about him. For Gisele it had simply been about the acquisition of knowledge. For with knowledge came control. With control came safety and the ability to steer her own destiny.

And he understood her imposed distance. This... attraction, or whatever it was that had ignited and begun to burn between Gisele and himself, was powerful and reckless and uncontrolled. Everything Gisele had spent the last four years avoiding.

Jamie stared at the empty bed. He still wanted her, now more than ever. His growing respect and admiration for this courageous woman only served to make his desire for her that much more intense. But he understood she wasn't ready yet.

And for as long as it took, he would wait.

Chapter 12 ————————————

Gisele slept fitfully and restlessly, finally abandoning the endeavor just before dawn. She had lain awake in the dark, straining her ears for the rattle of a carriage or the sound of a door, but so far removed from the streets and the apartments, she heard nothing but the groaning of the building's timbers and the rattle of the wind as it harried the roof.

Washing and dressing in the near dark, she crept downstairs, only to find Sebastien already rummaging in the kitchens, half a roll stuffed into his mouth.

"Where are you off to so early?" she asked in surprise.

"To renew some acquaintances," he told her. "Every servant from every residence will be out and about very shortly. I'd like to discover what we've missed these past four years. I've been told the Marquess of Valence has only a single scullery maid left in his employ, who also serves as his housekeeper and his cook. I thought it prudent I should pay her a visit sooner rather than later. See what she has to say about her illustrious employer."

"Ah. Then you've already renewed some acquaintances?"

"But of course." Sebastien gave her a wink.

"Did you see Jamie when he came home last night?"

She watched in fascination as a flush crept over Sebastien's collar.

"Did you even come home last night?" she teased.

"I will not ask whose bed you slept in if you return the favor," he shot back.

"Very funny." An unwanted frisson of desire at the mere suggestion caught her unaware. She pushed it aside. "So you didn't speak with him?"

"No." Sebastien eyed her. "Neither did you, I assume?"

"Of course not." She wished she didn't sound so defensive.

Sebastien shook his head. "When you do, be so kind as to remind James we have appointments all afternoon." He crammed the last half of the roll into his mouth as he shrugged on his coat. "As much as he may wish it, he cannot live in his boots and his riding breeches indefinitely," he added around a mouthful of crumbs. "I'll be back in a few hours. Please have James awake and fed by then like a good little lass." He gave her a cheeky grin and then disappeared.

Gisele began making herself a simple breakfast by setting water to heat. Above her head she could hear the sounds of a stirring city, though she knew it would be a long while before those who had been out at last night's entertainments stirred. She sighed in frustration and resisted the urge to march upstairs and shake Jamie awake to drag every detail from him, though at this time of the morning she was quite aware he'd probably had less than an hour of sleep. Gisele needed him sharp and coherent, not exhausted and dazed.

But all of this... waiting was going to be the death of

her. She was more accustomed to doing. Not waiting for someone to take action on her behalf.

Unfortunately, until she could come up with a better plan, she was stuck.

⁓

It was midmorning by the time she opened the door of the apartment, a tray heaped with plates of food carefully balanced in her hands. She placed it on the desk in the drawing room, glancing at the bedroom doors still shut against the morning light. Jamie was obviously still sleeping.

His shoes had been discarded near the hall, and Gisele retrieved them and set them neatly against the wall. Jamie's evening coat had been left draped over the settee, and as she picked it up, a whiff of tobacco smoke and perfume escaped the fabric. The scent was enough to remind her of the few balls she had been allowed to attend with the marquess, and despite everything, she remembered how she had loved watching the swirl of color and excitement. How she had longed to be part of the dancers or the little knots of women giggling and whispering about everything and nothing.

She ran her fingers over the shoulders of his coat. Jamie Montcrief would have been the most captivating man at that ball, titled or not, and she wondered if he had been forced to dance until the very last set by grasping girls and their watchful mothers. She wondered if Jamie had met Lady Julia. If he had danced with her and, as Gisele had suggested, plied her with pretty words and empty promises in an effort to turn her head. Perhaps Jamie had even managed to steal a kiss.

A vileness tore through her innards, curling ruthlessly

into her chest and leaving a toxic taste in her mouth. She froze, examining this new sensation for what it was. Jealousy, she realized. Pure, unadulterated jealousy.

Dropping Jamie's coat back on the settee, she paced to the window. She should be shocked, a little voice inside her nagged. Horrified. At the very least dismayed. Yet she wasn't any of those.

It was ironic she should flog Jamie with ideals of honesty when she couldn't even be honest with herself.

Because, in truth, Gisele wanted the man sleeping just beyond those bedroom doors badly enough for it to leave her breathless and weak-kneed and sleepless. She had kept her distance, and he had let her. Yet the more distance she'd put between them, the worse the wanting had become.

She had told herself she couldn't afford the distraction. But she was now realizing the futility of that argument. Jamie had been a distraction since she had sat down across from him in that tavern. He was a distraction just standing in a room. Riding a horse. Eating his eggs.

She pressed her forehead to the glass. So where did that leave her then? Trapped somewhere between desire and denial? Between needing to believe she could take what she wanted and not knowing if she would find the courage to do so? Hiding behind excuses and fear of the unknown?

It was the last thought that sent her striding across the room. Gisele Whitby had ceased being afraid a long time ago, she thought fiercely. Before she could consider the wisdom of her actions, she turned the knobs on the bedroom doors and silently slipped inside.

Jamie was stretched out on his back, a bedsheet

wrapped around his waist, his breath slow and even. The soft light filtering through the drawn curtains made his skin glow and etched the hollows and planes of his body in fluid shadow. Taut muscle flowed from his arms into his shoulders and across his chest, the expanse broken only by a faint scattering of hair that couldn't quite hide the furrows of scar tissue marring the perfection.

She studied him from the doorway, unobserved and unhurried. Mother of God, but he was beautiful. His honor and decency made him even more so. Her heart squeezed, and she took a step forward, teetering on the edge of folly.

"Good morning."

She jumped, nearly tripping backward.

He was watching her through sleepy eyes, a faint smile playing around his mouth. "Normally I'd be troubled, but this seems to be quite a regular occurrence for me of late."

"This?" she squeaked, her heart hammering in her chest.

Jamie gestured at the sheets. "Waking up naked in a bed to find you watching me."

Gisele could feel the color flood into her face.

"That wasn't a complaint," he teased. He pushed himself up on his elbows.

She couldn't seem to move. Couldn't seem to tear her eyes away. Couldn't seem to think.

Jamie shoved the pillows up against the headboard and leaned back, making space beside him. "You're wanting to know about last night." It wasn't really a question.

It wasn't entirely the right answer either.

He gave her a puzzled look at her lack of response. "Is something wrong?"

No. Yes. She had not the faintest idea what she was doing here.

"Gisele?"

She stepped closer to the edge of the bed, looking down at him.

"I met him last night. The marquess." Jamie was watching her carefully.

She froze.

"I can't imagine what you endured at his hand, Gisele, but know that no one else ever will. I promise that to you." His face was hard.

She caught her breath, a sense of inevitability prodding her from her silence. "You want me to tell you what he did—"

"No." Jamie stopped her before she could finish. "No."

"Why?"

"Because it doesn't matter. Because it is something that you've defeated. It no longer controls you. *He* no longer controls you. You are the master of your destiny now, Gisele. No man shall ever again dictate how you choose to live your life. Not your father, not the marquess, and certainly not me. No one can put you in a cage ever again."

Gisele let out a shaky breath, her truth exposed in a handful of simple words. Something deep inside her soared.

"Yes." She sat down on the edge of the bed next to Jamie, her legs suddenly unwilling to support her.

Jamie rested his head back against the pillows, a soft smile on his lips. "I missed you last night, you know. The waltzes were positively tedious."

Gisele gazed at Jamie, watching as his smile slowly

faded. His eyes darkened, yet he made no move to touch her.

"Jamie…" Gisele felt a slow burn start in her cheeks, move through her body, and lodge at the junction of her thighs.

His eyes were hot now, and the room suddenly became stifling. Her skin thrummed, and her breasts tingled and ached. Gisele curled her fingers into her skirts so he couldn't see that they'd started to shake, even as desire flexed violently at her core. She was staring into the depths of Pandora's box, uncertain if she had the strength or the willpower to close it.

"I can't—"

"You can." Jamie hadn't moved.

Oh, God. The idea was both empowering and excruciating at once. To taste what she'd believed was lost to her forever. Jamie was the leap of faith she'd never thought she would take.

He never took his eyes from her, nor did he reach for her. She was free to step away from him and this madness. And she was free to stay.

"I'm yours," he whispered, and she understood then what he was offering. It would seem Jamie Montcrief understood her more than she understood herself.

She leaned down and kissed him.

Softly at first, his head angling up to meet hers, his lips soft and inviting. She took her time, nipping and sucking at his lips, tracing the outline of his mouth with her tongue. She increased her demands, and Jamie obeyed instantly, opening himself to her. He groaned into her mouth, yet remained where he was, his hands clenched into the sheets.

She left his mouth, her lips exploring the underside of his jaw and the hollow of his neck at the base of his ear. She smoothed back the hair from the side of his face, feeling the rough stubble beneath the pads of her fingers. Slowly she slid her fingers down the sides of his neck to his shoulders. Under her touch she could feel the muscles tense, and she spread her hands over and around them, kneading the tautness.

She continued her exploration down his arms, stroking the steely sinew and strength. She twisted, kneeling beside him and splaying her fingers over the expanse of his chest. The ridge and valley of each rib passed under her touch, her fingers tracing the definition of the muscle straining across his abdomen. She reached the edge of the sheet at his waist and paused. His entire body was rigid now, and his breath was coming in painful gasps.

"Shall I stop?"

Jamie shook his head almost imperceptibly and shuddered.

Gisele dragged the sheet from his waist, letting it fall to the floor. In a single movement, she slid over him so that she straddled his thighs, her skirts bunched around her waist. She took his erection in her hand, feeling it pulse and throb. Jamie hissed, and his hips bucked. She placed her thumb over the tip, feeling the bead of moisture that had already gathered.

"Not yet," she whispered.

She leaned forward, her weight pressing him back, her lips finding his, kissing him deeply. She kept her hand beneath her, sliding it down his shaft to cup his balls. He rocked against her palm hard, and she could feel her own core throb in response. She dropped her mouth to his chest, sliding farther down his body. Her teeth scraped against his nipple, and he arched into her mouth.

"God, Gisele," he gasped.

She brought her hands up and slid them down the sides of his ribs, to the ridge of muscle at his waist and to the bones at his hips. His buttocks were straining now beneath her touch, his muscles trembling in an effort to remain still. But he had yet to touch her, yet to guide her. She looked up at him, her eyes meeting his, the whiskey-colored depths fevered, sweat glistening along his temples.

"Gisele—"

Very deliberately she bent her head, taking him fully into her mouth. She dragged her tongue along the length of his shaft, and Jamie made a tortured noise, every muscle in his body seizing. She swirled her tongue around the tip of his cock then and he shouted, his hips surging up against her as he lost all control. She felt her own body spasm as he pulsed, breathing hard.

She smiled against the flatness of his abdomen, pressing gentle kisses along the surface, feeling his body still shuddering beneath her touch.

"I'm sorry," Jamie said hoarsely. "I don't usually... that doesn't—"

"I'm flattered," Gisele said, a languid satisfaction stealing over her. She stretched herself forward, kissing his neck.

He caught her head with his hands then and drew her all the way up, claiming her mouth with his own. He kissed her desperately, holding her tightly against him.

Eventually Jamie pulled back, searching her eyes with his own. "No regrets?" he whispered.

Gisele shook her head, feeling more free than she had ever felt. "No regrets."

Jamie grinned at her before letting his head fall back against the pillows, his eyes closed in blissful lethargy.

Gisele rolled onto her back beside him, her head on his shoulder, and took a moment to revel in her newfound knowledge. The knowledge that she possessed the power to elicit the same reckless need in Jamie that he inspired in her. He had given up his control willingly and placed himself in her hands, and she understood that he had offered more than just his body. He had offered her his trust.

She glanced up at his profile. Jamie still had an expression of euphoric contentment on his face, and Gisele savored the thought that she had put it there. Her lips curled in wicked satisfaction as she considered what else she might do to provoke such an expression from Jamie Montcrief.

His stomach suddenly rumbled loudly. Gisele chuckled and rolled away from him, climbing from the bed and straightening her skirts. "Hungry?" she asked.

Jamie cracked open an eye with a wolfish grin. He rolled on his side to appraise her, and it was impossible not to notice his swelling erection.

"For *food*," she said, picking the sheet up from the floor and tossing it at him. The power was positively heady.

"Yes. And yes." He was laughing.

"Thank you, Jamie. For...that," she said suddenly, the words slipping out unbidden.

He stopped laughing. "I'm fairly certain that was supposed to have been my line." His eyes became serious. "You have no idea what you do to me, Gisele."

A bubble of laughter burst. "Oh, I have an idea." She dodged a pillow as it flew at her head.

They both froze due to a sharp banging on the door.

"Who is that?" Gisele asked.

"I don't have the first clue." Jamie was already out of bed and reaching for his breeches and shirt.

Gisele glanced down at her dress even as she hurried from the bedroom, closing the doors tightly behind her. It was one thing for the housekeeper to answer the door as she went about her duties—it was another thing for a housekeeper to be keeping company with a half-naked man.

She stopped in the hall, rearranging her face into an expression of polite servitude, and opened the door.

She had a brief impression of a rifleman's uniform before it blurred and she found herself enveloped in a pair of strong arms, her nose buried in new wool. She was lifted nearly off her feet and then set back, the object of intense scrutiny as a pair of coal-dark eyes raked her from head to toe.

"You should have sent me a message," the intruder barked. "I could have come immediately."

"You were busy." Gisele was gaping. "Why are you wearing a uniform? And why are you here?"

"Why are *you* here, Gisele?" the rifleman demanded, ignoring her questions. "I stopped at the duchess's, and she gave me this direction. I nearly expired. She told me you were currently posing as a London housekeeper and that you had hired a cavalry captain who was—" His eyes suddenly left hers to focus over her shoulder, and she knew Jamie had stepped into view.

"Who the hell are you?" Jamie demanded in a voice

Gisele had thought reserved only for infuriated monarchs. He moved forward, pushing Gisele behind him as though he believed her to be in imminent danger.

Both men had their hackles raised and their teeth bared.

Gisele looked to the ceiling for guidance she knew she wouldn't find and sidled out from behind Jamie.

"Gisele?" Jamie said, not taking his eyes from the soldier. "Do you know this man?"

"Umm, yes." Gisele took a breath. "James Montcrief, may I present to you Iain Ferguson."

Chapter 13.

Jamie studied the man as he was ushered into the apartment, noting the strange shuffling walk that did little to detract from his striking good looks. Iain was tall and lean, roped with long muscle Jamie recognized as the kind earned only by hard physical labor. He had dark hair, black eyes, and a rich, olive complexion. He was in regimental uniform, the garments clearly new, which Jamie thought strange, considering Gisele had told him Iain's injuries had removed him from service. She had also told Jamie that Iain Ferguson was in Scotland getting married, which was clearly not the case.

Jamie was aware he was glowering at Iain, and he made an effort to put a more pleasant expression on his face. This was her *friend*, he reminded himself, and he would try, for her sake, to remember that. Gisele turned and led both men into the drawing room, gesturing for them to sit. She perched herself on the edge of the settee and gave Jamie a look that pleaded with him to hold his tongue. At least for now. He gave her a tight nod.

"Please tell me why you are not in Scotland." Gisele impaled Iain with a level stare.

"Please tell me why you thought it was a good idea to be in London," Iain retorted.

"The marquess is getting married again, Iain. And it cannot be allowed to happen."

"I heard. You should have sent me a message when you found out, Gisele. You can't do this by yourself."

"Mr. Montcrief has volunteered his assistance," Gisele told him, rolling her eyes. "I was not about to attempt anything foolish alone."

"But you'll attempt something foolish with him?" Iain jerked his chin in the direction of Jamie.

"Oh, for pity's sake," Gisele muttered. "Why are you here, Iain?" she asked, and Jamie recognized her posture. She would not be dissuaded this time. "Did something happen? Is Helena all right?"

"She fine." A smile touched the rifleman's lips. "She's wonderful." The smile faded. "But I had to see you before..." He trailed off. "We're leaving."

"Leaving? For where?"

"Halifax."

"Halifax?" she repeated, sounding startled. "You're going to Canada?"

Iain leaned forward. "The bulk of my old regiment is to be deployed there. My captain asked me if I would consider coming with them. While my injuries obviously prevent me from participating in any engagements, they do nothing to impede my ability to load and fire a rifle. An ability which seems to have become legendary." He said the last almost regretfully. "I am told they are in dire need of skilled men to train and drill troops in the use of such weapons."

"I see." Gisele was twisting the fabric of her skirts in her lap, and Jamie had to restrain himself from going to her.

"It's not the only reason."

Gisele looked up at Iain sharply.

"She's not as strong as you," Iain said quietly. "Helena. She's been brave, but the constant fear of being recognized is eating her alive. Every time we meet a new person or get passed by a carriage, she flinches. She can barely bring herself to go to market or the theater. She can't live like that anymore." He paused. "And she won't have to in Halifax. It's a new beginning for her. For us."

Jamie watched Gisele. She was silent, regret and resignation touching her features.

"When do you leave?"

"Tonight."

"Oh, Iain."

"I'm so sorry, Gisele."

"I beg your pardon?"

"I'm sorry. I don't feel right about leaving you when all this is happening."

Gisele slapped her hand on the desk. Jamie and Iain both jumped.

"Leaving *me*? Are you bloody serious?"

"But I—"

"You are not responsible for me. Your responsibilities lie with Helena. You are responsible for seeing her safe to Halifax, for giving her oodles of babies to raise, and for loving her with a single-minded devotion. You are responsible for cherishing the happiness you two have found."

"Speak your mind, why don't you," he muttered.

"And when have I not with you?"

Iain winced. "Once would have been nice, perhaps."

Gisele laughed, though it ended abruptly. "Jesus, but I'm going to miss you."

Iain grinned at her. "Yes, you will. The duchess seems to think you are in good hands, however." The grin slipped, and his eyes slid to Jamie. "Perhaps you might give Mr. Montcrief and me a moment of privacy, Gisele?"

Jamie sat back, his forehead creasing in circumspection. Gisele was shaking her head.

Iain stared her down. "I'll be but a minute. Mr. Montcrief has survived Napoleon and the Grande Armée for ten years, Gisele. Surely ten minutes with me won't be a stretch."

Jamie cut his eyes to Iain. He wondered what else the Duchess of Worth had told Iain Ferguson.

Gisele seemed to be considering the same thing, her eyes narrowed in suspicion. Slowly, reluctantly, she got to her feet. Even more reluctantly she moved to the door. Jamie thought she was going to argue further, but instead she fetched the two coal buckets and left without another word.

Iain stood and went to the bookshelves, running his fingers along the titles. "What are your intentions towards Gisele?" he asked without turning around.

"My intentions?" Jamie blinked, instantly bridling. He'd been expecting a more military question.

"Yes, your intentions."

"Why would that be any of your concern?" Jamie asked, deflecting.

Iain turned back to Jamie and crossed his arms over his chest. "I wanted to die, you know," he said finally.

"I beg your pardon?"

"In Spain. I wished every day they had left me on that damned field to die. I woke up on the ground in a hospital tent and realized I was still alive, and I begged anyone who would listen to help me die. I was still begging them when they shipped me back to England, though by then it was obvious my wounds were healing and the likelihood of death had faded. My mother came to collect me and brought me home, and I spent the next fortnight staring at the wall and wishing I were dead."

Jamie shifted, unsure of the point of this conversation. "What happened after a fortnight?"

"The duchess brought Gisele to my mother's house to hide. She arrived a stranger—silent and pale and stinking of smoke and the Thames, and my mother bathed her, fed her, and tucked her into bed next to me where I was attempting to torture myself to death with self-pity." Iain stared down at his hands. "Gisele had written me to inform me of her engagement, but I had heard nothing from her after that, which was odd. But I was so consumed with myself, it never even occurred to me to ask after her." He shook his head. "My mother was a smart woman. It's hard to pity yourself when your best friend is in more pain than you."

"That's what Gisele said about you."

Iain snorted. "She would. But the truth was, I was a sniveling, selfish fool. I had convinced myself my wounds were insurmountable and my life was over. That I would never be able to find happiness as I had always envisioned it—as a husband or father, for what woman would want me? Less than a whole man?"

"She convinced you otherwise." Jamie wasn't sure he had managed to mask the possessive jealousy in his words. Even though he knew they hadn't been lovers, compassion and care had forged a bond between the two friends that had endured.

Iain gave him a hard, knowing look. "Aye, she did that."

Jamie refused to take the bait and stayed silent. Without Iain Ferguson, Jamie was well aware he would not have the gift that was Gisele. But it didn't mean Jamie didn't feel an irrational resentment that he hadn't been the one to help mend her then.

"But then, you already knew that."

"Yes. She told me," Jamie answered simply.

"She told you everything." The words were speculative.

"Not everything."

"Enough." It wasn't a question.

"Yes." Jamie bore the full weight of Iain's stare steadily.

"Why did you agree to do this? To help her?" Iain's words were critical.

"Oh, for Christ's sake," Jamie swore angrily. "I'm not going through this again. Sebastien. The duchess. You. I am sick to death of the doubt of my character, my moral compass, and my feelings for Gisele!"

"Do you love her?"

"I—" Jamie opened his mouth to deny it, but the words lodged fast in his throat.

"So that's the way of it then." Iain straightened abruptly.

Jamie swallowed, his mouth suddenly dry. Did he love her? He wasn't certain he did or even if he deserved to do so. Protect her, yes. Help her, certainly. But love her?

Iain didn't seem to notice his distress and instead sat down on the settee and winced. He reached down and rubbed his leg through the leather of his boot.

Jamie cleared his throat and tried to collect himself. "Does your leg pain you?" he asked gruffly. He was a soldier. He was a man not given to demonstrations of emotion. He still had dignity. Somewhere. The revelation of the depths of his feelings toward Gisele would be dealt with. But not now. And most certainly not with Iain Ferguson.

Iain gave him a sidelong glance. "Aye. Some days more than others." He struggled to adjust his boot, but the tight leather left little room to maneuver. He glanced in the direction of the door as if hoping Gisele would reappear.

"Can I help?" Jamie asked, unsure if Iain would resent the offer.

Iain hesitated. "I'd be obliged."

The conversation was almost normal, and Jamie latched on to the concept. Nothing else about the last hour had been normal. Nothing since he had met Gisele had been normal.

"What do you need?" Jamie asked.

Iain grimaced as he tugged at the top of his boot. "I need to take the damned boots off," he grumbled. "Sometimes it helps to rub the tightness from the muscle."

"I can do that." Jamie moved to crouch in front of Iain. The other man braced himself against the settee, and Jamie grasped the heel of the boot.

"Just give it a good yank," Iain suggested.

Jamie did as requested and the boot came free with a horrible tearing noise. Iain let out a bloodcurdling shriek and clutched at his leg. Jamie went tumbling back into the bookshelves, landing hard on his back, Iain's boot still in his hand.

"Jesus Christ!" Jamie wheezed in terror.

"My leg!" Iain yelled. "God in heaven, you've pulled it off!"

Jamie blanched, staring from his back among fallen books at the spot where Iain's leg should have been. It was gone. He scrambled to his feet, spinning and casting about in panic. A tourniquet. He needed something to bind the wound. He'd done it before on the battlefield. Something to stanch the blood. Before Iain bled out before him.

Or before Iain pissed his breeches laughing.

Jamie turned back to stare at the man, who was doubled over, his breath coming in huge heaving gasps.

"Shit, Montcrief, you should have seen your face," Iain managed before losing his composure again.

Jamie looked down at the boot he still clutched in his hand. A thick pad of fleece was set into the top, leather straps protruding from the sides. The solid portion filling out the boot itself was rock-hard and, on closer inspection, composed a cleverly crafted lower leg and foot carved out of wood.

The apartment door crashed open, and Gisele tumbled in.

"What's wrong?" she panted, her eyes flying from Jamie to Iain and back again. Then they dropped to the boot Jamie held.

"Dammit, Iain, what have I told you about doing that?" she scolded the man still laughing hysterically behind him.

Jamie did not miss the effort she was making to appear angry.

"One day someone is simply going to put a bullet in your brain in a misguided attempt to put you out of your misery." Her eyes were watering now as she struggled to smother her own laughter.

Iain finally got himself under some semblance of control. "I'm sorry," he lied.

"No you're not," Jamie said, rubbing his face with his free hand.

Iain bent over his other leg and unbuckled the straps on the top of his remaining boot. He pulled that leg free too and propped it up beside him on the cushions. He caught Jamie's stare and made a wry face.

"French gunner had good aim that day." Iain rubbed the stumps of his legs, just below the knees. "Damn cannonball."

"Perhaps you should have jumped higher." Jamie straightened his clothing and tossed Iain his leg. The rifleman caught it midair and stared at him before grinning. Jamie couldn't stop himself smiling back.

Seeing the standoff had ended, Gisele began giggling like a schoolgirl. Jamie looked at her, his heart turning over in his chest, and he realized then that Iain had been right.

The respect and admiration and desire Jamie felt for this magnificent woman had merged into love.

Chapter 14 ———————————

Iain stayed to help Jamie enjoy the food Gisele had brought up earlier. As soon as they were done with the meal, Jamie left, dawdling in the stables and annoying the grooms, allowing Gisele and Iain to say their good-byes in privacy. When he returned, Iain was gone, and Gisele was tidying, her eyes a little red, but her shoulders straight.

"You'll miss him," Jamie said, wanting to go to her, but unsure if it was his comfort she needed right now. She had just said goodbye to a man she had cared about her entire life, and intruding on that seemed wrong.

"Yes." She smiled sadly. "But it's the right thing to do—for both of them. Iain is right. The life Helena has been living is no sort of life at all."

"How did Iain come to marry Helena?"

Her smile lost its sadness. "After the explosion, the duchess sent Helena to a friend's manor in Bath to work as a governess. She didn't call herself Helena, of course, but Iain would visit regularly just to check on her."

"Ah." Jamie toyed with the crystal cups on the side-board, thinking about the hold the marquess had on Helena even now. How Valence's heinous actions years ago were still creating ripples in the lives of his victims.

It was, he realized with sudden clarity, what had brought Gisele to his bedroom that morning.

He hadn't fully recognized her motivations at the time, but he had recognized her need.

He had seen her need to prove to herself she had the courage to give her body in trust, without that gift's exacting a cost to her own identity. It was why he had given her absolute control. So that Gisele might understand that the passion between them was not something to be feared. So she might understand that no man could ever own her, any more than one could own the sea or the moon or the stars.

Before this morning Gisele had denied herself the possibility of happiness and pleasure, not because she was *indifferent*, but because the marquess and her father had taught her that everything came with a price. Jamie would teach her differently if it killed him. He smirked inwardly at the thought.

She'd come damn close to it this morning. And he couldn't wait to try again.

He set a glass down and turned to face her. Gisele was watching him expectantly. He sighed, knowing they had put this conversation off for as long as possible.

"I might have to kidnap Lady Julia," he said, aiming at levity.

His comment earned a faint smile before it faded. "So you met her."

"Yes."

"And did you sweep her off her feet?"

Jamie schooled his features at the last second. Was that jealousy he detected?

"She doesn't seem the, er, sweepable type," he said with regret.

"What does that mean? Did you dance with her?"

"Yes."

"Did you kiss her?" The question was brusque.

Jamie was almost enjoying this. "I did . . ."

Her face pinched.

". . . not kiss her."

"You're a bastard." She made a face at him, finally recognizing his guile.

"Yes, I am indeed," he replied cheerfully, his heart lighter than it had been in a very long time. Not only was she not indifferent, Gisele Whitby was *jealous*.

"But I was a dismal failure at provoking anything more than a blush and a 'Thank you, Mr. Montcrief' from the girl. Apparently I did not make a very convincing Romeo."

"Oh."

"The good news is that Lord Huston has expressed his misgivings about this marriage," Jamie told her.

"To you?" She looked at him in surprise.

"Yes. His exact words were that he believed Valence to be a little . . . off."

Gisele raised a brow. "However did you get the viscount talking about his sister's fiancé with you?"

"Apparently I am trustworthy. And sympathetic. And affable. Even though I am a bastard," he added, unable to help himself.

"Mmm-hmm." She sounded worried now. "But she still plans to marry him?"

"Yes. I am quite sure her sense of duty to both her father and her family name will trump any assaults on her tender heart. Or her brother's instincts."

"So we're back to where we started." He could hear the frustration bleed into her words. "We might really have to kidnap her."

"Or not kidnap her and think of something else."

Gisele didn't seem to hear him. She had picked up an envelope from a stack of invitations that had been delivered and was tapping it against her hand, frowning fiercely. "Maybe it would be for the best," she told him. "Even if it does destroy her reputation. At least she'd be alive. I could build her a new life, with every comfort and luxury she has come to expect and enjoy."

"With what money?" Jamie asked, pointing out the obvious flaw in that plan. "No amount of creative accounting could hide a sum like that missing from the duchess's accounts."

Gisele gazed at him, a small smile playing at the corners of her mouth. "You're right."

"Thank you," Jamie said, though he couldn't see what was amusing about it.

"Have you named your horse yet?" she asked after a moment.

"My what?" How did the woman manage to do this? He had missed a turn somewhere in the conversation. Again.

"I was thinking," she said, "you might want to call that gelding Diamond."

It took Jamie a full minute before he understood. "Holy shit," he breathed.

"Valence had made a collar out of them," she said distantly, "that he liked me to wear. It was the width and circumference of my entire neck. That night was the first and only time I was glad to be wearing it. Those diamonds have helped a lot of women."

Jamie shook his head, unbalanced. Not only by Valence's depravity, but by the realization that Gisele possessed a king's ransom in diamonds and had chosen to stay. She could have fled and gone anywhere in the world, and that fortune could have given her the lifestyle of a princess. She could have had anything and everything she ever wanted. But she had stayed and helped others who suffered as she had. Stayed and used her fortune to help take women and families out of impossible situations and give them a chance at happiness. At life.

"The duchess sells the diamonds for you," he muttered, a piece of the puzzle clicking into place.

"I can't very well do it, can I?"

"Gisele," he started, but found he was groping blindly for the right words. "You...I think..." Something warm had wrapped itself around his chest and was squeezing mercilessly.

She was eyeing him warily now.

"You are extraordinary."

She blinked. "Thank you. But I don't do it alone. And I don't do anything anyone else wouldn't do."

"No."

"No?" The wariness was back.

"There are very few people in this world who would do what you have done."

Gisele shrugged, looking uncomfortable, but he refused to let her look away.

"Why did you wait to tell me?" he asked.

Her eyes dropped. "I didn't know if I could trust you then."

"And now?"

She raised her chin again. "You know I trust you."

Jamie crossed the room in two strides and touched her cheek, unable to help himself. He heard her breath catch and then, because it was inevitable, he leaned over and kissed her softly.

After a moment she pulled away. "Sometimes I think it was shame," she whispered.

"What was?"

"Why I stayed."

"I don't understand."

She looked down, her fingers twisting the envelope. "I didn't stop him. I ran away instead. That wasn't extraordinary." She was quiet for a moment. "You hear stories of other women, and you never think it could happen to you. You always think you would be stronger. Braver. Better. But in the end you're not. You're scared and helpless and you let it happen."

"Gisele—"

"You were right when you accused me of trying to atone for something. I thought, if I could keep it from happening to others, I could make up for my cowardice."

Jamie forced her chin up. "Stop. You were in an impossible situation with impossible choices. But don't ever believe it was cowardice that brought you here."

She smiled weakly. "I won't allow it to happen again."

Jamie drew her back into his arms. "No," he agreed. "We won't. We'll think of something. I'm not going anywhere."

She was still for a moment before she spoke. "Sebastien said to remind you that you have appointments all afternoon."

Jamie groaned. What he wanted to do was spend the rest of the afternoon with Gisele. He did not want to leave her here, alone. "What will you do while we're gone?"

Gisele let her arms drop and looked at him unhappily. "Pretend to dust? Jump on the bed so I can remake it?" She bit her lip. "God, but I hate this feeling of helplessness. I'm stuck in these rooms, and all I can do is wait. Wait for you to leave. Wait for you to come home. Wait for that bastard to do something stupid. I can't stand not being able to do anything!" She stomped to the bedroom doors. "I can't just sit by and let this man destroy another woman. I might just turn lunatic in the process—" She froze, her expression intense. "That's it."

"What's it?" Jamie looked at her in confusion.

"I know what we have to do."

"You do?"

She had an almost feral gleam in her eye. "I know how to destroy him. Destroy Valence," she clarified unnecessarily.

"How?" He watched her warily.

"There is one thing that would prevent him from being able to marry. From being able to hold his seat in the House of Lords. From being accepted into polite society as a whole."

"You let me kill him?" Jamie suggested.

"Better."

"I'm not following."

"How does one lose a seat in the House of Lords?"

"He dies."

"Or?"

"Or he is deemed insane," Jamie said slowly, comprehension dawning. "If a person has lost his reason, he cannot sit."

"Nor can he get married."

Jamie considered her. "You wish to make him appear unsound of mind."

"He's already mad as a March hare, Jamie. We just need to bring the crazy out for everyone to see."

"How do you propose we do that?"

"What do you think he would do if he believed I might still be alive?"

"I beg your pardon?" Jamie gaped at her, certain now he didn't like where this was going at all.

"How would he react if he saw me? In the street? In the park? Random places, random times?"

Jamie was shaking his head, every instinct he possessed clamoring in alarm. "You are not going to expose yourself, Gisele. You are dead, remember? Dead and *safe*. I'd prefer to keep it that way."

Gisele crossed her arms in impatient annoyance. "Don't be difficult. No one is ever really safe. I could get run over by a carriage tomorrow."

"By a *what*?"

"I can't believe I didn't think of this before."

"I can—it's a truly terrible idea! What if Valence discovers you are, in fact, very much real?"

"I can't hide forever!"

"You could try."

"Would you?"

Jamie opened his mouth to argue, but found he had no words.

"If Valence thought he could have me back, he would never marry Lady Julia."

The words were like a gunshot, the report sharp in its truth and simplicity. Jamie stared at her, knowing he was losing ground. Because in the back of his mind, beyond his initial gut reaction, he knew she was right.

In his mind's eye, Jamie saw Valence's visceral reaction to the mention of Gisele. Remembered Eleanor's comments about the marquess's extreme withdrawal after the explosion. And the unsettling resemblance of Julia Hextall to Gisele Whitby.

She was silent for a long minute. "He killed his first wife so he could marry me," she said, suddenly subdued.

Jamie had already suspected that. "Are you sure?"

"Yes. He met me when she was still alive and danced an attendance on me that was unnerving. The marchioness was dead within three weeks. At the time I simply thought it was tragic. Now I know it was premeditated."

"She drowned?"

"Helena's mother did not like or trust the water, yet somehow ended up drowned along the edges of the estate ponds. She had apparently slipped and banged her head."

Jamie took a deep breath, making sure his voice was matter-of-fact and even. "Then you're right."

"I am?" She looked a little startled.

"If there was even a remote chance you were still alive, I know exactly what he'd do."

"You do?"

He crossed over to her. "He would move heaven and earth to find you. He would do anything to have you back. He'd make himself look like a raving lunatic trying to convince others to help him, and he wouldn't care." He paused. "You said your death was witnessed by a number of people. Would any of those believe you might have survived?"

Gisele was shaking her head. "No. No, the explosion was spectacular. Valence had put Helena and me on the barge that night for a spring solstice costume party at Vauxhall Gardens. He wanted everyone traveling over the bridge to be able to see us—he'd hired the barge and had it tricked out with ribbons and lights and fireworks and—"

"And a waterman named George," Jamie finished for her.

"That was the easy part to arrange."

"Why wasn't Valence with you?" The thought struck him belatedly.

Gisele sneered. "He was waiting for us on the far side like some pagan deity surveying the delivery of a sacrificial virgin."

"Of course he was," Jamie muttered. "But you're sure no one would have seen you escape?"

Gisele shook her head. "Before the barge blew, George created a smoke so thick and noxious, I could barely see my hand in front of my face. And it was dark that night. It would have been impossible for anyone to have seen us in the water."

"So it's safe to say you are well and truly dead." He was watching her carefully, knowing exactly how hard this was, to relive that night.

"Two hundred people saw me die. Yes."

"Good." He took her hands in his.

"We'll just have to make sure he is the only one to see me."

"Correct," he replied. His mind was racing. "But you have to promise me you'll not be reckless. We must be smart and careful and precise."

She nodded up at him. "I promise." She took a deep, slow breath before letting it out. "Thank you. For being my partner. Not my warden."

"You're welcome. Don't make me regret it."

She grinned up at him in determination. "Never."

Chapter 15 _____

The Marquess of Valence crumpled the newssheet in his fist and tossed it into the fire in annoyance. One line. He'd had one line in the entire social section, while James Montcrief had merited nearly an entire paragraph. A bloody nobody, strutting around with fine clothes and fabricated war stories to obscure the fact that he was a nonentity.

There was something not quite right about James Montcrief. Adam had always trusted his gut, and his gut was telling him Montcrief was not to be taken at face value. The captain most certainly had a hidden agenda, and the conversation at the card tables last night had given Adam pause. When the subject of his late wife's remoteness had come up, Montcrief had fallen just short of actually calling Adam a liar, for Christ's sake.

Equally troubling was the amount of time Lord Huston had spent in Montcrief's company last night. The viscount had not been a problem thus far, but if the former captain should lead the boy in the wrong direction regarding his sister, Adam might be forced to do something…distasteful. Nothing could get in the way of his wedding. He needed Boden's money, and he needed it fast.

Adam had enormous outstanding debts, and though the creditors had been stalled with assurances his coffers would soon be refilled, he knew they were waiting like scavengers to seize what was left of his property if he did not deliver. Adam's connections and title would hold them off for only so long. His last investment, like everything else these past four years, had failed, and at this juncture, Adam would go to any lengths to ensure he had Lady Julia wedded and bedded before Boden could reconsider.

The marquess stared unseeing into the fire. He needed more time with Montcrief. Time to determine what made the man tick. To determine his strengths, his weaknesses, his limitations, and his price, if necessary. Perhaps the man really was in London to find a wife. Or perhaps he was here for something else entirely. Adam would do well to find out more about this mysterious interloper. Before the House of Lords convened this afternoon, Adam would stop at the war office. He still had a contact there who would be happy to deliver a full report on Montcrief, including the unofficial account of his service. If there were any blemishes on the man's military record, Adam would know them later this afternoon.

It seemed like a good place to start.

Chapter 16 _____

Sebastien returned to the Albany a short while later and listened as Jamie explained their plan.

"It might work," the valet speculated.

"Of course it will work," Gisele scoffed.

Sebastien hesitated. "You're poking a hornet's nest with a stick, my dear."

"That's the idea."

"You don't know what will fly out."

Gisele scowled. "As long as *something* flies out, we're further ahead than we are now. Do you have a better idea?"

"Tell us what you found out this morning, Sebastien," Jamie interjected, putting an end to their debate.

Sebastien's lips thinned. "I spoke to Valence's last remaining servant. Everyone else left in the year following your demise, mainly because the marquess stopped paying them, but his scullery maid had nowhere to go. She's stuck and overworked and bitter because of it."

"Did she say anything useful about Valence?"

"Oh, she had all sorts of things to say about Valence," Sebastien assured her. "How useful any of it is..."

"Try me," Gisele said.

"He hasn't changed much, as far as I can determine,"

Sebastien started slowly. "He has his patterns and routines, and he sticks to them. House of Lords, White's, a careful selection of exclusive social events. He doesn't gamble often, rarely drinks, though he does use laudanum frequently at night. Apparently he's had a great deal of trouble sleeping since the passing of the last Marchioness of Valence."

Gisele nodded silently, assimilating. "Where will he be today?"

Sebastien frowned. "Westminster this afternoon. His club late tonight. Then home, I suppose."

Gisele stared sightlessly at the bookshelves. "The House of Lords sits today, correct?"

"Yes."

"The grounds and streets around the palace will be busy then. Especially midafternoon."

"Yes."

"I haven't seen Westminster in quite a while," she said, sitting back with a decisive air. "I'm in the mood for a little outing." She regarded both men, batting her lashes in mock innocence. "Would the two of you care to accompany me? And, now that I think of it, perhaps we should invite Margaret and Miss Hughes as well. Please send a note to the duchess, if you would be so kind, Sebastien. If we hurry, we can make it there within the hour."

"To do what, exactly?" Jamie's eyes narrowed at her.

"Why, to see the palace and its grounds, of course. It's a stunning example of architecture, art, intellect, and . . ."

"And?"

She dropped her voice to a whisper. "I've also heard it's haunted."

Chapter 17 ————————

Adam Levire made his way back toward Westminster, inattentively navigating the increasing crowds as he neared Bridge Street. His visit to the war office had been interesting, but he had no idea if the information he had obtained about former captain James Montcrief would prove useful in any way. Moreover, Montcrief's competence as an officer had been confirmed, much to Adam's chagrin. He had been hoping to start the day with better news.

He shifted the bulk of his robes over his arms, cursing his lack of a footman and doubly cursing his lack of a carriage and coachman. Soon, Adam told himself. Soon he would once again be wealthy enough to avoid attending to the menial details a man of his station should delegate to others. He wasn't a servant, like the droves of bodies scurrying around him. He shouldn't have to carry his personal belongings around with him on foot like so much baggage. It was humiliating.

He had no sooner finished the thought than a careless kitchen maid knocked into him, her market basket driving hard into his hip and throwing him off-balance. A few apples hit the ground and rolled in all directions. Adam swore angrily, staggering back, trying to keep his robes from tipping into the mud.

"Watch where you're going, whore," he snarled, his temper finding an outlet.

The cloaked servant looked up at him, her green eyes wide, her pale hair tumbling around her face within the confines of her gray hood. "Good afternoon, Adam," she said, before ducking back into the morass of humanity funneling across Westminster Bridge.

Adam stared, shock rooting him to the spot. Tiny spots of light danced before his eyes, and his lungs screamed for breath he couldn't seem to draw. He thought, for a terrifying second, he might faint. People flowed around him, jostling him.

Jerked from his stupor, he dropped his robes and charged into the crowd after her. After his wife. His Gisele.

Adam dashed out into the center of Bridge Street, narrowly missing being run down by a team of heavies pulling a wagon teetering with woolen bales. The driver yelled profanities at him as he maneuvered his startled horses around the marquess. Adam barely took note. She was here. Somewhere. He bolted toward the river, certain it was where Gisele had headed, but all he could see among the congestion of carriages and carts and coaches was dozens of unidentifiable bodies, all wrapped in drab cloaks and coats against the chill of the afternoon.

"Lord Valence?" Distantly he heard his name being called from somewhere. He ignored it. He couldn't afford the distraction. Not when she was so close.

Up ahead he saw a woman hurrying away from him, the same basket banging against her side, fair hair escaping from the edges of the same gray hood. Gisele! He sprinted after her, evading oncoming horses, and grabbed her arm desperately, spinning her around. She screamed, her basket dropping, her hood falling from her face.

He shook her, so certain it was Gisele that he was slow to recognize the woman had pale blue eyes, not vivid green ones. Her hair was too gold, and she was too tall. And she was still screaming incessantly. His Gisele never screamed. Ever.

Adam shoved the useless woman to the ground. He was losing time. With every passing second, Gisele was getting away.

He ran back out into Bridge Street, looking around wildly. A desperate shout finally broke through the fog, and he looked up to see a wall of flailing hooves coming directly for him. The driver was hauling back on the reins, but the horses were helpless to stop the momentum of the massive load of coal behind them.

He threw himself out of the path of certain death, landing painfully on his knees as the horses skidded by, the collier's cart veering on two wheels and finally tipping. The crash was deafening, coal spilling across the width of the street at the entrance to the bridge, the already-panicked horses heaving themselves against traces tangled hopelessly. The driver had been thrown and the overturned cart was being dragged farther down the street.

Adam struggled to his feet, ignoring the pain shooting from his knees, and clambered up onto a stone balustrade at the edge of the bridge. But he couldn't see her.

He still couldn't find her. No, no, *no*. This couldn't be happening.

"Lord Valence!" His name came again, and this time he looked down.

The Duke of Worth was staring up at him in horror.

"Are you quite all right?" the duke exclaimed.

"No!" Valence shouted. "You have to help me!"

"Have you been robbed?" Another lord, already dressed in his sessional robes, had joined the duke. "I'll set my men on the scoundrel, so I will! Which direction did the villain go?"

"Not a villain, you imbecile," Valence snapped, frantic. "My wife!"

Worth cleared his throat. "Er, I've just come from St. James, Lord Valence. Lady Julia was entertaining a number of callers with her sister. It is quite impossible for her to be here."

Adam swore in frustration. Goddammit, but was everyone this dull-witted? He was losing her, and no one seemed to understand. They were all standing around like sheep while his beloved wife slipped farther away.

"Not Julia," he cried. "Gisele!" Adam leaned forward in agitation and promptly lost his balance. His hands grasped at thin air, and for a sickening moment, he thought he would slip from the bridge and into the river far below him.

The duke, with lightning speed, caught the skirt of his coat and yanked him back to safety. His footing lost, Adam tumbled from his perch and landed hard on his back, the breath knocked clean from his lungs.

Spots danced before his eyes, and when they cleared, Adam looked up to find a half dozen lords, including

Worth, staring down at him, their expressions ranging from alarm to confusion to pity. Beyond them traffic had ground to a standstill, blocked by heaps of coal strewn across the road. Crowds of people were muttering angrily and giving him vile looks. Someone had caught the horses, and two footmen and a groom were trying to free them from the overturned wagon, while a gentleman was helping the dazed and bleeding driver to his feet. The servant he had accosted was sobbing loudly and pointing at him even as she was comforted by a lady and her maid who had climbed from their stalled carriage.

Adam could feel the color drain from his face. What had he done?

~

Jamie watched with interest as the marquess finally became aware of himself and his surroundings. If he had questioned Valence's obsession with Gisele, this reaction had erased any doubt. Sebastien joined him, slightly out of breath.

"She's safe?" Jamie asked, not looking at the valet.

"Long gone across the river," Sebastien confirmed. "Margaret is with her."

"Good." If Gisele wasn't safe with Margaret, she wasn't safe with anyone. "How did Gisele seem?"

"She seemed... very confident," Sebastien replied slowly.

Jamie nodded his head, fiercely proud of her. He returned his attention to the scene in front of them.

"Is Miss Hughes injured?" Jamie asked, watching as the tall serving girl Valence had accosted collected her basket and allowed herself to be led away by a well-meaning lady clutching a vinaigrette and offering it to

Miss Hughes every few steps. Miss Hughes's raven hair was hidden under a long blond wig of the highest quality, and where the duchess had been able to find such an excellent match for Gisele's color on such short notice was beyond Jamie's comprehension. Her Grace did indeed have some very odd and very useful resources at her fingertips.

Sebastien snorted. "Miss Hughes is a great deal more resilient than she might appear. I asked her to be noticeable and convincing."

"Well, I was duly convinced."

Sebastien made an indistinguishable noise in the back of his throat and surveyed the wreckage surrounding them. "This is quite impressive."

"Beyond my wildest expectations," Jamie murmured.

The marquess was being helped to his feet, shrugging off concerned questions and offers of help. Valence was breathing hard, his hair disheveled, his coat filthy, and his breeches torn at the knee.

"Shall we finish this little performance?" Sebastien asked.

"Indeed we shall." Jamie glanced at Sebastien. "Are you sure you're ready?"

The valet nodded, revulsion crossing his features once before it was gone, replaced with a perfect mask of mild disinterest. "This has been too long in coming. After you, Mr. Montcrief."

Jamie strode forward, the heavy robes flapping in his arms. "Lord Valence!" he called loudly. "A moment, my lord!"

The marquess stopped, a trail of uncertain aristocrats strung out in his wake. "Mr. Montcrief," he said, distaste ringing, even as his eyes darted from side to side. "Whatever are you doing here?"

"I was sight-seeing, my lord," Jamie said earnestly. "I've never had the chance to visit Westminster, though I certainly did not expect…this." He waved his hand at the carnage around them.

Valence's jaw clenched, and his eyes fell to the garment in Jamie's arms.

"You dropped these, my lord," Jamie continued, holding out the filthy robes Valence had abandoned. "I didn't imagine you meant to leave such a fine costume in the mud. It looks quite expensive."

Valence was looking at him intensely, ignoring his outstretched arms. "Then you saw her."

Jamie pretended to look confused. "Who?"

"My w—the woman who knocked into me."

"Oh." Jamie shook his head. "No, no, I'm afraid I didn't see anything," he lied. In truth, he'd been not five feet behind Valence, ready to tackle the marquess should Gisele not be able to make good on her escape. "It was my valet's quick thinking that saved your robes, my lord. I cannot take the credit." Jamie gestured casually behind him to where Sebastien stood, patient and stoic.

Valence's eyes bulged slightly before he recovered. "Sebastien."

"Good afternoon, Lord Valence," the valet greeted him with a short bow.

"I didn't realize you were back in London."

"Just recently, my lord."

"You know each other?" Jamie asked with feigned surprise.

"I had the good fortune to serve Lord Valence a number of years ago," Sebastien said.

The marquess's eyes went from Sebastien to Jamie and back again. "And you are currently employed by Mr. Montcrief?"

Sebastien gave a clipped nod. "Yes."

Jamie was impressed by how much dissatisfaction Sebastien managed to convey in a single word.

"I see." Valence seemed torn between addressing the reappearance of his former valet and the reappearance of his wife. "Then did you see her? The woman?" The ghost of Gisele emerged the victor, just as Jamie had known she would.

"No, my lord, I did not see anything." Sebastien stared straight ahead, his face a mask of stone. "Of course."

Valence's nostrils flared, and he snatched the robes from Jamie's hands. Without another word he stalked away from Jamie and Sebastien, to be swallowed quickly by the crowd trapped and milling around the destruction.

"Montcrief!" The Duke of Worth joined Jamie, scratching his head and glancing in the direction in which Valence had disappeared.

"Your Grace," Jamie said, adopting a look of grave concern. "What happened here?"

"I haven't the foggiest notion," the duke said, perplexed. "It would seem Lord Valence lost his sense of bearing and ran out into the middle of the street. He seemed to be convinced he was chasing his wife."

"Lady Julia?" Jamie asked. "Whyever would Lady Julia be in the middle of Bridge Street?"

"Not Lady Julia," Worth revealed. "Gisele. The last Lady Valence."

"His dead wife?" Jamie let that hang.

"Apparently."

Jamie barked out a laugh. "You're telling me all of this occurred"—he swept his hand at the disaster around them—"because the Marquess of Valence saw a ghost?"

The duke shrugged helplessly.

"Does he see his dead wife often?" Jamie asked.

"I don't think so." The duke looked at Jamie uncertainly. "But maybe?"

"Perhaps he's losing his mind." Jamie left it to the duke to determine if he was joking or serious.

The bells began tolling the hour, interrupting them.

Worth grimaced. "Bloody hell, but I'm late. Though at least"—he peered around at the small knots of men talking and gesturing excitedly—"I won't be the only one." He gave Jamie a grin. "Perhaps you might care to join Lord Huston and me tomorrow? We are to ride in Hyde Park. I've a new mare I'm considering breeding, and I'd not be averse to a qualified second opinion."

"Of course, Your Grace," Jamie said easily. "It would be my pleasure."

"Care to watch a session?" the duke asked, jerking his head in the direction of Westminster.

Jamie shook his head with regret. "I am afraid I am off to a number of appointments my valet assures me are necessary if I am to release you from your obligation of seeing me clothed for the remainder of my time in London."

Worth laughed. "I will send a note round then, Montcrief." The duke took a final look around, shaking his head in disbelief. Giving Jamie a brief salute, he hurried toward the looming edifice of the palace.

"That went well," said Jamie conversationally.

"Exceedingly." Sebastien stepped forward, kicking at a piece of coal that had rolled near his boot, his eyes fixed somewhere on the smoggy horizon. "Just for the record, James, if this fails, I will kill him."

"Get in line," Jamie told him pleasantly. "You may have whatever is left of Valence once I'm finished."

Chapter 18

Adam crashed into his study, not caring that his boots were leaving great streaks of mud on the expensive rugs. His hair was dripping, and his coat was filthy and wet. His housekeeper, or whatever she was calling herself these days, had fled upon his arrival. Yanking his coat from his shoulders, he threw the ruined garment on the floor as he stalked directly to the sideboard and poured himself a large glass of brandy, gulping it down in three swallows. It burned his throat fiercely and forced the marquess to take a deep breath. He poured another, his hands shaking less than they had a minute ago.

He had seen her. His Gisele.

She had looked at him, touched him, spoken to him. Called him by name, the way he had always encouraged her to do. *Adam.* His name had rolled off her tongue like quicksilver, in a way she had never managed to get right when she'd been married to him. How could he have let her slip away? Why had no one else seen her?

That thought brought him up short. Putting down his glass, he forced himself to close his eyes and regain control over the scattered thoughts that were pinging wildly inside his skull. Why had no one else seen her, indeed?

Because she died a long time ago, a little voice whispered cruelly from inside his head. *No one saw her because she doesn't exist.* He braced his hands on the sideboard, sweating. Had his encounter today been a manifestation of his imagination? Was the idea of his upcoming wedding so repugnant that his mind was seeking refuge in the memories of his lost bride—his most cherished Gisele?

No, he snarled to himself. His marriage was not to be abhorred but anticipated. Once he was married, all his problems would be solved. He couldn't afford gossip or scandal now. He couldn't afford Boden finding a reason to call off the wedding. Adam *needed* this wedding or he was ruined. Whatever had happened out there on that bridge this afternoon had been a mistake. A horrible, embarrassing mistake, but a mistake nonetheless.

It had all happened so fast, but the truth of the matter was that the woman he had believed was his Gisele had been naught but a lowly servant. He was an educated man, for God's sake. Too sophisticated to believe in spirits come back from the dead to stalk him in broad daylight in the middle of Bridge Street. It was obvious Adam had misheard what the servant had said as she'd passed him. Hell, it was likely she hadn't even been speaking to him, but to someone else in the crowd around him.

Adam groaned and rubbed his face with his hands. He would have to put some very serious thought into how he was going to handle the talk that would be generated by the unfortunate turn of events this afternoon. He couldn't have people whispering. Not now.

Another thought surfaced, leaving him stricken. Sebastien. His former valet.

Adam had thought the man long gone, perhaps even dead, yet here he was, back in London, with Montcrief of all people. The valet had never been anything but a paragon of discretion, yet the man had also been privy to the most private parts of his life. Adam was well aware others might not share or understand his tastes in pleasure, but those tastes had never been intended to be shared in the first place. Would the valet cause trouble?

No, Adam reassured himself. Sebastien would not be a problem. Not now, after so many years. At any rate, it would be a marquess's word against that of a servant. Adam could certainly brazen out gossip, but he would need to be vigilant. Careful. Discreet.

He would have another bride and her fortune in but a few days, and then nothing would matter.

Chapter 19 —————————————

Margaret had seen Gisele safely back to the Albany after her appearance near Westminster. The day, like so many others, had turned cold and rainy, but even without the heavy cloaks covering their heads and faces, two servants would have gone unnoticed as unimportant but necessary fixtures in the machinations of daily London life. Gisele built up the fire in the hall, the air damp and chill, and hung her cloak near the building warmth. Crouching in front of the hearth, she held her hands out to warm them and realized with no little surprise that they were steady.

Her heart had been in her throat as she had watched Valence approach, his face as dour as she had ever remembered it, and it had taken everything she had not to turn and run. And then she had knocked into him and sent him stumbling, and all she had seen was a man. Not a monster, not an indomitable creature, but just a man who no longer held the power to hurt her.

So she had smiled then, at the marquess, holding his eyes with her own, whispering his name and sinking the barbs deep into his soul. There was no fear or panic, only the knowledge that she, together with the people who loved her, could destroy this man's sanity with a weapon of his own making.

And then, in a heartbeat, she had melted back into the crowd, easily losing the marquess amid the congestion of the bridge entrance. She wondered what had happened afterward. What had happened after the marquess was presented with the living, breathing image of his dead wife. Her brow creased in consternation.

What if she was giving herself too much credit? What if she was overvaluing herself? What if the marquess no longer cared about her as much as she thought, and his obsessive nature had already moved on to greener pastures that included Lady Julia and all her money? What if— She forced herself to stop. She despised what-ifs. They never served any useful purpose, other than to torture their bearer.

They had all agreed it was better for Jamie to keep his afternoon appointments than to run to ground after their little performance at Westminster. Sebastien believed Jamie should be as visible in town as possible, if only to establish his own credibility. A gentleman who secluded himself in a small apartment all day would be suspect, but a gentleman who was seen spending money in the finest shops and establishments of London would be viewed by the ton as one naturally of their ilk.

Gisele grimaced. Her partners would be back eventually with the answers to all her questions. She just needed to have a little patience.

Early evening had descended when Sebastien and Jamie staggered in, buried under piles of boxes and wrapped packages. The valet unceremoniously deposited his burden in the hall and went immediately to Gisele, kissing her soundly on both cheeks.

"You were brilliant this afternoon," he told her, drawing her into a rare embrace.

Gisele met Jamie's eyes over Sebastien's shoulder. Jamie was searching her face, anxious and concerned. She flashed him a reassuring smile and he returned it, a softness to his features she hadn't seen before.

"Tell me," she demanded, pulling away from Sebastien. "Tell me what happened. Did Valence truly believe it was me?"

Jamie had crossed his arms and was leaning against the fireplace mantel, looking smug. "Which version do you wish to hear?" Jamie asked. "For we heard quite a few in the places we visited this afternoon."

Gisele looked at Jamie with incomprehension. "Versions?"

Jamie frowned in concentration, relating four slightly different reports of the events that had unfolded after Gisele had smiled and bid the marquess a good afternoon. In three of these stories, Valence had climbed up on the edge of the bridge with the intention of throwing himself into the river, only to be saved by the quick thinking and quicker actions of the Duke of Worth. In another, the marquess had thrown a hapless servant girl into the river. But in all, the Marquess of Valence had wreaked havoc and confusion, out of his mind in his desperate search for his dead wife.

"Oh." Gisele dropped to a chair unfeelingly, the success of their strategy startling. "I didn't expect..."

"It was the right place and the right time," Sebastien reflected after a moment. "Right before the House of

Lords convened. A great number of the right people witnessed Valence's, er, episode."

"Will it be enough?" Gisele asked.

"I don't know."

"Was the Earl of Boden there?"

"I didn't see him," Jamie said. "But I'm sure he's heard about it since then."

"Do you think—" A pounding on the door cut off her next question.

Jamie met her eyes, a twist of trepidation and alarm coursing through her.

"Do not even consider answering this door," Jamie hissed at her. "Close yourself in the bedroom and don't come out until I tell you."

Gisele didn't need to be told twice.

Jamie opened the door, coiled tightly.

Lord Huston staggered past him, ragged and sweating, coming to an abrupt halt in the middle of Jamie's hall.

"Why don't you come in, Lord Huston?" Jamie said as he closed the door.

"You must come to the park tomorrow." Huston was pulling on the fingers of his gloves in agitation.

"The park?"

"Yes, yes. Hyde Park. Rotten Row. The fashionable hour, and all that. And I can't—I need—"

The man was like a spooked horse. Jamie opened his mouth, then changed his mind. He held up a hand.

"Let me get you a drink. Brandy?"

The viscount gulped his assent.

"Sebastien?" Jamie called loudly. "Lord Huston is

here. Please pour, if you would be so kind. And did the housekeeper leave anything to eat?"

His valet appeared at the door silently. "Of course, Mr. Montcrief. I believe there may be some pies left from—"

"I don't want anything to eat," the viscount said. "Just a drink."

"Of course." Sebastien moved to take Huston's cloak.

The man seemed not to notice, nor did he notice when Jamie guided him into one of the chairs near the fire.

Sebastien reappeared with two glasses already poured, and Huston drank his in one nervous swallow. The decanter was left discreetly on the side table next to the viscount, and Sebastien exchanged a look with Jamie before disappearing back into the drawing room.

The brandy seemed to have settled Huston. "I am quite sorry to have barged in on you like this, Montcrief."

Jamie took a seat opposite the viscount, waving his hand dismissively. Men barging into his apartments was becoming a pattern today.

"May I be of assistance to you in some manner? I believe you said something about Hyde Park? The Duke of Worth indicated to me this afternoon you two had plans to ride. Is that what this is about?"

Huston shook his head and looked hard at Jamie. "I have been quite candid with you regarding my feelings towards the impending wedding of my sister to Lord Valence."

"Yes," Jamie said slowly.

"I'm not sure why."

"You've lost me."

"I don't know you, Mr. Montcrief. Not well at all, yet the brief time I've spent with you has convinced me you are a man of honor. That you have the ability to see people for who they truly are. I think this is why I have confided my doubts."

"Thank you." Jamie stared at him in confusion. "I think."

It was Huston's turn to wave his hand in dismissal, pouring himself another drink. That one disappeared as quickly as the first. "This afternoon…" He stopped, seemingly at a loss for words and consoling himself by cradling the decanter against his chest.

"Ah." Jamie sat back, arranging his features into an expression of encouraging sympathy. "You're referring to the unfortunate incident on Bridge Street this afternoon."

"You were there, I heard," Huston mumbled. "Even rescued Valence's robes from the muck."

"It was my valet who did that, actually."

Huston slumped. "My father insists we go out as a family tomorrow," he said through gritted teeth. "My father and mother. My sisters. And Lord Valence, of course." He flinched. "The earl wishes a show of familial solidarity that this…unfortunate incident has been shoved under the proverbial rug and forgotten. He wishes to reaffirm all is right in the world of the Hextalls."

"Your father is not concerned that the man his daughter is set to wed was seen standing on the edge of a bridge, looking for his dead wife?" Jamie was rude in his surprise.

Huston sneered. "My father assures me the stories are exaggerated. He insists the incident this afternoon has been blown out of proportion by spiteful, envious gossips. Lord Valence, he tells anyone who will listen, has always been an upstanding gentleman to his daughter and those around him. And if the marquess was overcome with shock at seeing a woman who was the doppelgänger of his dead wife, why, that only proves just how deeply he cared for her and his admirable commitment to his marriage vows."

Well, shit, Jamie thought, stricken. They had been counting on a far different reaction from Boden. It didn't matter what the rest of London thought; it was the earl's opinion that mattered.

"That is unfortunate," Jamie said, keeping his voice even. "What does the marquess have to say about all of this?"

"I wasn't there, but I was informed Lord Valence called upon my mother and father personally this evening to express his regrets over the events of the afternoon and to apologize for any embarrassment it may have caused the earl or my sister."

Dammit, Jamie thought angrily. Valence was obviously not yet ready to abandon the Hextall fortune based on the single appearance of a wifely ghost.

"What can I do?" he asked Huston.

"Perhaps you might speak with my father. Convince him my objections to this union are not born of petty biases and personal dislikes; that I wish to stop this marriage not for the purpose of lowering the social standing of my family, but to protect Julia from harm. Perhaps if he heard a few words of caution from a respected cavalry captain, he might think twice."

"I don't know what I could possibly say that a hundred stone of overturned coal has not," Jamie pointed out.

"Oh, God." Huston dropped his head into his hands. "This is a disaster. Valence can't be allowed into our family."

You have no idea, thought Jamie grimly. "I will do whatever I can, of course," he assured the viscount. "I, too, neither like nor trust the man."

"Thank you." Huston looked up. "I can't spend two hours trapped in polite conversation with Valence and pretend to be happy he is there. I might take a page from his book and throw myself off a bridge into the Serpentine. You will save me from myself." He tried to smile through his distress. "At the very least, Viola will be thrilled at your presence."

Jamie winced inwardly. "Then I look forward to it."

They arranged the particulars, and Jamie saw the much-restored viscount to the door.

"Thank you again, Mr. Montcrief."

"Don't thank me yet," Jamie warned. "I haven't done anything."

Huston sighed and hurried down the steps. "I have every confidence in you," he flung over his shoulder.

Jamie closed the door and leaned against it.

"That is extremely disappointing." Sebastien had come up behind him. "I was hoping Boden was smarter than that."

"I don't know what else it would take to convince the earl he cannot allow the wedding to proceed."

"Then we don't worry about the earl." Gisele's voice startled him.

Jamie looked up at her. She was in the doorway to the drawing room, her expression resolute and calm, any sign of the frustration he was feeling absent. "You heard everything?"

"Yes."

"What are you suggesting?"

"We focus on Valence. We can still discredit him publicly when the opportunity arises, of course, but it is Valence who ultimately will decide if this wedding happens."

Sebastien was stroking his moustache. "You think we can make the marquess dishonor himself and refuse to marry Lady Julia?"

"Not we. Me. And yes, I can. And he will still look like a lunatic."

Jamie pushed himself from the door. He'd seen that look on Gisele's face before, and it generally didn't lead to anything he liked.

"Valence needs to believe, beyond all reasonable doubt, that I am alive."

"I thought we accomplished that quite nicely today." Jamie was trying to head off whatever wild scheme was currently developing behind those beautiful eyes.

"He believed he saw me at the time. But does he still believe that now? He has no proof. And the Earl of Boden has provided him with a reasonable excuse and explanation."

"So we do it again," Jamie said. "What we did this afternoon."

Sebastien was shaking his head in resignation. "Gisele is right, James. We can torment Valence with glimpses of his lost bride for months, but that is siege warfare, and we're out of time. After today Valence will be more vigilant and less likely to react so recklessly in public. We need to change our strategy."

"Valence is using laudanum to help him sleep." Gisele was deep in thought.

"There is comfort in the familiar," Sebastien said. "He always did like the smoke."

Jamie watched Gisele and the valet exchange a long look.

"Opium is a tricky thing, isn't it?" Gisele said quietly. "In its various forms, it can inspire all sorts of strange, fevered dreams. Make men believe in ghosts."

Jamie jerked as though she'd struck him. "No."

"I beg your pardon?" She raised a fair brow.

"No."

"You don't even know what I'm thinking."

"Oh, yes I do. And this is the most idiotic, reckless idea you've come up with yet. And you promised me you wouldn't be reckless. It's one thing to appear to him surrounded by crowds in which you can hide, where Sebastien and I are but a step away. It's another to trap yourself in a room with a drugged madman. That's what you were planning, isn't it?"

"Yes. Though I hadn't planned on being alone," she said. "And I hadn't planned on being trapped. I've seen Valence use opium many times. He becomes exceedingly debilitated and lethargic."

"Oh, of course," Jamie seethed. "Amidst all your grand plans then, Miss Whitby, how had you planned to drug him?"

It was Sebastien who spoke up. "Leave that to me."

"You're not helping, Sebastien!" Jamie shouted. "You should be saying something like 'Gisele, this is too dangerous and borders on insanity and it will never work.'"

"He needs to see me, Jamie. See me in a setting thick with memories and unrealized desires and dreams. I have to make him remember. Make him *believe*. I need to leave him with touchable, tangible proof."

"Well, you'll be doing it chained to me then," Jamie

growled, "for it will be a cold day in hell when I allow you into his house by yourself to craft another one of your absurd dramas amidst a haze of opium and depravity."

"Yes," Sebastien breathed.

"I'm sorry?" Jamie and Gisele both turned to the valet.

"That's brilliant."

"You've lost me."

"It is one thing for Valence to see Gisele again. That alone will eat away at him." He turned a speculative look on Gisele. "But what if he saw you with another man?"

Gisele was staring at Sebastien with wide eyes. "I love how your mind works."

"That would push him over the edge like nothing else." Sebastien crossed his arms with what looked like smug satisfaction.

"Oh, for the love of God!" Jamie threw up his hands in utter defeat, disgusted with the both of them. "And I suppose you expect me to just go along with this?"

"No one will force you to, of course. Though you would be much more convincing kissing Gisele than I ever would," Sebastien advised. "You have added appeal in that I get the feeling Valence doesn't care for you overmuch. But I'm sure Joseph could get the job done in a pinch."

"Joseph?" Jamie's mind blanked. "The horse thief?"

"Coachman," Gisele corrected with minor annoyance.

"Jesus Christ," Jamie swore.

"We're out of time, Jamie," Gisele said, having come to stand beside him. "Will you help?"

"This is *insane*."

"You seem rather fond of that word lately."

Jamie took his hands from his face. "That is because

it's the only adjective that remotely covers everything that has happened since I met you."

Gisele looked at Sebastien. "Perhaps you should fetch Joseph—"

"Don't you dare!" Jamie snapped. "If you are going to be sneaking around in the dark kissing men, it damn well better be me. Besides," he muttered, "the boy would likely never survive the experience."

Sebastien's mouth twitched, and Gisele blushed.

"You're confident we can get in and out without being seen?" Jamie couldn't believe he was agreeing to this. But he knew she'd do it with or without him.

"Yes," Gisele said. "I spent a great deal of time plotting versions of my escape. I know that house inside and out."

"What about the maid?"

The valet shrugged. "Sleeps in the attic. She won't hear a thing, but even if she does, she won't expend the effort to investigate. She's told me she's learned to ignore all manner of oddities."

"And the opium—"

"Will be the easiest part." Sebastien set his jaw.

"Fine." Jamie conceded defeat. He turned to face Gisele. "But you are not to leave my side. And if I think something is not right—if there is even a hint the marquess is not as debilitated as he needs to be for you to be safe—then you defer to my judgment. Understood?"

"Yes."

"For the record, Gisele, housebreaking and haunting were never mentioned when you hired me. I think I'm going to need a raise."

Chapter 20

Adam had been forced to call on the Earl and Countess of Boden after the events of the afternoon, wanting to allay any misgivings the earl might be feeling after the incident at Westminster. Boden was doing his best to discredit the gossip currently flying around London's coffeehouses and assembly rooms, but privately he made it clear he was in no way pleased with the scandal Adam's strange behavior had wrought. The earl had even dared to go as far as to threaten Adam, promising such conduct would not be tolerated in the future—and the fool concluded his empty tirade by suggesting Adam's continued interest in his late wife was a slur to Lady Julia's good name.

Adam sneered. As if he could tarnish the reputation of a girl whose father had owned a third-rate soap factory before inheriting a title that should never have belonged to him. The upstart earl was no better than the filthy tradesman he used to be, and he would soon learn that no one threatened the Marquess of Valence. Not without consequences. So when Adam returned home, he'd admitted every acquaintance who showed up at his door harboring morbid curiosity poorly disguised as concern. During each audience Adam had let slip a reluctant offhand comment that he might be having second thoughts about elevating a merchant-class girl to the lofty role of marchioness. That he was reconsidering the suitability of any connection to the regrettably vulgar Hextall family.

By tomorrow morning it would be the earl groveling in his drawing room, begging Adam to marry his daughter. Begging him not to withdraw his suit and ruin Lady Julia. He took a grim satisfaction in that.

Adam had, however, chosen to avoid his club tonight, having no further interest in fielding tactless questions that ultimately served only as painful reminders of Gisele. But as he stared out the window at the darkness, he was lamenting his decision, for without the distraction, he'd found himself rattling listlessly about his house, unsettled. The yearning and frustration and grief he was usually able to suppress would not be quieted.

When the housekeeper informed Adam he had a visitor, his first instinct was to tell the slattern to throw the man out. It wasn't until she told him the caller insisted he had once been employed by Lord Valence that Adam had snapped to attention. He barked at his housekeeper to show the man in, and then took up a position near the fireplace, hoping he appeared calm and in control.

Sebastien glided into the room, as soundlessly as always. Damn, but Adam had missed the man's impeccable competence.

"Lord Valence," he said with a respectful tilt of his head.

"Sebastien. I must confess, this is a surprise."

"Forgive my presumption, my lord."

"Of course. I trust you are well?"

"As well as can be expected, given my current situation."

"Montcrief."

Sebastien grimaced slightly. "He is but a common soldier, my lord."

"You are looking for alternate employment?"

Sebastien met his eyes.

"Consider it done." Adam felt a spurt of pleasure. Not only would he be acquiring arguably the best valet in London, Sebastien would be back under his roof. Back under his control. "You may present yourself here, after my wedding."

"My humblest thanks, my lord." Sebastien paused. "About this afternoon, my lord," he said evenly.

Adam scowled. "This afternoon I encountered a woman who was the very image of my dear Gisele. I am afraid her uncanny likeness made me act in a way that was neither dignified nor appropriate. This afternoon was an unfortunate mistake."

"Perhaps. You knew your wife better than anyone," Sebastien said softly.

"Yes," Adam sighed, before he frowned. What was that supposed to mean? He studied the valet, but could see only compassion in the man's face.

His former valet drew a tiny pouch from his coat. "For this evening, my lord. I know this afternoon was difficult. I anticipated the night may be more so."

Adam took the proffered opium from Sebastien. "Thank you," he said hoarsely, moved almost beyond words. It was the first kind thing anyone had done for him in a very long time. "You remembered."

"I remember everything, my lord," Sebastien said, then bowed himself from the room.

The smell of opium smoke was strong up here, masking the faint scent of decay and dust that clung to everything. The house was silent, and Gisele knew Valence would be shut up in his rooms, alone with his pipe where he could be neither observed nor disturbed.

Gisele crept slowly and soundlessly down the hall, the feeling surreal. She had never thought to return to London, and she had never, in all her wildest imaginings, thought to return to this house. Contrary to her earlier bravado, if Jamie hadn't been right behind her, she doubted she would have made it this far.

Gisele had spent almost her entire marriage in this prison, the marquess declining ever to visit his ancestral holdings somewhere on the far western edge of the country. They'd rarely traveled, only when fashionable etiquette demanded, and even then, visits to country manors and estates had been brief and suffocating. She paused in the doorway to her old rooms, feeling more than a little suffocated right now.

"We can go back." Jamie's voice was gentle in her ear.

"No," she whispered. She could never go back. Not anymore.

She forced herself to look into the rooms she had once occupied, as if to prove to herself she was now safely on the outside looking in.

It was the gleam of silver in the depths of the room that caught her attention. The glow from the streetlamps through the open curtains created macabre shadows on the walls, and it was enough to give shape and detail to the contents of the bedroom. Gisele stared, uncertain if her eyes were deceiving her. She took a hesitant step into the bedroom, and then another. She reached the dressing table and picked up the object she had seen shining in the dimness.

It was her hairbrush, blond strands still caught in the bristles. Her mirror and her comb were there too, along with a tiny bottle of perfume. A pair of her earbobs lay forgotten on the surface, abandoned four years prior. Gisele turned, moving to the massive wardrobe that stood against the far wall. With a soft click, the door swung open. Her gowns hung before her—the finest fabrics, still shimmering and pristine. She fingered the silk and the gold muslin, the taffetas and the satins. The gowns glowed in the darkness, their pale colors ghostly reminders of the woman who had once worn them.

"Oh, God," she breathed, turning.

Her embroidered silk dressing gown still hung over the back of a chair, where it had been discarded in favor of a ball gown on a similar spring night.

"Everything is here," she whispered. "How it was left on that night."

Jamie had come to stand just inside the room.

Gisele turned in a slow circle, trying to identify what was churning through her. Faint nausea. Revulsion. Something that fell short of pity. "Everything is the same."

Jamie moved to stand in front of her. His hands cupped her face. "Nothing is the same." His eyes glittered in the darkness.

Gisele nodded, grasping Jamie's hands with her own, anchoring herself to Jamie's steady strength.

"Valence has been waiting for me to come back for four years, Jamie." She smiled a cold, brittle smile. "Let's not disappoint him."

⁓

The opium was of excellent quality as he'd known it would be—Sebastien would never have brought him anything less than the best. The laudanum Adam used regularly offered oblivion, but tonight he wasn't seeking oblivion. He reclined on his bedroom floor, inhaling the earthy smoke deeply, the familiar languid release creeping over him slowly but surely. God, but he needed this. Needed but a handful of hours to feel good about something again. To find pleasure in something. Needed an escape into a world of fantasy where he might find the only thing left that could bring him comfort. Memories of Gisele had traumatized him this afternoon on the bridge, and he would seek her out now, where he knew he could find her and where he knew she couldn't run.

His limbs became heavy, and sensation drained entirely from his extremities. He was floating now, the pipe clattering to the tray before him, his head falling back as he let go of the petty and inconsequential world around him. He sought her out, murmuring her name, waiting, hoping, *knowing* she would come to him.

Minutes or hours passed and, out of a mist, she was there.

"Adam." Gisele stood over him, her flaxen hair swirling over her shoulders, strange shadows cast over her face by the lantern light.

She was in sharper focus than she had ever been before, seemingly real enough that his pulse spiked in anticipation. And unlike in past dreams, Gisele was wearing the dressing robe he had bought for her as a wedding gift—a sheer silk gown embroidered intricately with tiny roses. He felt his body stir as he remembered just how he had made her take that gown off. He smiled at his wife, reaching for her, but she drifted away. Adam didn't mind. She never went far here.

"Come back," he murmured, beckoning her with his fingers.

She drifted around him, the edges of her gown brushing against his skin, playing with something in her fingers.

"What did you bring me tonight, Gisele?" he asked.

"What you lost," she whispered, as though this should have been obvious to him.

The object sparkled and flashed.

"My diamonds." This pleased him immensely, and in his dream, she bent so that the gem flashed before his eyes, a kaleidoscope of colors. The colors swirled and spun, and when they cleared, she was gone.

"Gisele?" Adam turned his head, unhurried. She was near his bed, standing at the edge, looking into the shadows.

Another rush of ecstasy filled him, and Adam could feel his cock harden. He had trained her so well.

The darkness Gisele had been watching suddenly shifted and took shape, and a man morphed out of the murk. He caught her head with his hands and kissed her, the specter's dominance of her screaming his possession.

Adam shifted in horror, his rapture ceasing, but too lethargic to formulate a solution.

"Gisele," he called out, but she wasn't listening to him anymore. She was kissing the faceless man, her dressing gown sliding lower over her shoulders, ignoring him.

"Gisele," Adam called again, but it was the man who looked at him, features sharp in the glow of the lantern.

"I found what you lost," Montcrief said to him, and then the room went dark, and Adam lost the sense of where he had last seen Gisele. He fought to orient himself but it was to no avail.

Shadows swirled, and Adam was sucked into the oppressive abyss knowing, somehow, that he had lost his beloved Gisele again.

Chapter 21 _____

Jamie had forcibly prevented her from returning to her attic rooms. Instead he had smuggled her into the apartment, ignoring her halfhearted protests, and ensconced her on the settee with a blanket and a very full glass of whiskey. Then he had gone about building up the fire so that the pervasive chill soon gave way to an almost overwhelming, drowsy heat.

Sipping the fiery liquid, Gisele tried hard not to think about Valence sprawled out on the floor, his eyes inflamed and glassy and heavily lidded. She tried not to remember her old rooms in their perfect order, as if Valence had somehow known she would be back. Simply being in that house had made her skin crawl and had settled a cold miasma deep in her bones. She shivered.

"It'll be warmer soon," Jamie said quietly, coming to sit beside her.

"It's plenty warm," she mumbled, staring into her drink. She closed her eyes. "That was...more difficult than I thought."

"But it's over."

"Yes." She tipped her head back on the upholstery. "Thank you, Jamie. For being there."

"I would never leave you."

Gisele shrugged, suddenly feeling more exhausted than she could ever remember. She just wanted to crawl into bed and put the covers over her head and pretend the world didn't exist for a very long time.

She looked at Jamie. "I should go. You can't have a woman in your apartment in the middle of the night. You'll get evicted if they catch you."

"You're staying here." Jamie was watching her with worried eyes. "I don't want you alone right now."

"I'm not going to throw myself in front of a carriage, Jamie, if that's what you're worried about."

"I didn't expect you would." He brushed a strand of hair back from the side of her face.

Gisele tried to find the energy to argue, but the whiskey and the warmth, coupled with her fatigue, were making it difficult. "Maybe just for a few more minutes," she whispered. The idea of a cold, dark, isolated attic room had no appeal at the moment.

She became aware that Jamie had somehow slid a pillow under her head, and she leaned against the softness. She felt him shift as he raised her feet up onto the settee, tucking the blanket carefully around her. He lifted the glass from her hand and pressed a kiss to her forehead.

Gisele sighed and closed her eyes.

~⁓~

The guns had yet to quiet. They continued to belch fire and death, and the smoke hung heavy over the killing ground, making Jamie's eyes water. Beneath him he felt his mare shift, the exhausted beast anxious to see this nightmare to an end. Her sides were heaving, her once-rich coat now lathered with sweat and blood. Jamie looked to either side, horrified to see how few remained. One more. One more charge and the French would break or what was left of his regiment would be shattered.

"Stay behind me," he shouted to Red, who gave him a cocky grin, his teeth ghoulishly bright against his blood- and dirt-streaked face.

"Let's finish the bastards," Red yelled, his horse crow-hopping and sidling as another cannon crashed. He raised his sword in salute to Jamie, and then they were charging once more. Through the pall came the crackle of guns, the sick slap of lead into flesh, and his mare screamed, her front legs buckling as she crashed to the earth, her gallop turning into a broken somersault of snapping bones. Jamie was pitched from his saddle, though it was as if he were watching from a great distance above. There was no pain, nothing until he hit the ground, then only a numb disbelief as the twitching carcass of his horse landed across his lower body and then stilled.

Frantically Jamie tried to lever himself out from under the dead mare. Except one of his arms wasn't working, and he realized with the same disbelief that he'd been shot, blood pulsing darkly against the crimson wool of his uniform. He collapsed back into the filth, clawing at the grass, knowing that if he couldn't escape, he would die.

Suddenly there were hands beneath him, pulling roughly, and Jamie shouted as a white-hot lance of pain winged through his shoulder and into his chest.

"Stop your bleating, Captain," came the raw voice at his ear. "You were tougher when you were ten!"

"Goddammit, Michael, what the hell are you doing?" Jamie yelled. "Get on your horse!"

"Damn thing had the nerve to die on me," Red gasped as he struggled to free Jamie.

"Then get back! Find another." Jamie was looking around in panic, knowing just how vulnerable a downed cavalryman was. "Goddammit, Red! Leave me! That's an order!"

"Can't hear you." Red gave him another grin, jerking his head to the side. "Damn guns are too loud—"

He stopped, the roguish grin replaced by a look of confusion. His skin went gray, and a French infantryman, barely more than a lad, yanked his bayonet back out from under Michael's ribs. He glanced at Jamie and, seeing only a dead man, turned and disappeared back into the chaos.

"No!" Jamie screamed and jerked upright.

He was breathing hard, his skin beaded with sweat, chilled in the darkness of predawn. He was not on the field, surrounded by dying men and dying horses, the ground beneath him saturated with blood and entrails and the stench of death. He was in an aristocrat's bed on a feather mattress, tangled in silken sheets, still dressed in the clothes he'd fallen asleep in.

He pushed himself to the edge of the bed, rubbing his shoulder and feeling the thick ridge of scar tissue beneath the linen. He was desperate for a drink. Standing, he moved to the doors of the drawing room and pulled them open, wincing as the hinges protested with a loud creak. He stumbled toward the sideboard and the decanters.

"Couldn't sleep?" came a voice out of the darkness, and Jamie nearly yelled.

"Jesus." His nerves were raw. The dream always left him weak and nauseous.

He peered in the direction of the settee, but realized Gisele was not there. Instead the silhouette of a woman was barely visible sitting on the bench near the tall window that faced the gardens.

"What are you doing?" he asked finally, his voice rough.

"Same thing you are." Gisele tucked her bare toes beneath the hem of her skirts and tugged her blanket tighter around her shoulders. "Once the dream wakes you, there is nothing that will ever convince you returning to that place is a good idea. It's much easier to wait out dawn."

Jamie made an indistinguishable noise, recognizing his own truth in her words.

"I think it was being in that house again. It's been a long time since I...dreamed." She didn't look at him.

Jamie moved away from the sideboard and lowered himself down beside Gisele, close enough to feel her warmth, but not close enough to touch her. She'd pulled open the curtains just enough to allow a sliver of moonlight in, and he watched her for a long minute as she stared out, unseeing, into the darkness. As strong as Gisele was, going back into that house tonight had cost her. She looked weary and drained, and the vivacity that usually surrounded her had diminished.

He realized he had underestimated or had not understood the effort it required for her to keep her own ghosts at bay. Tonight she had been forced to come face-to-face with them. But she'd done it.

They sat in silence, listening to the wind push at the panes of glass.

"I killed my brother." The words were gone before he could call them back.

Her breathing stopped for a moment before it resumed, though she didn't look at him.

"At Waterloo."

She turned and rested her cheek against her knees, her eyes shining in the shrouded moonlight. "I don't understand. Your brother is the Duke of Reddyck."

"My youngest brother is the duke now. Malcolm. There were three of us."

Gisele only watched him, a faint line marring her forehead.

"Michael inherited the title after our father passed. He was two years younger than me and the favorite of the family. Witty, kind, clever. My father refused to allow him a commission. Said Michael had duties and responsibilities to the title, not to the army. I always teased Michael and called him Red, short for Reddyck—the sum of his future."

"Your father let you enlist."

"I was never going to be the earl. A cavalry officer was a noble profession for a bastard son, and my father was lavish with his support and praise of my service. After he died, Red continued to supplement my officer's pay so that I might retain the distinction of captain. He thought I was a bloody hero."

Gisele closed her eyes, understanding written over her face. "That wasn't your fault."

"Yes, it was. I never convinced him otherwise. I sent letters regaling him with tales he wanted to hear, and I never told the truth. I liked the idea that my little brother looked up to me. When Napoleon escaped from Elba and raised another army, Michael's first order of business was to buy a commission. With my father gone and me unreachable, there was no one left to stop him. Just showed up one day kitted out with a fine Irish hunter, a uniform so new the color bled, and a sword so shiny it hurt my eyes. Told me he wanted to be just like me. Live a life of adventure and glory." The memory was so bitter it nearly choked him.

"Your brother was a grown man, Jamie."

"A grown man who thought war was a game. Who had never heard or seen artillery flense a dozen men into an unidentifiable mess of bone splinters and flesh. Who had never seen an infantry square broken by the last strides of a dying horse and then gutted from the inside out. Who had never had to earn his pay by killing." Jamie looked bleakly into the darkness. "It's funny, how you become inured to the business of death. In India, in Spain, I saw and did horrible things. Yet I never stopped to consider that they were, in fact, horrible until my little brother rode beside me, filled with illusions and misconceptions of reality, and I realized there was nothing I could do to protect him. There was no adventure or glory. There was only the interminable wait for death, interspersed with terrifying, ruthless moments in which you must kill or be killed."

"I'm sorry, Jamie."

"He was trying to save me when he died. My horse had me pinned, and I'd been shot." He barely heard her words. "He wouldn't listen—" He stopped, terrified he was losing whatever tenuous control he had left over his emotions. He took a shaky breath. "I had to go home and tell my mother I couldn't save him. That he died in front of me and I couldn't save him."

"Jamie—"

"I don't think my mother had ever really gotten over her grief at my father's passing, and she was already ill when I arrived. I think Michael's death broke her. She died two months later."

The wind rattled a loose pane, and Jamie concentrated on keeping his breathing even. Gisele was the first person he had ever spoken to about Red. And he had no idea what he had hoped in doing so. That by confessing his complicity in the death of his brother he would be absolved of his sins? That she would pat him on the back and tell him it was all going to be all right? That he would distract her from her own demons and she would be grateful? He was afraid to look at her, and he was afraid not to.

"And this is why I found you drunk in that tavern." It was a statement, not a question.

He couldn't even answer her.

"I'm not sure what you want me to say, Jamie." There was no inflection in her voice, and Jamie hadn't a clue what she was thinking.

"I don't know either." He turned to look at her then and found her eyes on him, staring hard.

"Is this why your brother hates you?" she asked.

Jamie sighed heavily. "Malcolm hates me because he holds me responsible for Michael's death. He hates me because Michael followed me into war, and my actions, or lack thereof, cost him a beloved brother and forced him into a life of responsibility he never wanted."

"That sounds very . . . small."

Jamie made a pained sound.

"I am sorry about Michael." She searched his face. "But you've punished yourself enough, don't you think?"

"No," he mumbled miserably.

"No?" Now there was passion in her voice. "You figured, if you drank yourself to death, then everything in the world would be put right?"

Jamie rubbed his face in agitation. "It wasn't— I don't—" He stopped. "It was my fault."

"What was? The war against France? I hate to tell you this, Jamie, but you're not so important as to incite a war between countries."

Jamie scowled at her. "I never said I was. But I should have been able to do something."

She sighed. "You can start doing something now by not carrying Michael's death around on your shoulders."

"And how do I do that? How do I convince myself that there was nothing else I could have done? That if I had been just a little faster, if I had stayed closer, if I had kept—"

"You cannot survive by wallowing in what-ifs." Her face was all sympathy, but the words were firm. She pushed aside the fabric of her skirts, swung herself off the bench, and got to her feet. "You were in the middle of a terrible, bloody war. You think your brother was there solely because of you? You think him so childish and immature he couldn't grasp what was going on around him? That he did not realize there was a chance he might die?"

Jamie gaped up at her. "But if—"

"Let's play that game then, shall we?" She cut him off unrepentantly. "*If* your father had known your mother was pregnant, then maybe he wouldn't have gone to London. *If* he hadn't gone to London, you would have been born the rightful Duke of Reddyck, and you wouldn't have become an officer. *If* you hadn't become an officer, then your brother wouldn't have followed you. So by that rationale, this was all your father's fault for not marrying his duchess fast enough. Or let's blame your grandfather. He was the villain in all of this, wasn't he? Or maybe we should blame your mother? She never revealed her pregnancy, and by the time she did, it was too late." The blanket dropped from her shoulders and went unnoticed. "You can waste your entire life wondering *if*, Jamie, and it won't change a damn thing. Bad things happen to good people, and the only thing you can do is to pick up the pieces and move on. I would strongly suggest you try it."

Jamie struggled to his feet, staring down at her. He could feel his pulse pounding at his temples, and he tried to identify the maelstrom of emotion coursing through him at the moment. Fury. Guilt. Admiration. Wonder.

He went with fury, because it was the only one he wasn't terrified to embrace. "You can't begin to understand what it was like," he snarled.

Her expression shifted then, and her features rearranged themselves into a grim mask. Without taking her eyes off him, she reached up and unpinned her rough dress and then released the laces of her chemise. Very deliberately she pulled apart the fabric and let the garments slide down her body to pool at her feet. The clouds parted suddenly as the wind gusted, and a pale beam of moonlight penetrated the room, bathing her bared skin in luminous light.

Jamie swallowed hard, the breath knocked clean from his lungs and his stomach clenching in agony. She was stunning, her body and its lines everything he had ever imagined. But what he hadn't imagined was the scars.

Markings of torture starting beneath her breasts and continuing across her belly and along her legs and the insides of her thighs. Some of the marks curved in long arcs, the length of his palm. Others were simply slashes lacking deliberation, denoting only cruelty. Very slowly Jamie stepped forward, coming to stand directly before her. He reached out a hand, realized it was shaking, and paused. Gisele was still watching him, her chest rising and falling shallowly. He touched a ridge of scar tissue running alongside her hip, feeling the uneven flesh, cool in the night air.

With quiet steps he moved beside, then behind her, his fingers never leaving her skin. Her back was a horror of crisscrosses, and Jamie recognized them immediately for what they were. He'd seen more than one man flogged by an officer for offenses. He gathered her hair in his fist, pushing it to the side, his fingers tracing the evidence each lash had left. He could feel a tightness in his chest he had never before experienced, and his vision had blurred at the edges.

"Never where anyone could see," she said in a voice so quiet he barely heard her.

"I'm sorry," he whispered. "Oh, God, Gisele. I'm so sorry."

"I don't want you to be sorry for me," she replied. "I wanted you to see that I do understand what it was like." She sighed heavily. "Sometimes bad things happen to good people."

Jamie struggled to take a deep breath. He reached down and retrieved the fallen blanket, wrapping it around Gisele gently. He ran his hands down her arms, twined his fingers through hers, pressing himself against her back.

He bent his head, and rested his chin against the side of her neck. She leaned into him, squeezing his hands.

"I'll kill him."

Gisele twisted then, turning to face him. "You will not. You will not risk everything you have and everything you are for nothing. You get caught and your life isn't worth the rope they'll use to hang you."

Jamie extricated one of his hands from hers and brushed the hair back from her face. "How did you do it, Gisele? How did you endure and survive and come out on the other side like this?"

She frowned. "Like what?"

"Beautiful. Strong. Gracious and good, and everything I'm not."

She pressed her cheek into his hand. "I had help. I had people who loved me. I saw that people could love and respect each other, even on the days they didn't much like each other. I grew up wanting that, understanding I might not ever get it, but knowing I did not deserve what Valence was doing." She caught his hand again in her own. "What happened to your brother was not your fault, Jamie. You think Michael would want you to punish yourself for the choices he made? To do so would be an insult to the man he had become. What's done is done, and no matter how much you wish it, you can't change the past. You have to let it go if you ever want a chance at living again."

Jamie squeezed his eyes shut, a suspicious lump in his throat. He gathered her in his arms and pulled her close, some unconscious part of him believing that if he held on tight enough, he could do what she asked.

"I'll try," he whispered raggedly in her ear.

"That's all you can do," she said, her head resting against his chest. "Even when it seems impossible."

He buried his face in her hair. "How do you do it?"

"I don't ever think of him. Of what he did to me." She took a deep breath. "But being in that house tonight brought everything I had thought I'd buried back. Brought back the nightmares. Tonight is one of those times that letting go seems a little bit…impossible." A mocking, mirthless laugh escaped, but it was devoid of self-pity.

Jamie couldn't even begin to fathom how she had come by such strength—an inner strength he could not begin to claim for himself. He had looked elsewhere for consolation and clarity, mostly into the bottom of a bottle, and it had always remained elusive. Until now. Until Gisele.

The feel of Gisele's body against his was a sweet torment, his heart's compassion warring desperately with his body's stirring desire. He wanted to make her forget. It was something he could do for her. Wanted desperately to do for her. But he made no move to touch her further, terrified he might betray the fragile links of trust newly forged.

"Thank you," Jamie said quietly. He pulled the blanket a little tighter around her beautiful, scarred body. "For trusting me."

She looked up at him for a brief moment before laying her head back on his chest. "Some secrets lose their power when they aren't secrets anymore."

Jamie knew she wasn't just talking about herself.

"Are you thinking about Valence now?" he asked.

"Trying not to."

He tipped her chin up with his fingers and kissed her with exquisite tenderness.

"How about now?"

Gisele smiled softly against his mouth. "Not as much," she whispered.

Encouraged, he deepened his kiss, letting his fingers thread through her hair, cupping the back of her head. He felt her own fingers curl into his shirt.

"Now?"

Gisele shook her head, her arms twining around his neck. "Take me to bed, Jamie Montcrief," she breathed.

He didn't need to be told twice.

~

Jamie scooped her up in his arms and strode into the bedroom, letting her slide down the length of him as he came to a stop at the foot of the bed. He bent to kiss her again, a slow, gentle seduction of tongues, but it wasn't enough for her. She wanted to forget. She wanted to lose herself in Jamie so irrevocably that the past and all its dark imaginings could never again find her. She wanted Jamie as she had never wanted anyone else before in her life.

She pressed into him, her hands unwinding from his neck and dropping to his throat, delving into the open collar of his shirt until she could run her palms across the broad expanse of his shoulders. Beneath her fingers she could feel his heart pounding at a rate that matched that of the pulse roaring in her ears. She pulled his shirt over his head, letting it fall to the floor.

Jamie shuddered beneath her touch and any remaining gentleness began to dissolve into urgency. Gisele's hands found the fall of his breeches and made short work of the buttons. He groaned as she knelt before him, shoving his breeches to the floor. She ran her hands up the backs of his legs and around to the fronts of his thighs, before taking his throbbing erection in her palm.

"Not this time, my love," Jamie whispered, pulling her up against him. "This time you're coming with me."

Jamie claimed her mouth again, demanding and relentless. He pulled the blanket away from her and lifted her up against him so that her legs locked around his hips and she could feel him hard and pulsing at the entrance to her core. She moaned softly, desperate to accommodate him, but he kept her trapped motionless against his body. With torturous deliberation, Jamie lowered her to the bed, coming to rest above her, his weight and his heat sharpening the anticipation.

His lips left hers, leaving a trail of fire down her neck, and then they moved to her breasts along with his hands, caressing and shaping their fullness. The entire time, Gisele could feel the head of his cock pressed just at her entrance, and she nearly screamed for want. She reached down between them, but he caught her hand, bringing it back up to his shoulder.

"Not yet," he said, with a devilish gleam in his eye, and pressed an inch into her.

Gisele arched against him, feeling the edge of the abyss rushing at her. She was throbbing and aching and she needed Jamie. Needed him inside her, buried deep. Her legs tightened around his waist, increasing the pressure of his erection against her.

"Please, Jamie," she whispered, knowing she was begging and not caring at all.

Jamie groaned then and drove into her, even as his mouth covered hers to capture her cry. He withdrew, just barely, before surging forward again, the muscles in his back straining beneath her hands. Gisele's hips rocked up to meet his, every nerve ending in her body igniting.

Her tremors started deep, pulsing and spiraling and tightening until the vortex combusted mercilessly. Her inner muscles spasmed, and she let herself fall, waves of pleasure crashing through her, and in an instant, Jamie grasped her hips ruthlessly and thrust into her once more, sending sparks scattering across her vision.

Gisele held on to him with every ounce of strength she possessed, riding the storm until they both lay spent, breathing hard, their skin damp. She let her head rest in the crook of his shoulder, trying to catch her breath. After a moment Jamie shifted his weight from her and reached down to pull the blankets over their entwined limbs. Drawing her up beside him, he encircled her in his arms, and Gisele wriggled into his warmth.

"Sleep now," Jamie whispered. "You're safe here with me."

She nodded into his neck. Jamie tightened his embrace and placed a soft kiss at her temple and Gisele had never in her life felt as cherished and protected as she did at that moment.

Yet Gisele did not fall asleep immediately. She lay quietly in the darkness, listening as Jamie's breathing eventually became steady and deep, a sense of peace and rightness settling over her limbs. With perfect clarity, Gisele understood that somewhere between here and a tavern south of Nottingham, she had gone and fallen in love with Jamie Montcrief.

Chapter 22 _____

Adam opened his eyes to sunlight streaming in through the curtains, an unwelcome awakening. His head was pounding, and his mouth felt dry and sour. He was still sprawled out on his bedroom floor, his opium tray and pipe near his side. He winced as he pushed himself to a sitting position, groaning as his muscles protested.

Adam did not feel rested at all. In fact, he felt even more listless than he had last night, which was odd. His dreams had not been the perfect euphoric bliss he usually experienced, but had been plagued by a darker undertone. Gisele had appeared to him, of course, but last night she hadn't come to him when he called. She'd been in the arms of another man. Montcrief.

Adam shook his head in denial. Perhaps it had been the upsetting events of yesterday. Perhaps even the sudden reappearance of Sebastien had triggered that manifestation. But just thinking about Gisele in the arms of another man left him white and shaking with an irrepressible rage—a response that time and death had not dulled.

Adam forced himself to breathe deeply. It had been a dream. A disturbing dream, but a dream all the same. He hauled himself to his feet, trying to shake the lethargy still clinging to his muscles. It was probably late already, and he should—Adam froze, his eyes fixated on his bed. A robe was draped over the end of it, soft silk embroidered with tiny roses. As if in a trance, he reached for it, feeling the coolness of the fabric slip through his fingers. He pressed it to his face, inhaling her scent. Gisele's scent.

What manner of trickery is this? he thought, anguish making his heart pound. What had happened last night? What sort of cruel bastard would use his dreams against him in such a manner? He staggered to the mirror, peering at himself in the glass as if his haggard reflection might provide the answer. Gisele had been wearing this robe last night. He had seen her, touched the edge of the silk as she had moved around him. He squeezed his eyes shut. But it hadn't been real. It *couldn't* have been real.

He opened his eyes again, slowly, trying to regain a foothold in reality. Whatever madness had taken hold of him these last days, it had to stop. Perhaps in his stupor he had fetched the robe and simply didn't remember. Still facing the mirror, Adam eyed his abandoned pipe, visible in the reflection behind him, and for the first time ever, he regretted his loss of control.

A brilliant sparkle on his tray beside the pipe, where a shaft of sunlight fell across the floor, caught his eye. Adam turned, frowning fiercely. Slowly, as if approaching a viper, Adam crouched, the object glittering brightly in the sun. He reached for it and picked it up, his hands shaking.

He retched suddenly, caught unaware, his entire body convulsing and heaving. Sweat pricked at his scalp, and he collapsed back against the bed, his entire body numb and shivering. Very deliberately he forced his hand open, looking down at the object.

It was a large diamond, cut in a very unusual pear shape, unique in its slight gold color. When he'd bought the gem from a French count, it had been obscenely expensive, but at the time Adam hadn't cared, for there was nothing he would deny Gisele. She'd been wearing it the night of the explosion. The night he had lost a staggering fortune in diamonds, this stone being the crowning showpiece of them all. The night he had thought he'd lost his wife.

But why? Why allow him to suffer for four years, believing she was dead? What was she trying to tell him? And where was she now?

Montcrief. The name spewed into his consciousness like poison, and Adam almost retched again. That part of the night remained blurry, and Adam roared in frustration, kicking the tray away from him with a resounding clatter and the crash of broken glass. He thought he had seen the captain, but he couldn't be certain now what had been real and what had been imagined.

Adam clenched his fist around the diamond still in his hand. This he had not imagined. What he held in his hand was hard, unremitting proof.

Proof the diamonds hadn't been lost that night. Proof Gisele was still alive.

Proof she'd come back.

*Chapter 23*_____

Gisele had no idea what time it was when she finally stirred. Opening her eyes, she realized she was still in Jamie's bed, though the man in question was not. Instead there was a note propped up on his pillow that simply read, "Gone with S, back soon," and Gisele was content for the moment not to wonder where he might be. Though the fact that Jamie had left without her hearing was faintly alarming, it was mostly gratifying. Gisele had not slept as soundly or as well for as long as she could remember.

She knew she should get up. Or at least she should not continue lounging decadently in Jamie's bed like some smug courtesan. Yet she couldn't bring herself to care. What she had shared with Jamie last night had been astonishing and wonderful and now, in the bright light of morning, she was left only with a lingering sense of happiness and security.

And the knowledge she was very much in love with Jamie Montcrief.

Outside she could hear the sounds of traffic, and Gisele reluctantly pushed herself out from under the soft warmth of the sheets. Morning was slipping away and she couldn't stay here forever, as much as she might wish it. Someone—and Gisele desperately hoped it had been Jamie and not Sebastien—had left her clothing draped neatly over the end of the bed, and she quickly dressed. She splashed her face with cold water left in the washstand basin and combed and braided her hair, pinning her cap securely atop her head. At least now, if someone arrived, she looked more like Jamie's very proper housekeeper and less like his kept mistress. Gisele snorted in regret. Housekeeping was highly overrated.

As if on cue, a hesitant knock came from the door. Wiping her hands on her apron, and adjusting the kerchief tucked around her shoulders and into her bodice, Gisele opened the door. A woman stood on the step, dressed simply in plain but well-made clothing, a baby tucked against her shoulder. The woman's reddish-brown hair was pulled back from a pleasing, open face, and bright blue eyes darted past Gisele as if expecting to see someone else.

"Is this where Mr. James Montcrief lives?" the woman asked.

Gisele frowned. "Yes," she replied shortly, seeing no reason to lie. The porter would already have said as much if the woman had but asked.

"Is he here?" She was looking hopefully into the hall.

Gisele noticed she had a copy of one of London's newssheets in her free hand.

"No, he is not." Gisele moved to block more of the doorway. Who the hell was this woman and what did she want with Jamie? As she tried to tamp down her irrational jealousy of this pretty stranger, Gisele bit her lip in dismay. She'd thought herself more sophisticated than that. For if she'd had any lingering insecurities, Jamie had eliminated them last night. Multiple times.

"May I pass along a message for you?" she asked, as she imagined a well-paid housekeeper might do.

"Ummm…" The woman glanced down at the news-sheet with indecision.

The child in the woman's arms squirmed and she shifted him to her other arm, giving Gisele her first look at his face. He was perhaps six or seven months old, a happy grin between his round cheeks, and his chubby hand clutching a wooden horse.

The resemblance was uncanny.

The boy had a head of fine blond curls, which Gisele knew would darken to a burnished gold as he grew older. His whiskey-colored eyes, ringed with a profusion of dark lashes, looked up at her in watchful delight as he held out his treasure for Gisele's inspection.

She stepped forward, coming closer to Jamie's son.

"That is a handsome horse," Gisele finally managed, her heart hammering in her chest. She was riveted by his innocent perfection. "He's beautiful," she said, meaning every word. "You must be very proud."

"Thank you." Obvious pride shone from the woman's eyes, but a there was a sadness beneath it as her fingers absently brushed the golden curls from the child's fore-head. She gestured to the paper still in her hand. "I saw James's name in the paper," she said. "And it said he was staying here. I've been looking for him."

I bet you have, Gisele thought, fighting the roaring in her ears.

"Can you tell him Sofia was here? And Richard? Tell

him his family misses him." She tousled the blond curls again. "He knows where to find us."

"Of course," Gisele replied, her stomach churning.

"Thank you." The woman smiled warmly, and Gisele was struck by her loveliness.

They turned to go, the child watching Gisele over his mother's shoulder with wide eyes, and Gisele waited at the door until she could no longer see them. Then, very slowly, she closed the door, pressing her back to its solid bulk and closing her eyes. Her knees finally gave way and she slid to the floor, gasping.

He knows where to find us rang through her head over and over and over. Goddammit, but she was a fool.

How long? How long before Jamie would have eventually told her? But then again, why would he? It wasn't as though the boy or his mother seemed to figure prominently in his life. In fact, they didn't seem to figure at all.

But the idea that he might yet be with this woman cut deep. Almost as deep as the idea that Jamie Montcrief had a beautiful, perfect son, for whom he cared so little that the mother didn't even know how to contact him.

Anger warred with betrayal. How could he? He had a *son*. Regardless of his relationship with Sofia, he had a son he should be taking care of. He shouldn't be here, with Gisele, any more than he should have been in that filthy tavern, drunk and destitute. Jamie had much more important responsibilities. Fury was rapidly flooding her heart and mind, and she embraced it because it wasn't nearly as painful as the alternative.

Gisele forced herself to her feet, her face grim. She might have been blindsided, but she wasn't helpless. She could do one thing about this whole mess. She would pass along Sofia's message and one of her own.

⁓

It started raining a little while later, the brief morning sunshine eclipsed by heavy dark clouds that turned the apartment into a gloomy cavern. Which suited Gisele fine. She paced the dim hall like a caged lioness, waiting for Jamie to return. She thought she'd worked out what she would say, had practiced it a hundred times in her head, but when Jamie walked through the door, she could only stare at him mutely.

Oblivious, Jamie took his time shaking the water from his coat and hung it near the fire to dry. He turned to greet her and stopped.

"Gisele?" His forehead creased. "What's wrong? Has something happened? Are you ill?" His eyes slid over her, looking for signs of a trauma he would never be able to see.

"Where were you?" she demanded.

He had a flat box in his arms she hadn't noticed earlier, made from gleaming walnut, and Gisele recognized it for what it was immediately.

"You bought a pistol?" She was momentarily distracted.

"And two blades. Sebastien has them at the smith now. He'll be along shortly." Jamie was eyeing her with concern. "I didn't like the idea of being unarmed. I don't expect Valence would do something so stupid, but I will not be caught unprepared." Jamie took a step toward her, and she took a step back. "Gisele, what is it?"

Gisele opened her mouth twice before she found her backbone. "You had a visitor this morning," she said.

"Who? Gisele, what's going on? You're starting to scare me." He reached for her hands but she pulled away again. "I knew I shouldn't have left you here alone—"

"It was a woman. She had a little boy with her. Not quite a year old." Gisele watched as Jamie's complexion drained of color. "She asked me to pass along a message."

Jamie was watching her, silent and ashen.

"She said to tell you Sofia and Richard had called. That they missed you. And that you knew where to find them." Despite her best intentions, the last came out like an accusation. She was terrified she was going to cry.

"Gisele—"

"How could you?" she whispered. "How could you abandon them like that? She didn't even know where to find you until she saw your name in a damn newssheet!"

"I didn't abandon them," he growled.

"Really?" Gisele hated the petty tone of her words, but she couldn't stop. "Then what?"

"You don't understand."

"You're right. I don't understand how you could ignore that little boy."

Jamie dropped his head and swore. "They have everything they need. Enough money, enough clothes, enough food—"

"And you think all of that makes it all right? They need *you*. That little boy needs you." Gisele wrapped her arms around herself.

"It's not that simple."

"They're your *family*, Jamie. What is not simple about that?" She wanted Jamie to say something. To offer her an explanation that made some sort of sense. "You brought them here. To London. When?"

Jamie closed his eyes. "Last year. Right after the war."

Well, that would certainly explain why he had lied to her earlier about the last time he had been in London.

"And then what? You bought a bottle and drank your way to a tavern in Nottingham?"

"It wasn't like that! It—"

A pounding on the door interrupted whatever he'd been going to say next.

"Goddammit, now what?" Jamie swore, stomping to the door and yanking it open.

A man filled the doorway, rain-drenched and dressed in a mud-splattered greatcoat, his hand raised to assault the door once more.

"Jesus Christ," Jamie breathed and took a step back.

"I'm sorry, Mr. Montcrief," puffed the porter, coming to a skidding halt behind the visitor. "You said to question any gentlemen callers but this man wouldn't allow me the privilege of his card—"

"I don't need a damn card to see my damn brother," the man growled. "And if this title is good for anything, then a damned duke doesn't need to explain himself to a damned servant."

The porter paled. "Forgive me, Your Grace." He turned and fled.

"What the hell are you doing here?" Jamie asked, making no move to invite the man in.

Gisele peered around Jamie's bulk and nearly stumbled. The duke was indeed Jamie's brother—there could be no mistake. The same jaw, the same whiskey eyes, the same golden coloring. The only thing that set the younger man apart was a slighter, shorter frame.

"Are you going to let me come in or are you going to

make me do this in the rain for all and sundry to hear?" the duke demanded. "Because, by God, I will."

Silent, his face set like granite, Jamie backed up, allowing his brother access to the hall. He slammed the door behind the duke with more force than was necessary.

"What do you want?" Jamie asked, looking positively hostile.

"What do I want?" the duke repeated, his expression a mixture of disbelief, chagrin, and what looked like regret. "You can't be serious."

Gisele took a silent step back. She had no desire to get in the middle of this, whatever *this* might be. This was between brothers and had no bearing on her. Whatever bone she had to pick with Jamie could wait.

She cleared her throat. "I'll just go now—"

"Stay," Jamie barked, not looking at her.

"I don't think—"

"I said, *stay*. Whatever my brother has to say, he will do it in the next ten seconds, and then he will leave. You and I, however, are not finished. Not by a long shot."

Gisele swallowed and stood frozen behind Jamie.

"Say whatever it is you've come to say, Malcolm. And then get out."

"Like hell I will," Malcolm hissed. "Do you know how hard it's been to find you?"

"I can't believe you've spent any time looking," Jamie sneered. "You were the one who told me, and I quote, that you wished it had been me who had died out there instead of Michael, and to take the whore and never come back."

The duke flushed a deep scarlet. "That was a mistake."

"A mistake? Forgive me if I don't quite believe you."

Jamie marched to the door and opened it again. "Are you done? Salved your conscience? Now get out."

"Sofia told me where you were."

Jamie's face went slack. "I beg your pardon?"

"Sofia told me where you were. She saw your name mentioned in the paper so she came—"

Jamie closed the door very slowly before turning on the duke. "If you have done anything to her or to—"

"Goddammit, stop talking and try to listen for a bloody minute!" Malcolm shouted. He took a steadying breath. "I'm trying to apologize to you. What I said to you that day, I said out of anger and grief. In a heartbeat I had lost my brother and had found myself saddled with a title and expectations and responsibilities I never wanted. I was selfish and infantile and I resented the time you had with Michael that I didn't. That doesn't excuse what I did. But I regretted it immediately, because with my words and my actions, I lost another brother."

Gisele could see a muscle ticking along Jamie's jaw. "You didn't just dismiss me, Malcolm, you dismissed the very thing dearest to Michael. And that was unforgivable."

"I know. Believe me, I know. I had men searching for Sofia before the week was out. They were able to locate her fairly quickly. She told me what you'd done for her."

Jamie looked away.

"You shouldn't have done it. That commission meant a great deal to you."

"What the hell else was I supposed to do?" Jamie snarled, anger blazing. "What the hell was *she* supposed to do? She was alone and penniless and pregnant. She was family, even though you denied it and turned your back on her."

Gisele was looking back and forth between the brothers, a strange feeling crawling through her. None of this conversation was making sense.

"You're right, Jamie. She's family, same as you are. Which is why we've been looking for you for almost a year. When she saw that article—"

"Who, exactly, is Sofia?" Gisele could stand it no longer.

Jamie's jaw was set, and she wasn't sure if he was going to answer her.

"Sofia was...Michael's."

Gisele felt the ground tilt a little under her feet. "His wife?"

"They weren't married."

"Why?" The question was out before she could stop it.

"Because the men in my family have spectacularly bad timing when it comes to the women they love."

"I don't understand."

Jamie sighed. "Sofia and Michael met the day he reported for duty, and they fell in love on the spot. She was a gunner's daughter and had grown up following the British army. She did mending and tailoring for the officers to supplement her father's pay. Michael wanted to take her home to marry her, but then they found out she was pregnant and decided to marry straightaway. Their wedding day had been planned for June sixteenth of last year."

The day the whole of the English troops had been frantically sent marching to the crossroads of Quatre Bras and Waterloo.

"And Richard is Michael's son," Gisele whispered unsteadily.

Jamie jerked his head. "He never got the chance to see him." He turned a glacial stare on Malcolm. "Where is she?"

"Still in the shop you bought for her. I invited her to come and live with me as soon as I found her but she declined. Said she would stay where she was so that, when you were ready, you would know where to find her."

Gisele put a hand out to steady herself against the mantel. "Oh, God. He looked just like you."

Jamie turned around for the first time since Malcolm had arrived. "Who?"

"Richard."

Jamie stared at her. "Good Christ, you thought he was *mine*?"

"He looks just like you," she repeated numbly.

"He looks just like his father," Jamie snapped. "And his father looked just like me, being my brother and all. Just like him." He jabbed a finger in Malcolm's direction.

Gisele rubbed her face. "I'm sorry, Jamie." She looked up at him, another truth blindsiding her then. "You sold your commission to support her. And Richard."

Jamie looked distinctly uncomfortable. "Of course I did. And Sofia's done quite well for herself since then. Even has a seamstress working for her now."

Gisele suddenly felt like weeping.

"Are we done here, Malcolm?" Jamie asked wearily, turning back to his brother. "This is pointless."

"No, we certainly are not done. Not after I have just found you."

Jamie ground his palms against his eyes. "You couldn't find me, Malcolm, because I didn't want to be found. I didn't want to look at Richard every day and be reminded he will grow up without a father because I failed to protect Michael. To look at Sofia and know I failed. To look at you and know I failed."

"Michael left you Foxhaven."

Jamie's head jerked up. "What?"

"Michael left you Foxhaven."

"He left me an estate? How?" Jamie was looking at his brother in confusion.

"What do you mean, how?"

"Where are you getting this from?"

"He left a will, Jamie. Michael wasn't six years old. He knew he wasn't playing war with sticks and rocks. He knew very well he might not survive."

"But it was my responsibility to see that he stayed out of harm's way. I should have—"

"Oh, for God's sake, Jamie. You always did fancy yourself the hero, even when we were children. Protector of all, savior of many, but honestly, this bloody martyr act is wearing thin. You—"

He never finished because Jamie's fist crashed into his jaw.

Malcolm staggered back, but didn't fall.

"Feel better?" Malcolm asked, straightening and rubbing his chin. He wiped a trickle of blood from his lip where it had split.

"A little."

"Do you want to do it again?" The duke was grinning.

"Maybe later. Outside." A small muscle was pulling at the corner of Jamie's mouth. "I can't afford to replace any of the furniture in here."

The grin slid from Malcolm's face. "I'm truly sorry, Jamie. I don't know how I can make it up to you, but I hope you can forgive me. You're my brother, and I can't bear to lose you too."

Jamie was silent for a minute. "I don't want to lose another brother either."

Malcolm's grin returned. "I'm glad to hear that."

"That doesn't mean I'm not going to hit you again."

"You always did have a good right hook."

"You used to be better at ducking them."

"I think I'm getting old." Malcolm snorted and peered around the hall. "What *are* you doing here, Jamie?"

Jamie crossed his arms. "Working."

"Doing what, exactly?" Malcolm looked at Jamie's expensive clothing and expensive apartment and smirked. "Or should I have said *whom*?"

"Don't be a bastard," Jamie grunted with no venom.

"No, that's you," Malcolm said lightly. "Though from the gossip columns, that seems to be helping rather than hindering. Seriously, Jamie, you don't need to be here. I've nearly concluded my business in town and will be returning home in a few days' time. Come home with me. Foxhaven is yours, and I would like my brother back. I need you. Do you know what a bloody headache it is to be a duke?"

"I can't."

Malcolm misunderstood. "Sofia and Richard would join us—"

"I can't," Jamie repeated. "Not yet."

"Why?"

"Because I made someone a promise and I need to keep it."

"To whom?"

"Me." Gisele stepped forward, finally finding her voice.

"And who are you?" The question was cautious.

Gisele looked to Jamie, having no idea how to answer that question. A good part of her still felt like collapsing in a puddle of tears in response to the revelations of the last few minutes. The utter selflessness and loyalty of the man standing before her were making it hard to breathe. She should never have doubted him. She never would again. She loved this man with an intensity that defied reason.

"I love you, Jamie," she said suddenly, not caring who heard it, not caring if Jamie returned the sentiment. But he had to hear it. She had to say it.

Jamie moved to stand before her, his forehead touching hers, his eyes closed. He cupped her cheek with his hand and kissed her softly.

"Gisele . . ."

She put her fingers to his lips. "Shhh." It didn't matter. Nothing he could say or failed to say would change anything.

Behind them Malcolm cleared his throat tactfully.

"He's my brother," Jamie whispered to her. "We can trust him. But what we tell him is up to you."

Gisele squeezed his hand. She stepped away from Jamie and looked the duke in the eye. "I am the Marchioness of Valence."

Malcolm blinked and looked at Gisele askance. "The one who was on a barge when it blew up in the middle of the Thames?"

She knew her own expression now mirrored the duke's.

"A good memory runs in the family," Jamie muttered under his breath.

"Is this a joke?" Malcolm asked his brother.

"No, I can assure you it's the farthest thing from."

Malcolm swung his attention to Gisele. "But you're dead." His eyes went back to Jamie. "And you're kissing her."

"Umm..." Gisele winced.

Another series of sharp raps sounded on the door, and it was Gisele who moved to answer it, if only to delay the awkward explanations that were looming.

The Duchess of Worth swept in, a troubled look on her face, and the hall suddenly shrank to minuscule proportions.

"We have a problem," Eleanor announced without preamble. She was brought up short by the sight of Malcolm, still dripping in the middle of the hall, his lip bloody and rapidly swelling. "Good gracious, there's two of you." She peered at Malcolm. "The Duke of Reddyck, I presume? Whatever happened to your face?"

"He walked into my fist," Jamie said.

"My reflexes aren't what they used to be," Malcolm added cheerfully.

Eleanor blinked. "I can see that."

"May I present my brother, Malcolm Montcrief, Duke of Reddyck. Malcolm, this is Her Grace, the Dowager Duchess of Worth."

"A pleasure." Malcolm offered a polite bow.

"What are you doing here?" the duchess asked in response.

If Malcolm was perturbed by her rudeness, he showed no sign. "Looking for my brother."

"It would appear you've found him." She cut a sharp glance at Jamie in question.

"I'd like to help," Malcolm offered.

The duchess turned an assessing eye on the duke. "And what is it you believe you can help with, exactly?"

"My brother was just kissing a dead marchioness," Malcolm said calmly. "Now, I do not claim to be exceedingly clever, but even I can recognize what's at issue here."

Eleanor crossed her arms, but not before she sent Jamie and Gisele an arch look that flooded Gisele's face with heat. "Kissing, you say? Was he indeed?" She paused and turned back to the duke. "How much do you know?"

"I only know that I've spent a year trying to find my brother, a situation born purely of my own stupidity. And now that I have him back, I'll not walk away from him ever again." Malcolm looked Jamie in the eye.

"He hasn't yet been told the...details," Gisele explained to Eleanor. "We hadn't quite yet got to that part when you arrived."

Eleanor *harrumph*ed. "Well, then I would suggest you share the details sooner rather than later. Perhaps Reddyck might indeed be of assistance with our problem."

Jamie gave Malcolm a composed and steady account of what had brought him and everyone standing in the room together. The duke looked alternatively shocked, horrified, indignant, and furious at appropriate intervals. It would seem Jamie's decent upbringing had not been limited to the eldest son.

"And which of these myriad problems do you believe I can assist you with?" Malcolm asked the duchess when Jamie had finished.

"My son is holding a ball."

"A ball?" Gisele worked her tongue around the word as though it were the first time she'd been presented with the concept. That certainly wasn't what she had been expecting.

"Yes, the boy has been a constant burr under my

backside this week, snooping about, talking in slow, measured sentences about how delightful it would be if I gave up my home and came to live with him. And if that weren't trouble enough, today Worth, bless his meddling heart, has taken a notion to host a ball. And a masked ball, of all things."

"I don't understand." Gisele was frowning. "Why?"

"The events of yesterday afternoon have caused a tidal wave of talk, just as you planned. Unfortunately, the undertow of that gossip seems to have caught his dear friend Lord Huston and his two lovely sisters in its wake. It would seem it is now Lady Julia's fitness that has been called into question, based on her untitled upbringing and Valence's preference for the ghost of his dead wife to a living, breathing debutante."

"Oh, for God's sake," Gisele cried in horror. "What is wrong with people?"

"That is exactly what Worth said to me this morning. So he's holding a ball. An engagement party of sorts just prior to the wedding, in honor of Lady Julia and Lord Valence. A public quashing of petty gossip. A declaration from a duke that anyone who takes exception to the good name of his best friend and his family will deal with him."

"When?"

"Tonight." Eleanor crossed her arms over her chest in disgust.

"Tonight?" Jamie was staring at her. "As in tonight-*tonight*?"

"I thought we had addressed this comprehension issue," the duchess chided Jamie.

"How can the duke host a ball tonight?" Gisele asked.

"Balls take weeks to plan. You need invitations and food and decorations and—"

"Money. And when you're a duke and you have lots of it and you're willing to spend it to make something happen, it does. Right now society matrons and maidens are in a dither, frantically rearranging their social calendars to accommodate the Duke of Worth." Eleanor said it with no arrogance or pride, just as a simple statement of fact. "Because to cut a duke, and a popular, eligible, wealthy one at that, would result in social consequences no one would wish to consider."

"So everyone will attend," Gisele said evenly.

"Yes."

"And by their presence, they will be validating the assertion that Lady Julia is above reproach."

"Yes." Eleanor was nodding.

"And if the Marquess of Valence were to be absent?"

The duchess looked taken aback. "Then despite my son's efforts, her reputation would suffer a substantial blow. For what honor-bound bridegroom would not attend his own engagement party, hosted by his social superior, unless he was sending a very harsh message? Since Lady Julia does not suffer from any obvious physical deformities, it must be assumed she has acted in such a manner as to render her unacceptable for marriage to a marquess. Unacceptable for marriage to anyone."

"Shit." It was Jamie who said what Gisele had been thinking.

"Language, James," Eleanor reproached before looking between them warily. "Why on earth would you think Valence would not attend? I would have thought after the events of yesterday afternoon, Valence would be falling all over himself to reassert himself into the good graces of society."

Gisele exchanged a look with Jamie. "I went to see Valence last night," she said.

Eleanor's face went comically blank before her eyes bulged from their sockets. "You did *what*?"

"Lord Huston arrived here last evening, most distraught, as you might imagine. He told us that his father had dismissed Valence's actions." Gisele sighed. "I had to do something."

Eleanor was trying to formulate words. "Define *something*."

"Last night Valence took refuge in opium, just as I knew he would, just as he's done a hundred times before when faced with emotional turmoil. I waited until he was insensible before I . . . appeared to him."

Eleanor whirled on Jamie. "Where the hell were you?" Her voice was shrill.

"Right beside her." Jamie's jaw was set.

"I thought to provoke Valence with the idea I no longer belonged to him," Gisele said wearily.

Eleanor's shrewd blue eyes went from Jamie to Gisele and back again. "Dear God in heaven." Harried color bloomed across her cheeks.

"Valence seemed quite convinced," Gisele interrupted the duchess. "Though with the opium, it's difficult to predict how much he will remember. So I left the diamond."

Eleanor sat down with a graceless thump on the chair nearest the hearth. "Diamond?" she croaked.

"The strange yellow one. The one you didn't want to sell for fear it would be recognized."

"Oh, dear God."

"Valence knows now that what happened yesterday on Bridge Street was not a figment of his imagination. I left him proof."

"Oh, *shit*," the duchess breathed, and Gisele would have laughed at the incongruity of that statement had the matter not been so bleak.

"Whatever happens, Lady Julia's reputation cannot be destroyed," Gisele said quietly. "She's done nothing to deserve this."

Jamie fixed Gisele with a strange look. "Wasn't it you who suggested I ruin her in the first place?"

Gisele shook her head. "You were right to refuse, Jamie. Even though Lady Julia would be physically safe, she would be destroyed, and Valence would still win. We cannot let Valence ruin her."

Eleanor scowled. "I don't know how it will be avoided." She slanted a glance at Jamie. "James might as well have the Hextall girl on a blanket in the middle of Piccadilly for all it will matter if Valence is absent when the cream of London society is at a ball held in the happy couple's honor. Now that Valence has proof Gisele is alive, it is almost certain that his obsession with her will cause him to abandon his engagement, his fiancée, and her dowry, for Gisele is worth far more to him. We can hope he searches publicly, which would, of course, bring his soundness of mind back into question, but if he goes to ground, the Marquess of Valence will simply be seen to have cast aside the Lady Julia for reasons left to the cruel imaginations of society. And she will be ruined."

Gisele pressed her forehead into her hands. "It wasn't supposed to happen like this," she moaned.

"Then tell the duke," Jamie said, pushing himself away

from the wall. "Tell him the truth. The truth about what the marquess did to his last wife. Why Lady Julia would be better off if Valence did throw himself off a bridge. Your son would never go through with the ball if he knew."

"To what end? Invitations to the ball have already been delivered. To cancel now would send out a message the duke no longer supports Lord Huston or Lady Julia." The duchess spread her hands out before her. "It's not Worth we need to convince. It would be the whole of London society that would need to believe. Short of producing Gisele for their inspection and perusal, which will never be allowed to happen for all the obvious reasons, it would be damned near impossible to sell such a tale."

"Valence would come to the ball if he thought Miss Whitby would be there." Malcolm spoke up for the first time.

All eyes swiveled to the duke.

"If what you say is true, everyone who will be at the ball tonight saw Miss Whitby die four years ago. In their minds that is a nonnegotiable truth. If Valence were to show up tonight, searching for his dead wife, no amount of distortion and twisting of words could make him appear anything other than mad. Especially after yesterday. But he would need to be provoked into another very public search at the ball. And if that were to happen, Boden would be forced to refuse to allow his daughter to marry a man sunk in insanity, and the earl would have the support of everyone there. Lady Julia's reputation would remain intact."

"True." The duchess considered Malcolm. "But how would Valence be convinced Miss Whitby would be at the ball?"

"Perhaps, if your son would be so gracious, His Grace

might be persuaded to make this ball a celebration of two engagements? Lady Julia and Lord Valence. And my dear brother, Mr. Montcrief, and his mystery bride, to be announced at midnight. It is a masked ball, after all. A little intrigue always ensures an impressive attendance."

A slow smile crept across Eleanor's face. "You do yourself a disservice, young man," she said. "You are exceedingly clever."

Malcolm smiled faintly. "I must be content with my lot in life. Not everyone can be blessed with a stellar right hook." He prodded his face gingerly.

The duchess was thrumming her fingers on the edge of her chair. "Why, everyone will be talking about it. Mr. Montcrief's sudden and thrilling engagement to a woman of exceptional beauty. A woman who, I will say when asked—and I will be asked—bears a *shocking* resemblance to the late Lady Valence." Eleanor stood abruptly, her breathless, mocking demeanor vanishing. "But whether or not you actually make an appearance tonight like the one you made yesterday afternoon, Miss Whitby, will remain to be seen."

"Of course I will," Gisele intoned.

"Of course she won't," Jamie said at the same time.

Eleanor tapped her chin. "A masked ball may indeed work in our favor. Regardless, I need to speak with my son immediately. And I need to make a number of calls. And send out a number of notes. The sooner people start talking the better. I must excuse myself immediately."

"Do I get any say in my impending fictitious nuptials you and my brother have so thoughtfully planned?" Jamie called after the duchess as she headed for the door, sounding a little overwhelmed.

"No," Eleanor replied brusquely. "You don't." She smirked. "Just try and look happy. As I would imagine you look when you're kissing a dead marchioness."

The door slammed behind her, and Gisele was torn between the need to laugh and the need to cringe.

Jamie sent Malcolm an exasperated look. "I hope you're enjoying this."

"Incidentally, I am." His amused expression slid from his face. "What that man has done is reprehensible. And I have a great deal to make up to you, Jamie. Please let me help." He included Gisele in his plea.

"Thank you," she said, meaning it. Just the knowledge that Jamie had someone watching his back was a considerable relief. "I'm glad you're here."

"Very well," Jamie said, coming to stand behind Gisele and wrapping his arms protectively around her. "If you want to help, I am supposed to go riding in Hyde Park this afternoon. Valence is to be included in our party."

Malcolm looked at his brother in question.

"You may accompany me and prevent me from killing him."

*Chapter 24*_____

Adam accepted the note delivered to him by his surly housekeeper and read it carelessly, tossing it into the fire when he was finished. *Just as well they all canceled*, he thought, glancing at the torrents of rain pounding against the windows, for he had never intended to join them. He wasn't about to waste time riding in Hyde Park with anyone, and certainly not the bloody Earl of Boden and his simpering daughter. Not when his Gisele was out there, just waiting for him to find her.

Adam's study was in disarray, records and dusty sheets of paper stacked on every surface. He was going back through every correspondence, every scrap of information he had from the last four years, trying to discern some clue as to where his beautiful wife might have gone. The explosion had been horrific, and it was possible she had been rendered insensible from the blast. He'd heard of that before—people suffering memory loss after a trauma. It was undoubtedly what had happened to his Gisele.

He wasn't entirely sure why she hadn't simply presented herself to him, but he was too happy to care. Perhaps Gisele was hesitant about reentering society. There would, after all, be an outlandish amount of gossip and speculation. Or perhaps her memory was not yet completely restored. Adam pulled the miniature of Gisele from his pocket, where he'd taken to keeping it with the yellow diamond, close to his heart, and smoothed his fingers over her beautiful face.

God, what he would do to help her remember.

Another knock on his study door had him scowling at the interruption.

"It's the man from yesterday, my lord," the housekeeper said wearily. "Says he's your valet?" She paused, a small flicker of hope in her eyes. "Didn't know you had a valet, my lord."

Valence straightened abruptly, sending a flurry of papers to the ground. Sebastien was here again?

"He says it's regarding your wife," she added as if it was an afterthought.

Adam froze for a split second before he shoved past the startled housekeeper, taking the stairs two at a time down to the servants' entrance. Sebastien was waiting just inside the door, his usual unruffled composure slightly askew. Adam came to a skidding halt, a thrill of anticipation firing through him.

"Good afternoon, my lord," Sebastien greeted him nervously.

"Tell me," Adam demanded.

Sebastien looked around warily, as though he was afraid of being overheard. "I can't stay—Montcrief does not know I am here. But I had to come."

Adam bobbed his head, nearly dancing from foot to foot.

"I am afraid you might think me crazy, my lord,"

Sebastien started hesitantly, his voice so low Adam could barely hear him. "But I saw her."

He had known, but the confirmation by another sent a rush of intense joy and possessiveness flooding through his body. "Where is she now?" He was nearly coming out of his skin.

"I don't know." The valet appeared to be struggling for words to explain. "But I know she will be at the ball tonight. The one the Duke of Worth is hosting in your honor."

Adam searched his memory blankly before recalling there had been an urgent missive delivered earlier with the Worth crest stamped on the front. He hadn't bothered to read it, let alone respond. "In my honor?"

"For you and Lady Julia, my lord." Sebastien didn't seem to notice his ignorance. "But at the ball, Mr. Montcrief is planning to announce his own engagement and introduce his bride to the ton."

"I don't understand." Adam felt the first pricking of apprehension.

"It's her, my lord. Lady Valence."

"Who?" The apprehension grew into dread.

Sebastien glanced around nervously again, his face pale. "The woman Mr. Montcrief intends to marry. I saw her today. With him. He's kept her hidden all this time, but today I saw her. It's Lady Valence, my lord. I'm sure of it."

A black rage filled Adam so quickly it blurred the edges of his vision, and he had to steady himself against the cool plaster of the wall. It all made sense now. The sudden appearance of Gisele coinciding with the sudden appearance of Montcrief. Adam had never believed in coincidences, and this only proved the merit of his intelligence. His vision cleared.

After all these years, Adam had finally found Gisele, and tonight he would fetch his bride and bring her home.

"You were right all along, my lord," Sebastien was saying. "It was Lady Valence you saw yesterday on that bridge. She's not dead at all. She's with *him*."

A vision of Gisele, dressed in her silk dressing gown and locked in a passionate embrace with Montcrief, dropped into his mind's eye.

And for the second time in two days, Adam thought he might faint.

Chapter 25 _____

Gisele was sitting at the window of her room, staring out at the bruised sky hanging low over the grounds and the treelined drive of Breckenridge, the Worth ducal manor that sat perched on the southwestern edge of London. Below her was a steady stream of wagons and carts and horses, all making their hasty deliveries of food and drink even in the relentless rain and mud. Inside, the scene was even more chaotic. She could hear an army of servants, frantically swarming about the ballrooms and kitchens in an epic effort to cram days of preparations into hours.

Eleanor had sent Joseph and her carriage to collect Gisele and bring her to Breckenridge by midafternoon. Gisele could not pretend she wasn't relieved to be hidden in the anonymity of the manor's vast warren of rooms. Sebastien had returned from Valence's grimly satisfied, and while they were confident Valence would make an appearance at the ball tonight, they weren't entirely sure he wouldn't try to make one at Jamie's apartment first. Jamie hadn't been able to push her out the door and into the carriage fast enough.

Gisele's eye was caught by a rider coming up the drive, bundled against the rain, his horse eating up the ground in easy, fluid strides. In an instant her pulse raced, and butterflies soared. God in heaven, her reaction to Jamie Montcrief was getting worse every time she saw him. It was a wonder she was able to string more than four words together in his presence.

She didn't know what she was going to do when he left.

Gisele shoved that thought from her mind. She would have far more pressing things to worry about in the next hours than the inevitable ending to whatever this was that she and Jamie shared. Gisele waited where she was, knowing he would seek her out as soon as he was able. Even though the planned excursion to Hyde Park had been put off because of the miserable weather, among all the comings and goings of the day, Gisele and Jamie had had little time to talk. And there was a great deal that needed to be said before tonight.

It didn't take long. She heard his footsteps in the hallway, and the door banged open and he was standing there, windblown and flushed from his ride.

"Dammit, but this is a bloody big house," he said. "Sebastien was able to recall the location of the green guest room with somewhat less than his usual perfect accuracy." His eyes widened as he took in the luxurious rugs and wall coverings and the massive antique draped bed, all decorated in shades of emerald.

"Did anyone see you come up?" Gisele asked.

Jamie made a wry sound. "An entire regiment could have marched through the house below and no one would have noticed unless they had come bearing crystal and pressed linens."

"Close the door then, Jamie," she said with an impish smile. "I have no desire to scandalize any errant soldiers."

Jamie kicked the door closed, taking a precious few seconds to turn the key in the lock before Gisele was in his arms, and he was kissing her with an ever-increasing intensity.

"I can't seem to get enough of you," he breathed, even as Gisele shoved his riding coat from his shoulders.

"You don't know the half of it," she whispered back.

The pins in her hair scattered everywhere, and the top of her gown slipped.

"I'm supposed to be furious right now," Jamie told her, his lips against her neck.

"Oh?" Her hands lifted his shirt neatly over his head, and she smoothed her fingers across the broad expanse of skin on his chest.

He hissed in pleasure at the sensation. "You're distracting me."

"You have my sincere apologies, sir."

"I am trying to believe you will not be so foolish as to try wearing that ball gown currently hanging behind you," he told her.

"Mmmm." She ran her fingers over his shoulders, his skin hot and smooth beneath hers.

"I don't want you here."

"Liar." She pressed into the evidence of his want.

"I never said I didn't want you. I said I didn't want you *here*." She found herself pulled up against the hard length of him, his eyes searching hers. "Gisele, we have to talk about what you have planned for tonight. This is important."

"Must we really have this conversation now?" She sighed.

"We have to."

"No, we do not."

"Gisele, I love you."

She stared at him, her breath caught in her throat.

He cupped her face in his hands. "You have come to mean everything to me," he said, and his voice was hoarse.

"Oh, Jamie. I love you too."

"I should have told you sooner because I think I fell in love with you the moment you bought me that first God-awful pot of ale. But the man I was in Nottingham had nothing to offer you—nothing you would want, anyway."

"You're wrong. I never wanted things," Gisele said softly. "I only ever wanted you."

"I know that now. After seeing Malcolm today, and after hearing of how Sofia and Richard searched for me, I realized a person may want my love even if I haven't fully earned the right to give it. And... I'm afraid you are stuck with me regardless, for I find I can't live without you." He shook his head slightly. "Gisele, I want you safe."

"I know. And I will be. I'll be with you." She wrapped her arms around his waist and laid her head against his chest, listening to the steady beat of his heart.

"So you are going to wear that damned dress."

"Yes." She pulled back to meet his eyes. "Because tonight, it ends for good."

～

It was pointless to argue. Everything that had happened from the moment Gisele's father had offered his only daughter to the Marquess of Valence had set the wheels of fate in motion so that they had arrived at this point.

"Where's Malcolm?" Gisele asked.

"He went back to his rented rooms to get his affairs in order and dress for the ball. While my father avoided London, Malcolm does not. He and Sebastien will be here by early evening. He said he doesn't dare miss out on a moment of his brother's engagement party." A rumble of rueful laughter echoed through his chest.

"Good." Gisele grinned up at him. "What did the duke say when his mother told him you were engaged?"

"He sent me a note offering me his sincere congratulations. And that he understood now why I dodged the rather enthusiastic overtures of Lady Goddard at the Baustenbury ball. He also wondered how much time I might be allowed to spend in his stables in the future before my wife objected."

Gisele laughed. "You're probably entitled to a raise, you know," she told him.

"Indeed?"

"I feel certain that sham betrothal was not among the potential duties we discussed when I hired you."

"True. But I wasn't entirely forthcoming about my various skills at the time."

"I agree you left a great deal out." Her finger traced the ridge of his collarbone, coming to rest on the scar across his shoulder. "It was Sofia who pulled you out from under your horse that day, wasn't it?"

Jamie caught her hand in his. "Yes. She followed Michael to Waterloo, and when he did not return from the battlefield after it was all over, she immediately went looking for him. She found both of us, though it was I who still lived, if barely."

"What you did for her and Richard—selling your commission—was very noble."

"It was the right thing to do and I would do it again in a heartbeat." Jamie traced the outline of her lips with his thumb. "But if we're comparing noble acts, you've set a high bar."

"I might have been persuaded into your bed far sooner had I known you could meet it so effortlessly," she teased.

"Touché," he whispered, bending to kiss her properly. "I shall report all my good deeds straightaway in the future. In fact, I believe I may have helped a kitten from a tree on the ride from town."

She laughed, twining her arms around his neck as he kissed her deeply and pulled her forward until they bumped into the canopied bed. Her hands moved from his hair to caress the sides of his face, and then his own fingers caught hers, pulling them down to rest on his shoulders. He ran his hands down the smooth lines of her waist and gathered the fabric of her skirts, pushing it up her thighs.

"What are you doing?" Her kiss suddenly stilled.

"Oh, pardon me," he growled. "Perhaps I forgot to mention I also helped a footman carry a rather weighty delivery of petit fours downstairs. Need I go on?"

Jamie felt her smile against his mouth. "Why, Mr. Montcrief, could this be your attempt to ply me with pretty, persuasive words?" Gisele was watching him, wicked amusement dancing in her eyes.

"Do you think you can do better?"

"I am very adept at pretty words," Gisele told him, shivering slightly at his touch. "I even had a tutor for such a thing. I am likely far more literary than you."

"Mmm-hmm." Jamie let his fingers roam along the impossibly soft skin of her inner thighs.

"You don't believe me?"

"No, I don't believe you," he said, dipping his head to kiss the underside of her jaw. He heard her suck in her breath, and he grinned. "But you can try me. Say something inspired." He kissed the hollow of her throat as his fingers moved in slow circles, exploring her damp folds.

"I—the—by—hmmm," she sighed against him.

"That's very scholarly," he teased, though the sounds she was making were beginning to make it hard for him to concentrate. His hands slid around her backside, pulling her up hard against his erection.

"That's cheating," she panted. "I can't think."

"Admit defeat." He was rapidly losing what little restraint he had left.

"Never."

"Last chance."

Her mouth was against his ear. "I think you should have me, Jamie Montcrief," she whispered. "Every way you can think of and some you can't."

A wall of lust slammed into him and he nearly came undone where he stood.

"You win," he groaned.

He let go of her only to help her rid them both of their clothes, her fingers as frantic as his. In a minute his body was bare to the chill of the air, and he pushed her back on the bed, her skin hot against his own. He came down on top of her, kissing her with a savage need. Her hands were at his back, on his hips, pulling him toward her, her body straining to meet him. He entered her in a single thrust, and the pleasure of it left him nearly insensible.

She was whispering his name, writhing under him, urging him deeper, and he tried desperately to regain control but any semblance had slipped away a long time ago. Jamie had his hands beneath her, raising her hips to meet each of his thrusts, feeling her very core as he surged against her. Her legs wrapped around him, her head tipped back, and she stiffened, her body convulsing around him, and he drove into her once more before his world came apart.

He left his head on the pillow, his nose pressed into the side of her neck, breathing hard. He was aware his weight was likely crushing her, yet when he attempted to move, she tightened her hold on him.

"No," she said. "Stay." He could still feel her spasms, felt her quiver in her own eddies of passion.

He kissed her again for long minutes, a slow, sensuous exploration. Presently he rolled to his side, and this time she let him go. "That wasn't fair, you know."

She smiled. "I told you I was adept with pretty words, even if I must steal them from naked, drunken cavalrymen I've only just met."

"I love you, Just-Gisele." Jamie wanted this moment to last forever.

She laughed breathlessly, a beautiful sound that made his heart turn over. "I love you too, Jamie Montcrief."

"Promise me that tonight you will not be noble," Jamie said suddenly. "Promise me you will be smart and safe. Promise me that I will be able to tell you how much I love you tomorrow and for all the days after that."

"Only if you promise the same."

Jamie kissed her. "I promise I will love you forever."

Chapter 26

It was Miss Hughes who came to help Gisele dress. Nearly all of the duchess's staff had been commandeered from her town house to help with the ball at Breckenridge, and it wasn't a surprise to see Eleanor's companion poke her head into the room. What was a surprise was that Jenna's attire was nearly identical to her own and that her dark hair was once again hidden underneath a pale-blond wig. Wearing masks, the two women might be easily confused at a glance.

Jenna caught Gisele's stare. "Her Grace told me what you are planning to do," she said. "I want to help."

Gisele remained silent as Jenna went about the task of helping her into her gown.

"You don't have to," Gisele said, meeting the woman's pale-blue eyes in the mirror once she had finished.

"I know." Jenna motioned for her to sit so that she could dress her hair.

"It might be dangerous."

Jenna smiled faintly, gathering Gisele's hair into a simple, elegant twist. "I know."

"Then why are you doing this?"

"Because at some point in the evening you might need me to be noticeable and convincing again."

"That's not what I meant."

Jenna's hands stilled, and her eyes grew cold. "Because people like the Marquess of Valence ruin lives without thought, and they are allowed to do so simply by the accident of their birth. And that is not acceptable."

Gisele watched her for a moment, wondering if she might say more. But Jenna fell silent, concentrating on the last pins and curls.

"Thank you then," Gisele said.

Jenna inclined her head. "You're welcome." She rose and saw herself to the door. "I'll let Her Grace know you're ready."

Gisele returned her attention to the mirror.

The woman looking back at her was unrecognizable as the woman who had last been dressed this way. Four years ago the ashen reflection staring back had been draped in pearls and diamonds and satin from the top of her perfectly styled hair to the toes of her slippers, none of which had hidden her despair. On this night she was again draped in silks and jewels, yet it was there the likeness ended.

She'd thought she would be nervous. She was playing with fire tonight, exposing herself more than she ever had in the last four years. But there was no doubt. No anxiety, no fear. All that stared back at her was a visage of determination and resolve. An immovable courage quietly fueled by the knowledge that she was not alone.

"You look more beautiful than you ever have," Eleanor said from the door.

Gisele turned, meeting her eyes. The duchess was already dressed in a deep-rose gown, powdered and pampered and ready for battle.

"Aren't you forgetting something?" Gisele teased, trying to lighten the mood.

"*Hmpph*," Eleanor huffed. "I'm thinking of abandoning the chickens. They are truly stupid, stupid creatures. No wonder everyone prefers them with sauce on a plate." She tapped her chin in consideration. "I was considering moving on to badgers."

"Badgers?" Gisele nearly slipped from her chair.

"They *are* delightfully stripy. And I have been given the impression they are quite aggressive. I wonder if they could be trained to bite on command?"

"Trained?" Gisele asked faintly.

"I'm joking, dear. I think." She closed the door behind her and crossed the room, her face becoming serious. "Are you sure you are ready to do this?"

"Yes. I have been waiting a long time to do this."

Eleanor sighed. "This is a risk. The setting is uncontrolled. Things could go wrong."

Gisele laughed a humorless laugh. "Things went wrong a long time ago. This is about stopping the cycle. And if the worst happens? If I am revealed, then what?"

Eleanor went pale beneath her powder. "That won't happen."

"It might. I've acknowledged that. And if it is a choice between Lady Julia and me, it won't be a choice. At least I have my eyes wide open."

"James will kill Valence before that happens," the duchess snapped.

"No," Gisele said fiercely. "If the worst happens tonight, have Jamie tied up, knocked out, or drugged, I don't care. But he cannot sacrifice himself for me. Promise me you will not let it happen."

Eleanor stared at her.

"He has a family."

"Of course he does. The Duke of Reddyck is his—"

"No." Gisele took a steadying breath. "He has a nephew. Richard. He's not even one yet, but he looks just like Jamie, and in eighteen years, he will have become a strong, kind, decent man because his uncle will have taught him how. He will need Jamie more than anyone because Jamie will be the one person who will be able to tell the boy just how generously his father loved and how brilliantly his father lived right up to the day when he died trying to save another's life."

The duchess put a hand to her chest.

"Promise me I will not need to tell Richard that his uncle died in the same way. Trying to save my life."

Eleanor nodded silently.

"Jamie protects what and who he loves, and he assumes that responsibility to a fault. He will go to extremes and think nothing of it. It's why I love him beyond measure, and it's what scares me the most. I am terrified he will do something irrevocable if pushed too far."

"I understand."

There was a knock on the door. "Your guests have started to arrive, Your Grace," came the disembodied voice of a servant through the heavy door.

Eleanor held Gisele's eyes for a long minute before reaching for her hands. "It will turn out all right," she said. "Just promise me you won't blow anything up. Inside Breckenridge, at least. I'm rather fond of this heap."

It earned a weak smile. "I promise, Your Grace."

The duchess stood then, straightening her skirts.

"Thank you," Gisele said as Eleanor reached the door.

"Thank you for everything you've done. For everything you are doing."

The duchess looked directly at her. "No, the gratitude is mine. You are an inspiration."

~

Because Adam no longer owned his own carriage and coachman, or even his own horse, he was forced to accept the assumed invitation to travel to Breckenridge with the Earl of Boden and his insufferable family. But Adam reminded himself that to endure a single carriage ride for his Gisele was a small price to pay.

The Earl of Boden had commandeered the early conversation, a loud dissertation on the miserable weather and the miserable crops that were sure to follow. Boden's countess, perched like a nervous magpie, her head swiveling back and forth among the carriage occupants, chattered loudly to fill any conversational gaps the earl might have left behind. Huston sat in stony silence, his eyes occasionally lighting on Adam in critical hostility, while his sisters carried on breathless speculation about the identity of the mystery woman the dashing Mr. James Montcrief was to wed.

All of which might have driven Adam to the edge of violence on any other night, but now, so close to his Gisele, he found himself indifferent to all their suspicion and stupidity. He didn't need to hear the gossip that Montcrief's bride-to-be bore a shocking resemblance to his late wife or that she was an exceptional beauty. He already knew very well who the woman was, and Adam felt feverish and flushed with anticipation at what waited for him. Four years of grief and pain and aching loneliness and tonight he would realize his dream of having his Gisele back where she belonged.

As soon as the carriage stopped in front of Breckenridge's wide stone steps, the marquess snapped open the door and took the stairs two at a time, not bothering to look back, even as Boden bellowed after him. His future was not behind him, stuffed into the crested carriage. The heart of his future waited for him somewhere inside Breckenridge. And it was time to go and find her and bring her home.

Jamie paused in the hall outside Gisele's door. He was dressed in his suffocating evening clothes again, though tonight he barely noticed them. Instead he felt much the same as he did waiting for dawn to break over a battlefield, waiting for the light to lay bare the enemy he would be forced to conquer. Anxious, determined, and more than a little terrified it would all go wrong, and that, as he had been a year ago, he would be helpless to keep the one he loved safe.

Jamie took a deep breath. Twenty minutes. Thirty minutes, tops. And then Gisele would be back upstairs, locked safely away from the madman. And if this did not work—if the marquess did not seize upon the notion that he might have his beloved Gisele back and render himself suitably unfit for anywhere or anyone save Bedlam, Jamie would do the next best thing. He would call the bastard out for what he had done. Swords or pistols, it mattered not. He was more than competent with both, and either would end with the marquess dead. He would do whatever it took to keep Gisele safe and her identity a secret.

He tapped on the door lightly.

"Come in," she called, and he let himself into the room.

She rose from the chair in front of the dressing table. And in that moment, he could understand the marquess's complete obsession with possessing this woman. She was an ethereal angel, serene and composed, watching him with luminous eyes. Jamie had had a whole array of clever and witty compliments on his tongue in preparation for seeing her dressed in all the trappings of a lady for the first time, yet every one died unspoken, unable to justify the vision before him.

Her gown was of the palest gold silk, the fabric caressing her body like the touch of a lover. The front of her bodice traveled low across the tops of her breasts, which had been pushed up to display them to their full advantage. Her hair had been swept back, ringlets trailing down, exposing her graceful neck and shoulders and framing her face with flaxen perfection. Long gloves covered her arms, and she wore only a simple pair of earrings, dainty emeralds that emphasized the green in her eyes. Eyes that were looking at him with a love that stole whatever remained of any rational thought.

He shut the door behind him and strode over to where she waited. He searched her eyes and her face before bending to kiss her reverently.

"You're beautiful," he whispered, knowing how insubstantial those words sounded.

"Thank you," she replied anyway.

They stood there in silence for a long minute, neither wishing to relinquish the last seconds of solitude. Finally Jamie moved away from her, certain that if he didn't do something purposeful he wouldn't be able to go through with this. Wouldn't be able to allow *her* to go through with this.

Jamie picked up the mask sitting on the dressing table. He moved to her back, watching her in the looking glass, and very carefully he fitted the mask to her face, pulling the ribbons tight around the back of her head. It covered almost her entire face, making her unrecognizable to anyone who didn't already know who she was.

Jamie pressed a kiss to the side of her neck. "Are you ready?" His voice was hoarse.

"Yes."

At least one of them was.

"I love you, Jamie," she said, turning to face him. "No matter what happens, no matter what has happened, I love you." Her eyes glittered with emotion.

"I love you too," he said. "And I won't let anything happen to you tonight. You'll just do as we discussed. No more, no less. And you'll let me do the rest. Malcolm and Sebastien won't be far, and if things get thoroughly catastrophic, then the duchess can always throw another chicken into the crowd."

Gisele laughed softly and he held out his elbow. Her fingers curled around his forearm. "Lead the way, Mr. Montcrief," she said, and he heard the determination in her voice. "Let's go and create a scandal the likes of which London has never seen."

Chapter 27 ─────────────────

Gisele entered the ballroom on Jamie's arm and immediately there were whispers. She almost laughed at the sheer lunacy of it. A woman who had faked her death and stolen a fortune in diamonds, on the arm of a penniless, illegitimate ex-cavalry captain, and they were the most talked-about couple in London society.

Gisele caught sight of the Duke of Worth, standing just inside the ballroom entrance welcoming his guests. Even behind his simple black mask, his height and dark coloring set him apart. And if there was any further doubt, he was looking around at the ballroom with boyish delight at the stunning greenery and ribbons and flowers and twinkling lights as though he couldn't believe that he had pulled it off. Or rather, that his staff had pulled it off.

"Mr. Montcrief!" the Duke of Worth exclaimed, catching sight of Jamie and Gisele. He clapped a hand on Jamie's back, beaming. "I almost didn't believe it when I was informed you were to be married. I had no idea. And a love match at that! Congratulations!" His attention focused on Gisele. "And this, I must believe, is the beautiful woman who has made the captain here a very happy man."

Gisele extended her hand, and Worth took it politely. "An honor to make your acquaintance, Your Grace," she said.

"Might I have the pleasure of your name?" he asked Gisele.

"Not until midnight," said Jamie with an easy smile, drawing Gisele a little closer to him. "The intrigue will help divert attention from any unpleasantness that may still linger from yesterday and give the gossips something else to talk about."

Worth sent Jamie a look of gratitude before a shadow passed over his face. "I just don't understand," he said in a low voice. "Lord Valence is acting very strangely, and Boden has dug in his heels. And it is Huston and his sisters caught in the middle, and I can't see that they have set a foot wrong in any of this."

"Then you've done a good thing here," Jamie told the duke. "Having this ball. Standing up for what you know to be right. Standing up for the people you care for."

The duke straightened. "Thank you, Montcrief." His face creased into another easy grin. "Now, please, enjoy yourselves. And if you have time on the morrow, Mr. Montcrief, I would still like your opinion on that mare of mine."

"Of course," Jamie replied, and the duke drifted off to greet another group of guests.

"Have you seen Valence yet?" Gisele asked as they turned toward the crush of people milling before them in Breckenridge's impressive ballroom. Her insides twisted uneasily despite her determination to remain composed.

"No. But Sebastien tells me he is indeed here. The marquess arrived with the Earl of Boden and his family."

"Well, then at least Lady Julia's reputation is safe for the moment." Gisele closed her eyes, a temporary feeling of relief combating her disquiet.

"Yes."

Gisele surveyed the swirl of color and glitter and light before her with a sense of irony. She'd been to a handful of balls just like this when she was newly Lady Valence. She'd been isolated then, watching everything at a distance, yearning to be part of the excitement. Tonight Gisele found herself again at a ball, the Marquess of Valence also in attendance, but on this night she would not be watching from the side. Four years later Gisele would get her wish. She would indeed be part of the excitement.

⁓

They'd made it not a dozen steps into the dazzling room when Malcolm joined them, flanking Gisele. Jamie had never been so relieved to have his brother at his side as he was at that moment.

"You clean up well, little brother," Jamie said casually, even as his eyes raked the crowd around them.

"I like to think so." Malcolm grinned at a group of young ladies who drifted by, giggling and shooting not-so-subtle glances in the duke's direction.

"I am under the impression you are very popular tonight, Your Grace," Gisele said dryly between them.

"But of course. Charm, wit, and dashing good looks run in the family. And since Jamie here has gone and gotten himself engaged and disappointed every daughter who aimed to take him to the altar and every widow who aimed to take him to bed, the women of London have had to settle for me." He leaned closer to Gisele. "And I even come with a title thrown in for good measure," he whispered loudly. "Do you wish to reconsider your choice?"

"My thanks for your kind offer, but I am quite happy with the Montcrief I have."

She grinned at his brother and Jamie was relieved to see it. Her grip on his arm was crushing, and Jamie knew she wasn't nearly as at ease as she pretended. Which was probably just as well. Her apprehension would serve her well and keep her safe.

"Have you seen the man?" Jamie asked Malcolm.

"Indeed. The duchess pointed him out to me." The teasing manner disappeared.

"And?"

"And he is skulking around the ballroom like a hunted cockroach. I am made to understand he's barely said a word to anyone since he's arrived. People are talking."

"Good." The bastard was leaving here tonight in either chains or a coffin.

"Ah, Reddyck, there you are." The address came from just behind Malcolm, and they all turned to find a distinguished-looking gentleman with silver hair smiling pleasantly at the group.

"Havockburn," Malcolm said with pleasure. "I did not expect to have the good fortune to see you again so soon." He stepped forward. "Since I am sworn to keep this lovely woman's identity a secret, at least for the next hour, please excuse my awkward lack of presentation." He winked at Gisele. "However, I am delighted to present to you my brother, Mr. James Montcrief. James, His Grace, the Duke of Havockburn."

The gentleman smiled and pushed his mask up off his face. "Happy to make your acquaintance, Mr. Montcrief," he said. "And best wishes on your upcoming wedding."

"Thank you very much, Your Grace," Jamie said with a slight bow.

"I must confess, when I saw Reddyck, I was rather hoping you would be here with him, Mr. Montcrief. If I might impose on your time for a moment? I wish to speak to you regarding a matter of . . . er, a sensitive nature."

"Of course," Jamie said, distracted. He met his brother's eyes over Gisele's head and sent a silent message.

"If you would do me the honor of a dance?" Malcolm made a ridiculous bow to Gisele, and she smiled prettily, though she glanced up at Jamie in question.

Jamie nodded briefly. She would be safe enough with Malcolm for the moment. Valence wouldn't be looking for Malcolm. Valence would be looking for Jamie.

The pair moved off to join the dancers in the center of the ballroom, and Jamie turned back to the duke.

"I understand I am in some debt to you," Havockburn said bluntly.

Jamie started, surprised. "You have no debt to me, Your Grace."

"Well, perhaps not me, per se, but my son. I believe he lost his head at a card game against you some nights past."

"Ah." Jamie understood. "You may rest assured, Your Grace, your son owes me naught. His wager has been settled in full."

Out of the corner of his eye, he saw Gisele and Malcolm twirl by before being swallowed by the crowd of dancers again.

The silver-haired man barked a gruff laugh, though he

shook his head. "My son did not pay his wager in full as it was made, Mr. Montcrief. Your principles allowed him to walk away from that table with his honor and his pride intact. As well as his property." The last words were spoken grimly.

"We were both young once, Your Grace, and I think we both can recall times when our judgment may not have been at its finest," Jamie said lightly. "And besides, as I told him, I have not the means to maintain or keep such a finely matched team, nor the vehicle they were meant to pull. Owning such fine horses would have beggared me, for I wouldn't have had the heart to sell them. He did me the favor."

The duke gave Jamie a look that told him he didn't believe a word. "You are still entitled to the value of his wager, Mr. Montcrief. As such, and knowing you are a superior horseman, I have brought one of my most exceptional stallions with me tonight in the hopes you will accept the animal in payment. The horse is of excellent conformation and breeding and has been raced most successfully these past three years. Indeed, it is one of the fastest horses I have ever owned."

"While I appreciate the gesture, Your Grace, I cannot accept," Jamie repeated stubbornly.

Havockburn shook his head. "Then we will have to agree to disagree, for—"

"Montcrief!"

Jamie's name was almost snarled, and it interrupted the duke mid-sentence.

"I was wondering when you were going to show up here," Valence said, shoving through the crowd and coming to stand directly in front of Jamie. The marquess hadn't bothered to don a mask, and even in the soft glow of the lanterns and candles, he looked pale and haggard.

"Good evening, Lord Valence," Jamie said evenly, forcing his eyes to remain on the marquess and not dart out in the direction of the dance floor. He desperately hoped Malcolm was watching. "Is there something I can assist you with?"

"Where is she, you bastard?" the marquess hissed.

"I say, Lord Valence, are you quite all right?" Havockburn was frowning fiercely at the marquess's rudeness.

Valence ignored the duke. "I know you have her, Montcrief. And I want her back. She belongs to me."

"Perhaps I can get you a refreshment, Lord Valence?" Jamie asked with feigned concern. "You look a little pale."

"I don't want anything from you, Montcrief, except my wife."

Jamie stared at Valence. "I have no idea what you are talking about, my lord."

"Don't push me too far, Montcrief," Valence threatened. "You have no idea what I am capable of."

"Lord Valence, calm yourself!" Havockburn was thoroughly annoyed.

"I will not calm myself," Valence snapped. "Not when this man thinks he can steal my wife from me."

"Lord Valence," Havockburn said sternly, clearly trying to head off what he believed to be the makings of a duel, "Lady Julia is currently standing with her brother near the refreshment table. I can attest Mr. Montcrief has not laid an eye, much less a hand, on her. He is here with his own fiancée."

Valence's eyes took on a reptilian sheen. "And where might this woman be right now?"

Jamie forced himself to remain calm. *Dear God, Malcolm, look this way, please, please see what is happening.*

"Why, she is dancing with the Duke of Reddyck."

No, no, no! Jamie watched as Valence whipped his head around to stare at the dancers. The marquess made to move, but Jamie stepped in front of him, his eyes blazing.

"Is there something in particular you wanted with my lady?" Jamie asked.

"Get out of my way," Valence hissed.

"I don't believe I will," Jamie replied. He was aware a number of people were staring now.

In a sudden movement, Valence shoved a nearby woman at Jamie and charged into the throng of dancers like a Smithfield drover. Jamie cursed, righted the woman among a number of startled screams, and set after the marquess.

He could see Malcolm's head above the crowd, dipping in time with the music, though he couldn't see Gisele. He hoped the duke didn't mind blood on his polished ballroom floor. For if Valence touched a hair on Gisele's head, he would kill the marquess where he stood.

A number of angry protests preceded Jamie as Valence pushed and shoved his way toward Malcolm. Jamie arrived just in time to see Valence crash into his brother with his shoulder, sending him staggering back. The dancers around them scattered as Valence reached for Gisele and yanked her around by her arm, grabbing for her mask.

Jamie was still three steps behind, his heart in his throat, and he was preparing to do whatever it took to stop Valence from hurting Gisele.

Except it wasn't Gisele.

The woman's mask fell to the floor, broken beads clattering on the wooden surface. Valence, so caught up in what was to be his moment of victory, had yet to release his captive and was hanging on for all he was worth. In a movement so fast it defied believability, the woman stomped on Valence's instep and, as he doubled over, sent her elbow smashing into the marquess's face with an audible crunch.

Jamie stared in shock as he then watched Jenna Hughes extricate herself from her attacker and press her hands to her heaving bosom, blinking rapidly, the perfect picture of innocent outrage and injury.

The Duke of Worth crashed into the clearing on the dance floor, his eyes flashing in fury as he stared down at the marquess. "Just what the hell do you think you're doing, Valence?" he demanded.

Valence was still doubled over, gasping, his eye already beginning to swell. A buzz had started in the ballroom at the excitement, and the music stopped discordantly as, one by one, the musicians abandoned their efforts to play over the disturbance.

"Are you all right?" Worth had turned away from Valence in disgust and was now gently addressing Miss Hughes.

"Yes, thank you, Your Grace," she replied breathlessly, looking extraordinarily fragile for a woman who, just seconds ago, had effectively stopped a raging marquess. "It was just so ... unexpected."

The duke bent and retrieved her mask and handed it to her, completely tongue-tied.

Malcolm had no such problems. "That was most

uncalled for, Lord Valence," he said loudly. "If you want to dance with a lady, I would suggest you simply ask next time. Though I'm not so sure you'll find many who are brave enough."

Laughter rippled through the crowd.

Across the floor Jamie caught sight of the duchess. She met his eyes and gave him a tight nod. Relief flooded though him. Gisele was still safe.

Valence straightened and glanced around him, pressing his hand to his face and once again realizing he was the center of attention. He faltered slightly before recovering, a vindictive glint touching his eyes.

"Your Grace, the Duke of Reddyck, I presume." Valence transferred his gaze from Malcolm to Jamie. "The one brother the celebrated captain here didn't manage to kill."

There were a few gasps around them, and Jamie recoiled. "I beg your pardon?" he managed.

"Your brother. The tenth Duke of Reddyck, for as pitifully long as that lasted. Young Michael Montcrief."

Jamie stared at the marquess mutely, afraid he might be ill. Malcolm's face too was a frozen mask of horrified shock.

Valence smiled a cold, cruel smile. "Oh, I know all about you, Montcrief. The guilt you must live with every day knowing it should have been you who died on that battlefield must be excruciating." He was playing to the audience now to divert the unwanted attention and everyone knew it. "Yet here you are in London, reveling in the high life while he lies in a cold grave. How do you live with yourself?"

Jamie took a deep, shuddering breath. The guilt rose

up again like a foul mist, although he thought he had over-come it. Jamie wished desperately Gisele were beside him. Her presence alone was enough to help him drive those demons back into the past where they belonged.

But she wasn't here. Because of the man standing in front of him.

And nothing Valence could say or do to Jamie could ever compare to what he had done to Gisele.

The air around them was electric. Malcolm took two menacing steps toward Valence, but Jamie stopped him with a raised hand.

"You're right," Jamie said quietly, and the crowd craned forward to hear. "You're absolutely right."

Valence shifted uneasily, his eyes darting from Jamie to the onlookers.

"Not a day goes by when I don't think of Michael," Jamie said, everything fading strangely around him. "That he was killed so young is a tragedy, but no more so than the death of any other man killed on the battlefield serving king and country. He chose to fight a brave fight, to fight for something he believed in." Jamie paused. "My brother died saving my life. He died a hero. *My* hero. I owe him everything. I loved him, and I will not do him the dishonor and disservice of wallowing in self-pity, though some days I miss him more than I can stand. He paid the ultimate price for our freedom. Mine and yours." He pointed a finger at Valence scornfully. "I have not forgotten that. Nor will I take it for granted. Ever."

Jamie stopped, feeling disoriented. In the background the orchestra started up again, though all around them was silence, until someone sniffed. A man turned and offered the woman his handkerchief, and then suddenly time resumed, and the air was punctuated with murmured agreement and admiration.

Jamie swallowed with difficulty and blew out a breath he hadn't been aware he'd been holding.

Valence, sweating profusely, turned on his heel and stomped away. Slowly the rest of the crowd moved off as well.

Malcolm laid a hand on Jamie's shoulder. "That was cruel and unnecessary. You should never have had to defend yourself in such a manner," his brother said gruffly.

"No," Jamie replied slowly, looking at Malcolm. "That was entirely necessary. I loved my brother, and it was not my fault that he died."

It was the first time Jamie had actually believed it.

Chapter 28 _____

Adam downed the rum punch he didn't remember taking and pressed the cool glass to his face, staring at Montcrief through the one eye that hadn't swollen closed. The bastard was like a fucking cat, always landing on his feet. His brother was dead because of him, and somehow Montcrief still came off as a hero. Well, not for long. Soon Adam would prove to everyone Montcrief had stolen his wife. His Gisele. And then who would be the hero?

He wasn't entirely sure what had happened out there on that dance floor, or how Gisele had gotten away from him again, but she was here. Adam had seen the fear in Montcrief's eyes when Havockburn had told him where Gisele was, and that fear had told him everything. Montcrief had her, and he was terrified Adam was going to take her away.

Adam tossed his glass onto a chair along the wall and stalked through the crowd, ignoring the whispers and the stares that followed him. Boden had tried to corner him, furious, of course, but Adam didn't care one whit. And in a crowd such as this, it was easy to avoid him. Adam didn't want any distractions. He needed to be fully focused on Montcrief. For it was the captain who would lead Adam to Gisele. He pulled out her miniature and the diamond and stared at them both in his hand.

"Soon," Adam whispered to the painting, pressing a kiss to her beautiful, perfect face.

He curled his fingers around the diamond and felt the edges of the stone bite into the flesh of his hand. A gray-haired matron was watching with appalled concern, and he glared at her, sending her scurrying.

Soon, Adam repeated to himself.

He just needed to be patient.

❧

Eleanor was pacing by a long row of potted ferns as Gisele, seated on a low chair concealed by the foliage, watched her.

"Hettie just told me she saw the marquess kissing a miniature and talking to himself," the duchess said. "I would think that would be adequate proof of Valence's descent into delirium. I'd like to see you upstairs now, locked safely away."

"Not yet." Gisele shook her head.

"Valence nearly caught you," Eleanor hissed through her garish mask of chicken feathers. "If it hadn't been for Malcolm and Jenna—"

"Has Boden called off the wedding?"

The duchess's nostrils flared. "I'm sure it's only a matter of time."

"Not good enough," Gisele said. "I've heard the whispers. Valence is said to be acting strangely. *Strangely* isn't good enough."

"You can't risk it!"

"It will be all right, Your Grace."

"Worth wants James to introduce his mystery bride at midnight. Fifteen minutes from now. What are you planning to do about that?" Eleanor demanded.

"Jilt Jamie with seconds to spare?"

"This isn't funny," the duchess snapped. "You've done all you can. You need to go."

"I agree." Jamie was suddenly at Gisele's side.

"One waltz," Gisele said suddenly. "I will dance one waltz with Jamie. And then, before the stroke of midnight, I will disappear like a secret princess in one of those children's fairy tales."

Eleanor eyed her uncertainly.

"We've brought Valence to the very edge," Gisele said quietly. "He just needs a little push. This is our one chance." She stood and held out her hand. "So you may ask me to dance, Jamie Montcrief, or I will find someone who will."

No sooner had she finished speaking than the first strains of a waltz started.

Jamie stared hard at her. "Very well then." He took her hand and tucked it under his arm, sounding completely at ease, yet the feel of his rigid muscles beneath her fingers told a different story. "If you'll excuse us, Your Grace, we have a hornet's nest to stomp on."

Eleanor was watching them with worried eyes. "Straight upstairs to Sebastien," she warned Gisele, "the second the damn dance ends or the second things go sideways. Do you understand?"

"Understood." Gisele nodded.

They turned and made their way to the center of the ballroom, where couples had begun to dance. Jamie pulled her into his arms as they joined in.

"This is insane," Jamie muttered under his breath.

"Quite likely." Gisele pressed a kiss to the back of the hand that held hers.

"What was that for?" Jamie asked.

"For everything you said tonight. Michael would be proud."

"I didn't know you heard."

"Every word." She looked up at him, her throat thick. "Did I mention how much I love you?"

He squeezed her hand. "Once or twice."

Her gaze fell back on the edges of the crowd spinning by. "Do you see Valence?" she asked as Jamie effortlessly guided her across the floor.

"Not yet." His eyes were scanning the room from above her head. "But he'll be watching, looking for me."

Gisele caught sight of Eleanor watching them from the edge of the onlookers. Her eyes were barely visible behind her mask, but she jerked her head subtly in the direction of the terrace doors.

Gisele peered over Jamie's shoulder, following the gesture, and felt the gooseflesh rise on her skin.

The Marquess of Valence was indeed watching.

⁓

Adam Levire stared hard at the woman dancing with Montcrief. This time he was sure it was Gisele and not that other blonde Reddyck had tricked him with. The blood was roaring in his ears, and his heart was beating in a painful staccato against his ribs.

It was Gisele. It was her, it was her, *it was her*. He knew it with every fiber in his body.

Adam took an involuntary step closer before stopping, realizing what he was doing.

He needed proof that Montcrief had stolen his wife. Adam wasn't a fool—he was going to need proof to justify his actions, both past and future. One could not be faulted for defending one's honor, and if ever Adam's honor had been insulted, Montcrief's theft of Gisele had done it. He could not have his marchioness disappear again like a wisp of smoke in a gale, leaving him bereft and tortured anew.

⁓

"Is he still standing there?" Gisele asked in low tones.

"Yes." Jamie had spun them around so Gisele was hidden from view.

She could feel the malevolent force of Valence's stare, and the tiny hairs on her neck were standing on end.

"I think you should go back upstairs now," Jamie said, and there was real urgency in his voice.

"Not yet. He has to be completely convinced."

"He's looking very convinced," Jamie snapped. "Gisele—"

"It's not good enough," Gisele said quietly. "He has to be pushed past the point of no return. Past the ability to think and act rationally."

"Gisele, I want you safe. Now. This is too risky—"

Gisele could feel a rage boiling up inside her chest such as she had never before experienced. An uncontrollable fury at everything Valence had done to her, to Helena and her mother, at what he would continue to do to others for as long as he was able.

"No. I will not run." She could hear the fierceness in

her own words. "Not until he can never hurt anyone ever again. Do you understand?"

Jamie took his eyes off Valence to search hers. "Yes," he said simply.

"Thank you," she whispered.

"I love you," he said, and in a heartbeat Jamie pulled her closer to him, never breaking stride.

His fingers spread across the small of her back, and he curled her hand in his until she was pressed against the length of his body. His heat suffused her, the hard strength beneath his skin reassuring and electrifying all at once. She never took her eyes off him, gazing up at him as if they were the only two people in the room, yet she was aware of the disturbance they were creating around them.

Their dance went from standard to seductive, their bodies one, their movements one. Jamie dipped his head, his mouth inches from hers. Gisele smiled softly up at him, her hand moving from his shoulder to curl around the nape of his neck. He spun her across the floor, to all appearances heedless of the gawking stares. She heard the last strains of the waltz begin, and she realized Jamie had maneuvered them as close to the doors leading out into the hall as possible. As the music came to an end, Jamie closed the last inches between them and kissed her with a scorching, desperate passion that created a ripple of shock clear across the room.

A commotion had erupted on the far side of the floor amid angry protests and shrieks.

"Go," he hissed against her lips. "And don't look back."

She kissed him hard, one last time, and then she was gone.

Jamie watched for a brief moment as Gisele slipped from his warmth and fled through the doors and into the hall. Her exit went unnoticed, everyone's attention now riveted in the direction of the dance floor, where the Marquess of Valence was frantically shoving his way through the crowd in an effort to get to Jamie. Unobtrusively Jamie faded back along the wall, coming to a casual stop near the refreshment table, as far away from the doors as he dared without making it obvious.

Valence had caught sight of him and, changing direction, charged through a dozen unlucky dancers to skid to a tumultuous stop before him.

"You have her," Valence snarled, "I know you do. So where is she?"

"My lord?" Jamie adopted a look of concern.

"You have her, Montcrief. I saw you with her. Everyone saw you with her!"

"I don't have the slightest idea what you are talking about, my lord," Jamie said as evenly as he could.

Valence swept the neatly stacked china and crystal from the table, the deafening crash causing the orchestra to falter, then stop altogether again. An apprehensive silence fell across the ballroom.

The Duchess of Worth approached then in full mettle, flanked by her son and Malcolm. The Earl of Boden and Lord Huston also materialized out of the stalled dancers at the sound of Valence's raised voice.

Eleanor met Jamie's eyes briefly before narrowing her own.

"Just what is the meaning of this, Lord Valence?" she demanded.

"He has her!" Valence howled.

"Has who?"

"My wife! I saw him. He had his fucking hands all over her." The last slithered out like poison.

"My lord!" Eleanor gasped loudly.

"I will rip this house apart until I find her!" Spittle flew everywhere.

The Earl of Boden had gone a ghastly gray. "Lord Valence!" he pleaded. "What is wrong with you?"

Huston was looking on with a savage satisfaction, knowing the events unfolding were effectively ending any alliance between his family and the marquess. He met Jamie's eyes with wondering conjecture and a slight inclination of his head.

"There is nothing wrong with me!" Valence yelled. He grabbed at Jamie, who dodged back, the crowd behind shrinking away from the two men. "This man has stolen my wife!"

"Lord Valence, I must remind you that it is my daughter—"

"Shut up!" he screamed at the earl. "I don't want your daughter no matter how much money you're willing to pay me. I want Gisele back. And he has her!"

The crowd gasped in unison.

"Your wife is dead, Valence." Eleanor's voice cut through the crowd like a knife. "Most of the people in this room saw her die."

"She isn't. She isn't, isn't, isn't." He pointed a trembling hand at Jamie. "He has her."

Jamie watched Valence dispassionately. The marquess was sweating and shaking, in either rage or confusion, it mattered not. His clothing was disheveled, as was his hair, one side of his face was swollen and bruised, and he was breathing like a winded racehorse.

"If your wife were still alive, my lord, one would wonder why she would be hiding from you." Jamie finally spoke.

That brought Valence up short, and his eyes narrowed. "So you admit my wife is alive."

Jamie barked something resembling a laugh. "Of course not. But it is a concern to everyone that your wives don't seem to survive long."

Valence lunged at him again. "I love my wife," he wheezed. "And she loves me. She is mine. Gisele is mine! No one else's. *Mine!*"

"Is that why you used your crop on her?" Jamie asked tonelessly. "Is that why you used your knives and your twisted mind and brought her to within an inch of her life?"

"I never gave her a punishment she didn't fucking deserve!" Valence screamed. "And she knew it. But I love her!" Abruptly he stilled, his mind registering the implication of Jamie's words even if he didn't recognize the consequences of his response. "You fucking bastard. You have her. You've seen her."

Jamie stared at the ruined man, knowing nothing he said now would make a difference either way.

"I'll kill you." The marquess reached into his coat, and suddenly there was a pistol in his hand.

Jamie forced himself not to react, even as the room erupted into panicked screams and shouts. He cursed himself for not having anticipated this.

"Dear God, Valence, put that thing away before someone

gets hurt," the duchess demanded, shoving her way past onlookers who were doing their best to shrink as far away from the two men as they could without missing a word.

"There is no need for this!" Worth moved to protect Eleanor. "Lord Valence, stand down!"

Jamie knew it wouldn't make any difference. He had taken away the one thing that mattered to Valence, and they both knew it. Only one of them was walking away from this. And Jamie was willing to risk everything for the woman he loved.

"You're going to shoot me, Valence?" he asked tiredly. "Go ahead. The French have been doing it for ten years, and they haven't had much luck." A few nervous titters rippled through the crowd.

But it would be hard to miss from this distance, Jamie knew, even given the pistol's unreliability. He was watching carefully for an opening. The last thing he wanted was to tackle this man only to have the pistol discharge and injure or kill someone else.

"I want her!" the marquess roared, the pistol swinging wildly. "You can take me to her and live. Or you can die right here and I'll find her anyway. Choose, Montcrief."

"Don't be an idiot, Valence," Jamie said. "I'll not play your games."

Like a viper the marquess spun and lunged forward and grabbed a girl who was cowering at the edge of the crowd. With a strength born of desperation, he twisted the girl's gown in his fist, dragging her up against him. Very deliberately he turned the pistol and let the barrel rest on the temple of the terrified girl.

Jamie froze, and the girl began sobbing softly.

"I said choose," Valence rasped. "My wife or the girl.

Or I'll choose for you." The barrel pressed harder into the girl's skin.

"It's not his choice, Adam."

Gisele's voice carried across the space like a gunshot and Jamie died inside.

Chapter 29————————————

Gisele hadn't gone upstairs as she'd promised, to lock herself in the safety of Breckenridge's vast rooms. She had circled back at the top of the stairs, creeping along the upper hallways where, in between the columns, she could see the ballroom below her. Standing alone in the shadows, she'd heard the shouting and the screaming. Then Valence had produced a pistol, and she'd watched in growing horror as he waved it first at Jamie and then at the sobbing girl who had nothing to do with anything. Another innocent victim who would be hurt at the hands of the marquess. And Gisele knew then she could no longer stay in the shadows.

This fight was no one's fight but hers. It was not Jamie's, though he might argue with her. But there was a little boy who needed Jamie more than he might be able to understand or imagine at the moment, but Gisele understood. Adam Levire, Marquess of Valence, could not be permitted to ruin any more lives. This was hers to finish, and she had always known there might come a time when she would need to stop hiding. And this was it.

"No," she said more loudly this time, and she saw Valence's eyes widen as he finally saw her and heard the buzz of the crowd as they pulled back, allowing her access.

She walked up to Valence, who had frozen, and pushed the barrel of the pistol away from the shaking girl's head.

"You don't need her anymore, Adam," she said. "You need me."

"Don't do this," Jamie said behind her.

It was everything she could do to ignore him.

"Adam," she whispered again, "take me home."

"Who are you?" he gasped, suddenly uncertain now that she stood before him.

"I'm your wife, Adam. How can you not remember?" She beseeched him with her eyes through her mask.

He was motionless for a second more before he shoved the girl from him and reached instead for her. Gisele allowed herself to be pulled up against him.

"It's you," he hissed, his breath hot and foul on her neck. He grabbed a fistful of her hair and yanked her closer to him. The gun caressed the side of her face. "You left me."

"No," she said. "I never did."

"Yes you did!" he screamed, half sobbing. The barrel of the gun banged against her ear.

"Valence, put the gun down." Jamie was advancing steadily on them, his voice even but his expression feral.

"Or what?" Valence demanded wildly.

"Leave the lady out of this."

"She's not yours."

"She's not yours either." Jamie had stopped.

"Yes, she is. She's mine. But if I can't have her, no else will." The edge of hysteria had abated, and now Gisele heard only desperation. "Come one step closer and I'll kill her." He began backing up, dragging Gisele with him. "I'm leaving with what is mine, and I'll shoot anyone who tries to stop me."

"Do what he says," Gisele said. She needed to get Valence out of the crowd, where he couldn't hurt anyone. And away from Jamie.

Jamie was shaking his head, his face pale and his eyes wild.

"I'll be fine," she told him. "But no one else can get hurt."

Valence managed to maneuver the two of them to the doors, backing away from the horror-struck crowd. Valence waved his pistol at a terrified servant, who sprang to open the door, and then again at a coachman who was lounging at the bottom of the steps, waiting for his master with his equipage.

"Get the hell away from the carriage," he snapped at the coachman, pointing his pistol at the man's face. The coachman stumbled back.

"Where are we going?" Gisele asked, hoping the servants could hear her. Or, more important, Valence's answer.

"My sweet Gisele. My perfect, perfect Gisele." Valence was crooning to her. "I've missed you. You can't imagine how much I've missed you." He pressed his lips to her throat, his hands still pulling her hair painfully.

Gisele flinched. "I'm here now. Can we go home?" She tried in vain to look behind her.

"Maybe," he murmured. "But not quite yet. You left me," he said, fury bleeding into his words suddenly. "You left me, and now you need to be punished."

A blinding pain struck the side of her head, and in an instant, her world went white and then black.

Jamie had barely reached the doors as the carriage careened into the night.

"Get me a horse," he yelled at the stunned coachman still standing at the bottom of the stairs.

The man stood dumbly before him, but a young footman was already running in the direction of the long line of carriages still waiting in back of the manor. Sebastien burst out into the night, looking as though he might throw up. Huston and Malcolm were hard on his heels.

"Where is he taking her?" Jamie demanded. "Where would he go?" The carriage would be out of sight by the time he got to the end of the drive.

"Back into the city." Sebastien was making a monumental effort to remain calm.

"Where?" Jamie was nearly coming out of his skin. "Dammit, I need a horse!"

"To his town house. Or..."

"Or where?"

"He owns a warehouse. Or what's left of one. On the docks near Battersea Fields. West of the marshes. It's wretched, suitable only for trolls and rats—it's impossible to miss. It's not far from here at all."

"Why would he take her there?"

Sebastien looked at Jamie, and he had his answer with a sick certainty.

"Take Lord Huston and go to his town house in case he changed his mind," Jamie ordered. "Tell Malcolm to follow after me as soon as he can."

"Find her," Sebastien begged, even as he headed toward the stables.

The footman had returned with a sleek horse as dark as pitch dancing at the end of its reins, its nostrils flared and its ears pricked at the commotion.

"I will beg you to reconsider your willingness to accept the stallion," the Duke of Havockburn urged, hurrying down the stairs behind Jamie. He took hold of the horse's bridle, and Jamie realized the footman wore the Havockburn livery.

"Yes," Jamie gasped.

"He hit her, my lord," the servant said. "Not so to kill her, but she's not sensible, aye?" The man made a disgusted noise. "I was too far away to stop him."

Jamie hissed in fury before nodding his appreciation, both for the information and the man's practical anticipation.

"Godspeed," Havockburn said grimly, and Jamie vaulted onto the horse's back, not allowing the startled animal a chance to react but immediately driving it into the night after the fleeing carriage.

He was too terrified and furious to wallow in self-recrimination and regrets. No one could have predicted what had happened tonight, and none of it mattered anymore. All that mattered was that Valence had Gisele, and he had to be stopped.

Jamie had a rough idea where the docks were, just east of Battersea Bridge. He pushed the horse recklessly, straining to catch a glimpse of the carriage, but it had disappeared into the darkness. The stallion's muscles bunched and stretched beneath him with seemingly inexhaustible stamina. The first two miles passed in a blur, and then the ground ahead of him opened up, the marshy scent of rotting vegetation rising in the air to couple with the ever-increasing smell of the Thames. It had started raining again in spurts, clouds scudding across the sky, just enough to give Jamie brief intervals of weak moonlight before the land around him was again swallowed by blackness. The ground beneath the horse's feet became a quagmire of mud that sucked and splashed with each step, and Jamie was forced to slow the stallion. Against the slight shimmer of the river, looming black structures were taking form. He must have reached the westernmost docks, but it was nearly impossible to see anything.

His horse suddenly pricked its ears and called. Jamie immediately allowed the stallion to stop, trusting the animal's senses. An answering whinny cut through the air, startling a handful of marsh birds from their roost, and Jamie could have wept with relief. They were close. Jamie gave the horse its head, relying on the stallion to lead him to its mates, still in the traces of a stolen carriage.

Desperately hoping he would not find Gisele too late.

*Chapter 30*_____

Gisele blinked and groaned, her head throbbing. She was stiff all over, and everything hurt. She tried to bring her hand to her head, but her arms wouldn't move. With a spurt of panic, she realized they were tied behind her.

"Ah. My lovely, there you are." A hand tipped her chin, and the mouth of a bottle was put to her lips. Liquid fire burned her throat, and she choked and coughed, spitting it out.

"Ungrateful bitch. Get up." The gentleness disappeared, and rough hands pulled her to her feet.

Gisele swayed, nearly retching, her vision still fuzzy. The shock of the liquor had helped clear her mind, however, and the events of the evening flooded back with perfect clarity.

The marquess was standing before her, peering into her face, his expression unreadable. He held a half-empty bottle of brandy in his hand, along with something else, and as her vision cleared, Gisele recognized it as her mask.

"Did you really think you could hide from me?" he said, tossing the mask to the floor and crushing it beneath his heel. "I knew it was you tonight, just like I knew it was you on the bridge that day." He ran a hand along the tops of her breasts, and it was everything she could do not to flinch.

"You ruined me," he said, "when you left me."

"I didn't leave—"

"Don't lie to me!" Valence yelled.

Gisele tried to control her breathing while she took stock of her surroundings. A sharp unpleasant odor—sulfur, perhaps—overlain with the unmistakable stench of the Thames. The sound of rain, scattering across the roof, echoing loudly in the cavernous space, but a more rhythmic sound of water beneath them. A small warehouse of some sort, built over the docks jutting out into the river. And darkness everywhere, except for the tiny pool of light in which they stood, flickering from a lamp set on a table beside him. Next to the lamp, the pistol lay forgotten.

"You ruined me when you left," Valence repeated, pointing the brandy bottle at her face. "And now"—his voice rose to a peculiar pitch—"you've ruined me now that you've returned."

"The explosion—"

"I didn't tell you to speak!" he roared, hurling the bottle against the wooden floor at his feet, where it shattered, alcohol soaking his legs and splashing everywhere.

Gisele fell silent. Behind her back she twisted her hands desperately, trying to dislodge the ropes.

Valence took off his coat and laid it beside the pistol.

"Do you know what all this is?" he asked, gesturing around him.

Gisele shook her head.

"Gunpowder," he said. "For cartridges. I borrowed

heavily to purchase it, as I was assured there is a demand for powder fine enough for use in rifles."

She felt herself pale. They were standing in the middle of a bomb.

"But like everything since you left me, it's no good. It's been packed in barrels that *leak*. The powder, I've been told, is useless now because of the damp that's gotten in. It will not ignite." He was unbuttoning his waistcoat now. "I was advised it could be dried, though the quality may be compromised, and in any event the process is a very long and tedious one, and the results are not guaranteed."

Gisele looked around her, feeling her insides crawl. Even if there wasn't much, even if most of the powder was damp, it would take only a small percentage to turn the building into an inferno.

Valence was divesting himself of his waistcoat, and his eyes were glazed.

"I was supposed to get married tomorrow, you know," he told her. "The bride's father was going to give me a great deal of money." He moved closer to Gisele, shoving her back against a heavy post. The rough edges scraped the exposed skin of her shoulders. "But I can't get married now, can I? Because I have you back."

He was alternating between anger and delight indiscriminately, and his shifting emotions were unnerving her. He had never been unpredictable before, only predictably cruel and ruthless, and this, more than anything else, was scaring her.

"But it doesn't matter. Nothing matters anymore now that I have you back." He giggled, a crazed, maniacal sound. Her kernel of fear grew.

His hands kneaded her breasts through her gown, and

he crushed his mouth to hers. Gisele shuddered in revulsion but held her ground. She needed time. More time to figure a way out of this.

"You're my perfect Gisele," he was whispering. He licked the side of her neck and bit her ear. "Tell me you want me."

"Yes," she whispered.

His eyes closed in pleasure, and he stroked himself through his pantaloons. "God, it's been too long," he moaned. "No one else can do what you do to me."

"Yes," she whispered again. She was using the post behind her to saw at the rope around her wrists, and the cord was starting to fray. She redoubled her efforts, blood becoming sticky against her skin.

She suddenly gasped at the shock of cold metal on her chest as he pressed the blade of a small knife just below her collarbone.

"Not there, my lord. They'll see," she said, trying to fight her growing dread. That he would break his rule and mark her where it might be visible later was alarming. It insinuated there was never going to be a later.

"It doesn't matter anymore, lovely," he confirmed. The blade bit, and she felt first the sting and then the warmth as blood welled.

"Ahh," he breathed, longing and satisfaction blending. His fingers traced the thin rivulet of blood where it had begun soaking her bodice. "I've missed this." His other hand was fumbling with her skirts, tearing the thin fabric as he shoved it up her thighs.

She twisted, making it more difficult for him to push her skirts out of the way. He snarled and backhanded her across her face.

"You left me!" Valence raged, letting the knife fall to the floor with a clatter. "And you ruined me. And now I can't go back. *We* can't go back to our old life. And it's all your fault for leaving. So now I'll make sure we're together forever."

With a violent jerk, he ripped the delicate layers of her skirts and clamped his hands around her hips in a vise grip. Using strength she had not realized he possessed, the marquess pulled Gisele's body against his own with such force that the rope binding her wrists finally snapped.

Wasting no time, Gisele heaved the man back with a vicious shove and he stumbled, astonished, to the ground. Diving forward, she grabbed the pistol from the table and turned to point it at Valence.

He stared at her in stunned confusion before a slow grin spread beneath empty eyes. "You can't shoot that in here," he told her. "You'll blow this place to kingdom come."

"Maybe."

Some of his arrogance faltered. "You won't do it."

She pulled the trigger.

The flint fell on the frizzen, but the powder in the pan had obviously become wet in the rain during the flight to the warehouse, and nothing happened.

The marquess's face went ashen before it turned a livid red.

"Bitch!" he screamed, and launched himself at her. He missed Gisele by inches, instead hurtling into the table, sending the lantern and his discarded coat crashing to the ground. The space went black for the briefest of seconds before a burst of light flared as flames shot from the broken lantern, feeding on spilled brandy and fabric.

Valence was screaming, thrashing on the floor, fire

licking ravenously at his clothing. Gisele backed away in terror, knowing her life would now be measured in minutes unless she could get out of the building. She looked around her in desperation, but her eyes, blinded by the intensity of the flames, could make out only blackness beyond. She swallowed a sob and staggered forward, but was brought up short by an unforgiving wall.

A loud crash had her whirling and she thought she might have heard a voice calling her name. She stumbled toward the sound, her eyes and lungs burning now as the smoke spread. She was disoriented and desperate and angry. After everything, everything she had done, everything she had overcome and defeated and accomplished, she was going to die here. In a bloody explosion. She would have laughed at the bitter irony had she not been so furious.

Suddenly there was someone at her back and she was swept up into a pair of strong arms. She clung to him as he sprinted away from the glow of the fire, through an open door, and into the night, where the shock of the freezing rain, coming down in torrents, had her gasping. She found herself back on her feet, scrambling away from the warehouse, her hand locked tightly with his. They hadn't made it more than fifty yards from the building when it disintegrated in a firestorm of shattered wood. She threw herself to the ground, Jamie landing heavily on top of her and covering her with his body.

The dock crumpled into the Thames, pieces of burning wood hissing as they were swallowed by the river, and the remaining blazes were extinguished by the sheets of water falling from the sky. Within minutes all that remained was a noticeable hole where a building and a dock had once stood, their ruins scattered in chaotic disarray.

Jamie sat up, pulling her with him. His hands cupped her face, ran over her shoulders, her arms, her waist.

"Are you hurt?" he demanded, barely audible above the sound of the rain. "You're bleeding."

"It's nothing." She shook her head numbly. "Is he dead?"

Jamie made a funny sound in his throat. "Yes."

"I'm not sorry."

"Are you—did he—"

She shook her head again, more forcibly this time. "I'm fine."

He enveloped her in his arms, crushing her to him. "I'm not," he said. "You scared the life out of me. I should be furious. I will be furious. Just give me a minute and I'll get there."

She could feel him shaking.

"How did you know where I was?" she asked, her voice hoarse from the smoke and the terror.

"Sebastien. Sebastien remembered this place. Said it was the only wretched thing Valence still might own on account it was rotting from the inside out and no one save a troll would ever dare step inside voluntarily."

"What does that make you then?" she blurted, looking back through the darkness at the gaping hole. She suddenly found herself laughing and crying, tears streaming down her cheeks to mingle with the rain.

Jamie's arms tightened around her, and a tortured sound somewhere between a laugh and a sob escaped. "That's the last straw, Gisele. I can't work for you anymore. Your humor offends me, and these are the worst labor conditions imaginable."

"I beg your pardon?"

"I quit. This is far beyond what I'm being paid for."

"You can't quit. I love you."

"That's why I've decided to marry you instead. It seems safer."

She pulled back to stare at him.

"You're asking me to marry you now? *Now?*"

"Would you prefer I come back later? Say two o'clock?"

"Oh, God." A new flood of giggles overtook her. "What would being married to you entail?" she asked when the spasms had subsided.

"I'm not sure," he said, wiping gently at the water sluicing down the sides of her face.

"Would I have to steal something?" she managed.

"You've stolen it already." He pressed her hand over his heart.

She hiccupped, a fresh stream of hot tears starting.

"You'll never be a duchess, you realize."

Gisele sniffled. "Thank God. Every time I put on an expensive ball gown something seems to explode."

"I knew there was a good reason I didn't dress you up and take you out sooner." He smiled before he sobered. "Was that a yes?" He was searching her eyes now.

"Yes." She pressed herself into him, love leaving her breathless. The rain hammered down and the wind gusted and the mud sucked at her legs, yet the only thing that really mattered was the feel of his warmth around her.

"Jamie?"

"Mmmm?"

"Take me home."

Chapter 31 ————————————

There was only one invitation delivered that next week.

Jamie brought it to Gisele as she lay watching him from the bed, a shaft of sunlight kissing her skin and hair, putting him in mind of a sated nymph. He bent and kissed her, the mattress dipping beneath his weight as he settled himself next to her.

"You've lost your edge," she said, plucking the single plain paper from his fingers. "Last week there were stacks."

"Society is in a snit," he informed her. "Not only have I refused to identify the magnificent woman I danced with at the ball or name her as my fiancée, it appears that the manner in which I danced was quite unacceptable to most matrons."

"I'm sorry."

"No, you're not. And neither am I." He grinned suggestively. "I'm quite looking forward to our next waltz."

She grinned back.

Jamie studied her for a moment, his smile fading. "Where do you want to go?" he asked abruptly. "Even with Valence dead, we can't stay in London."

"No," she agreed. "Nor do I want to."

"I hear Halifax is nice," he said casually.

Gisele stared at him and Jamie watched as she grasped

what he was offering. "Oh, Jamie." She leaned forward and brushed the hair from his forehead.

He waited.

"No. My life is not in Halifax. My life is with you."

"Good Lord, I wasn't going to send you by yourself," he huffed. "I'd planned to accompany my wife."

She smiled at him and passed him the paper she still held in her hand. "Open it."

Jamie pulled the paper apart. "We've been invited to a picnic at the Reddyck family seat," he read. "By Sofia and Richard. They are removing to the country to live with Malcolm."

"That's where I want to go."

Jamie squeezed his eyes shut.

"Your family is there, Jamie. And they love you and want you just as you are. And so do I. With you I am not defined by a title or a label or a past. I am...just Gisele."

"And I am just Jamie, an almost-duke."

"*My* almost-duke. That's all I'll ever need." She pressed a gentle kiss to his lips. "Perhaps we can bring Richard something when we go on our picnic?" Gisele asked. "He has a little wooden horse that he adores. Perhaps we could find him another?"

"I'd like that," Jamie replied. He grinned at her, loving the way her eyes darkened and her breathing became shallow in response. He pressed her back against the pillows. "But there is something else Richard needs that I'm a touch more eager to give him."

"What's that?"

He leaned over, kissing her with a heat that left her gasping.

"Cousins," he said. "And lots of them."

Jenna Hughes uses her cover as a lady's companion to swindle the rich—and help the poor. But when this lovely Robin Hood targets a handsome yet rakish duke, who will be playing whom?

Please see the next page for a preview of

A Good Rogue Is Hard to Find.

Do you suppose the duke will have me hanged?"

The Duchess of Worth had been poring over a map of Quatre Bras, bold arrows clearly illustrating the advance and retreat of English and French troops. She set it down and leveled a stern look at Jenna. "No one is going to be hanged."

"So just transported then."

"No one is going to be transported anywhere," said Eleanor with an exasperated sigh.

"Have you forgotten what it is I do?" Jenna kicked the edge of the rug in frustration.

The duchess's nostrils flared. "Dramatics do not suit you, Miss Hughes."

"I am not being dramatic, I am being pragmatic. Every successful thief is pragmatic."

"You are not a thief. You use a unique set of skills to recover. Recoup. Retrieve."

"I steal."

The duchess made a derisive sound. "No more than anyone else."

"Except when the ton does it, it's not called steal-ing. When an earl or a viscount or a marquess steals the rightfully earned income of his tailor or cobbler, it's called *entitlement*."

"That may be so, Miss Hughes, but nothing has changed from yesterday. There has always been risk."

"Yes, but now there is a duke. And a damned decent one at that."

"He would be pleased to hear you say so."

"He would not be so pleased if he discovered what I do."

Eleanor's lips thinned but she remained silent.

"Tell me that your son would look the other way if he caught me swindling his friends and fellow peers out of their money. If he caught me fleecing his social contemporaries for what would appear to be my own gain. He wouldn't care who I was."

The duchess looked disturbed. "No, he wouldn't," she agreed quietly. "Strange, since it is the very opposite of how his father would approach a similar dilemma. Status and connection were the only things that mattered to my husband, and in his eyes, rank would excuse almost anything. And since you are connected to me, the old duke might have been tempted to overlook your transgressions. Particularly if he could personally benefit somehow. My son has a much better-developed sense of right and wrong."

Jenna groaned. "I hear Botany Bay is nice. I've always fancied living near the ocean. And at least the winters would be warmer."

"Don't be ridiculous. I'd never allow that to happen."

"I don't know that you'd get much of a say, Your Grace," Jenna mumbled miserably.

The duchess returned her attention to her map, her brows furrowed. Jenna knew Eleanor did her best thinking when she retreated into her massive collection of military maps, and if there was ever a time when the duchess's shrewd wisdom was needed, now was it. Because the man currently sleeping in the gold guest room upstairs was going to be a problem on an epic scale, and at the moment, Jenna had no idea what to do about it.

Jenna had spent a great deal of time studying the Duke of Worth. Well, specifically his horses, but by default, the duke as well. It was her job to educate herself about the owners and the trainers and the jockeys and who out of the lot would offer up real competition each year. It was her responsibility to know who could be bought, and for how much. Who would be willing to drug a horse, lame a horse, or ride that same horse anyway. Who could be paid to steal a horse, replace a horse, or pull a horse to keep it from running to its full potential. In her experience, everyone had their price. Everyone, that was, except the Duke of Worth.

In fact, the Duke of Worth, for all his obvious disinterest in politics and the governance of the Empire, was an unexpected leader at the tracks. He was involved with the Jockey Club, advocated for the accurate development of a stud book, and, to the best of her knowledge, had never accepted a bribe for anything. All things Jenna would normally admire.

But these were also things that would make her job at Ascot that much more difficult.

For all his sterling qualities as a horseman, Jenna knew William Somerhall would never understand what she did. And he would never forgive her absolute disregard for the rules of the track and the dignity of thoroughbred racing in fair Britannia.

"Do you think if we get rid of the chickens, he'll leave?" Jenna asked, trying to keep the desperation from her voice.

"I'm quite sure that will not be sufficient. Though I must admit the idea has appeal. Those damned birds are becoming tiresome. As is my supposed eccentricity," Eleanor muttered under her breath, riffling through a pile of notes and pulling out a page. "Why do you think the Prince of Orange didn't order square when the French cuirassiers attacked?" she asked abruptly.

"Because he was an idiot."

"I can't use that word in my thesis. It sounds inexpert."

"How about *uninformed*?"

"No, he certainly had the information he needed to issue the appropriate order."

"Perhaps he was distracted by the shiny tassels on his uniform?"

The duchess gave Jenna a long look.

Jenna sighed. "Perhaps *unwise*?"

"Better." Eleanor crossed out a word and replaced it.

"He'll want to see our stables." Jenna wasn't talking about the Prince of Orange anymore.

The duchess winced. "Yes, he will." She tapped her quill against the table. "There is no avoiding it, but I am hoping he will be too focused on his own mounts to pay much attention to ours. When the time comes, and it will, I am confident we can explain away my horses. Sadly, I do not think we will have the same success if we try to explain away your role with the horses. You'll need to appear to be simply my companion."

Jenna could do that. She'd posed as Eleanor's companion many times in the past and knew she did a damn convincing job of it. But that didn't mean she couldn't search for another solution to the problem that was the Duke of Worth. Every problem had a solution if one was resourceful enough and willing to think creatively. And Jenna had always been good at creative thinking.

"What if we bought him a new horse?" Jenna demanded. "Something he could not resist racing. Something he would feel compelled to take to Epsom immediately. Lord Bering has suggested he might be selling that Eclipse colt he bought as a yearling a few years ago."

"And how would we explain that?"

"A birthday gift?"

"His birthday is in January."

"An early birthday gift?" Jenna was reaching.

"My son believes I can't tell the difference between a donkey and a draft horse. He would only become more suspicious."

Jenna cleared her throat. "Well, how about a woman to distract him then? Perhaps I could find him a mistress," she suggested, though somehow that thought rankled.

Eleanor shook her head. "He won't take a mistress, mostly because a mistress is an encumbrance. The last one he had was well over a year ago, and from what I understand, she could not accept that he spent more time at the track and in the barns than he did in her bed. She had a vilely destructive temper. He hasn't had one since."

Jenna groaned in frustration, well and truly backed into a corner with no discernible way out. "How about we get Margaret to tie him up and lock him in the dungeon until after the Cup? Please tell me the dower house has a dungeon."

The duchess sighed in sympathy. "I believe dungeons went out of style a few centuries ago, dear."

Jenna sank into a stuffed chair, defeated.

Eleanor watched her a moment, then approached, perching herself on the wide arm of the chair and putting a hand on Jenna's shoulder. "We'll find a way, Miss Hughes, and Worth will be none the wiser. We'll set him at the accounts first. If we're lucky, he'll give up after a day and leave on his own."

"And what if he doesn't? Leave, that is?"

"Then we'll still depart for Windsor and Ascot Heath as planned."

"You don't think the duke will find it suspicious that we depart so early?"

"And therein lies the beauty of my bizarre behavior. Who can explain what I do?" Eleanor's eyes twinkled.

Jenna rubbed at her eyes. "This has the makings of an utter disaster."

The duchess patted her on the shoulder, and her features became wistful. "I'd like to think my son would understand what it is we—you do. Maybe, given enough time, maybe, given enough evidence of why we do it, he would eventually even empathize. He has a good heart— that I believe with all my soul." Her voice dropped even lower. "But time is something we do not have the luxury of right now. And I am not close to William the way a mother should be. That is my fault, and I will regret it until the day I die. For I fear now it is too late."

Jenna reached up and squeezed the duchess's hand.

Eleanor cleared her throat brusquely. "I want you to keep track of Worth while he's here. I don't think it is in our best interests to have him wandering around the property unsupervised. If and when he starts putting two and two together, it would be better if we had some warning."

"And what would make you think he will agree to my constant presence?"

The duchess smiled faintly. "My son has scores of

women vying for his attentions, either for his money, his title, or bragging rights. But you, Miss Hughes, are an enigma, if only for your clear disregard for all three. Like any man, he'll want to determine why."

"That's not true. I quite like the idea of his money."

"But not for yourself."

"That's not the point."

"That's exactly the point, dear." Her expression became grave. "Now, listen carefully, Miss Hughes. The duke is going to have a great number of questions, especially when he gets a look at what lies beyond those oaks out back. Whenever possible, tell the truth. I've always found the truth is easier to remember. Establish yourself in the role he already assumes you fill. If he digs his heels in and decides to stick this out, there is only one thing that will enable you to do what will be required in just over a week."

"What is that?"

"As long as the duke believes you are simply my hired companion, no matter what happens at Ascot, you will be above suspicion."

Jenna forced herself to cast aside her discontentment, thinking of the people who were depending on her. She would succeed in outwitting the Duke of Worth because failure was simply not an option. Perhaps, if the fates were kind, the duke would reconsider his decision in the hours before dawn.

And leave before breakfast.

~

Sometime in the small hours of the morning, Will reconciled himself to his impulsive decision of the night before. He'd miss the stakes races at Epsom, that was true, and that still needled. But after witnessing the aftermath of his mother's ill-fated dinner party, he fully understood that the sacrifice was nonnegotiable.

He'd never liked Ascot. The turf itself was fine, as far as tracks went, though he found the longer distances of many of the races did not often suit his own mounts. It was everything else that he rebelled against. To start with, Ascot hosted only four consecutive days of races out of the entire year—four days that seemed more dedicated to pomp and pageantry than to the pure sport of racing. Society descended en masse for the first races and then stayed for the entire four days, Ascot being just a little too far from London to allow for daily return. At least at Epsom on Derby Day, most people came, watched, and left by nightfall.

Ascot was of value to the ton only as a place to see and be seen. They used the damn turf as a promenade in between races, for God's sake, and it required hired men to push them back behind the rails so that they didn't get trampled by the racehorses or—more important, as far as Will was concerned—cause injury to a horse or rider in their wanderings. It was one thing for them to conduct their social dramas at Almack's or Rotten Row or Vauxhall, but that they made the racetrack just another backdrop for narcissistic theater maddened Will. The track was supposed to be where he could escape the political and matrimonial maneuverings of polite society. And it was for precisely that reason that he'd preferred to avoid Ascot entirely. Until now.

Though maybe this was meant to be, for this year was unlike any other. This year Will had a champion in his stable, a horse he had bred and trained himself. A horse that would, with success, prove to everyone beyond a doubt that the Duke of Worth was to be taken seriously. Another peer might buy himself a winner. William Somerhall, on the other hand, had made one from scratch, and that was worth more than any amount of money.

He couldn't deny that the Ascot Gold Cup was a very prestigious race. The distance was punishing, the competition fierce, and it took a rare horse to overcome both. A win on the track at Ascot would establish him as one of the preeminent horsemen of England, and that could only lead to great things. Yes, Will thought, warming to the idea, perhaps Ascot was indeed a blessing in disguise.

And the extra time would allow him to deal with whatever was amiss in the dower house. He would devote himself to straightening out his mother's finances, reviewing her staff, and, most important, reshaping her reputation. His first order of business would be a heart-to-heart with Miss Hughes. If she was to remain as his mother's companion, she would need to be more vigilant. Will planned to establish certain parameters for his mother's behavior, and it would be up to Miss Hughes to enforce them.

Though after last night's performance, he wasn't certain the captivating Miss Hughes could manage the burden. Will suspected she was too much of a renegade herself to keep the dowager firmly in check, but perhaps he was wrong. At the moment, both the woman and her motives were absolutely inscrutable.

Though if he was being honest, Jenna Hughes was a mystery he was very much looking forward to solving. Especially if the delectable Miss Hughes should prove willing to reveal more than just her secrets.

In the next instant, Will gave his head a hard, disgusted

shake. He couldn't allow the woman to distract him from his duty. He owed it to his mother—hell, he owed it to himself—to fix what was clearly broken. Staring sightlessly up at the ceiling in the predawn dark, Will realized that, between saving the duchess from disgrace and winning the Gold Cup, the former was going to be the more daunting task.

Fall in Love with Forever Romance

I'VE GOT MY DUKE TO KEEP ME WARM
by Kelly Bowen

Gisele Whitby has perfected the art of illusion—her survival, after all, has depended upon it. But now she needs help, and the only man for the job shows a remarkable talent for seeing the real Gisele...Fans of Sarah MacLean and Tessa Dare will love this historical debut!

HOPE RISING
by Stacy Henrie

From a great war springs a great love. Stacy Henrie's Of Love and War series transports readers to the front lines of World War I as army nurse Evelyn Gray and Corporal Joel Campbell struggle to hold on to hope and love amidst the destruction of war...

Fall in Love with Forever Romance

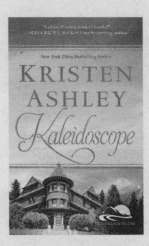

KALEIDOSCOPE
by Kristen Ashley

When old friends become new lovers, anything can happen. And now that Deck finally has a chance with Emme, he's not going to let her past get in the way of their future. Fans of Julie Ann Walker, Lauren Dane, and Julie James will love Kristen Ashley's *New York Times* bestselling Colorado Mountain series!

BOLD TRICKS
by Karina Halle

Ellie Watt has only one chance at saving the lives of her father and mother. But the only way to come out of this alive is to trust one of two very dangerous men who will stop at nothing to have her love in this riveting finale of Karina Halle's *USA Today* bestselling Artists Trilogy.

Fall in Love with Forever Romance

DECADENT
by Adrianne Lee

Fans of Robyn Carr and Sherryl Woods will enjoy the newest book set at Big Sky Pie! Fresh off a divorce, Roxy isn't looking for another relationship, but there's something about her buttoned-up contractor that she can't resist. What that man clearly needs is something decadent— like her...

THE LAST COWBOY
IN TEXAS
by Katie Lane

Country music princess Starlet Brubaker has a sweet tooth for moon pies and cowboys: both are yummy—and you can never have just one. Beckett Cates may not be her usual type, but he may be the one to put Starlet's boy-crazy days behind her... Fans of Linda Lael Miller and Diana Palmer will love it, darlin'!

Fall in Love with Forever Romance

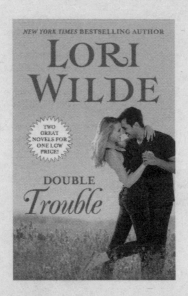

DOUBLE TROUBLE
by Lori Wilde

Get two books for the price of one in this special collection from *New York Times* bestselling author Lori Wilde, featuring twin sisters Maddie and Cassie Cooper from *Charmed and Dangerous* and *Mission: Irresistible*, and their adventures in finding their own happily ever afters.

3 1901 05712 0588